DOG HELPS THOSE

A GOLDEN RETRIEVER MYSTERY

BY NEIL S. PLAKCY

My beloved Samwise accompanied me on my amazing journey to publication, whether he was curled up protectively behind my computer chair or exuberantly tugging me down the street on our long walks together. I miss him every day.

Brody came into our lives a few months after Sam left, a bundle of adorable golden retriever puppy energy wrapped in soft white fur. He has staked his claim to our hearts and begun to put his own paw prints on my books.

I wouldn't be where I am today without Marc's love and support. A big sloppy golden thank you to Miriam Auerbach, Mike Jastrzebski, Christine Jackson, Christine Kling and especially Sharon Potts, for their help in bringing this book together. Puppy kisses to Jackie Conrad, DVM, for advice about cobra venom. Gratitude also to my professors at Columbia Business School, who gave me enough insight into the world of high finance to be able to write about angel investors and stock funds—though as usual, any mistakes in this book are my own errors and no one else's.

1 – Agility Training

"And you said I went dog crazy when Rochester came to live with me." I shook my head and looked around my friend Rick's fenced-in back yard. He had arranged poles, tubes, and a kids' teeter-totter to form an obstacle course. "What is all this stuff?"

"It's for agility training," Rick said. "Before you go any farther, Steve, I know. I'm puppy whipped. This is all for Rascal."

I adopted my golden retriever, Rochester, when his previous owner, my next-door-neighbor, was murdered. Seeing me and Rochester together made Rick want his own dog. Just after Christmas, he brought home Rascal, a black and white Australian shepherd from the Bucks County Animal Shelter in Lahaska. And now, barely five months later, he was as crazy about his dog as I was about mine.

"What's agility training?" I asked Rick, leaning up against the chain-link fence.

Rick and I went to high school together, and met up again when I returned home to Stewart's Crossing after a marriage, a divorce and a brief incarceration for computer hacking. Rick become a patrol cop, then police detective; he'd put on a few pounds in the twenty-some years since high school, but hadn't we all. He had bags below his eyes and a couple of laugh lines around his mouth. Otherwise he looked the same; unruly mop of brown hair, broad shoulders, athletic build.

"It's an obstacle course that Rascal and I run together."

"You climb through that tunnel?" I pointed at a long polystyrene tube with intermittent ridges that held its shape.

Rick shook his head. "I lead him through everything and reward him when he does it right."

The two dogs were lolling next to each other in the

shade of a big maple tree, lush with new buds. They had sniffed each other, then raced around the yard for a while, until they collapsed together, their tongues hanging out.

It was hot out back in the bright sunshine, so I peeled off my windbreaker and tossed it on the fence. "Show me."

Rick reached into his pocket and pulled out a dog treat in the shape of a tiny T-bone steak. "Rascal want to play?"

The shepherd jumped up and rushed over to Rick, sitting on his haunches at my friend's feet.

"Let's show Steve and Rochester how you climb the seesaw." He led the dog to the board and motioned Rascal to begin climbing. Delicately, the shepherd raised one black-and-white paw and placed it on the board. Then he stepped up, one paw after the other until the board began to rise behind him. He paused when the board was nearly balanced.

Rochester sat under the tree, watching the action.

"Come down," Rick said, standing at the far end of the board, holding out the treat. Quickly, Rascal scampered down the board as it fell to the ground, then jumped up to snatch the treat from Rick's hand.

"What a good boy," Rick said, reaching down to scratch behind Rascal's ears.

"Uh-oh, here comes Rochester," I said. The big goofy golden bounded up to Rick and Rascal but ignored the possibility of a treat. Instead he hopped right on the lower end of the board and began to climb up.

He hesitated only for a moment when the board came level, then bounded down and ran up to me, his mouth wide open in a doggy grin. "Rochester doesn't even need the treat for motivation." I reached down and scratched his neck. "Do you, boy?"

He woofed.

"Maybe not motivation, but reward." Rick held a treat out to Rochester, and my traitorous dog grabbed it.

Like Rick, I was forty-two, though I was an inch or

two taller than he was, with a body made for sitting behind a computer, not chasing criminals. We had originally bonded over the mutual bitterness of our divorces, but now we came together because of an underlying friendship and the love of our dogs.

"Come on, Rascal and I will go through the course, and then you and Rochester can follow." Rick led Rascal over to the gate, and then took off at a run, the dog right behind him.

"Go on, through the tunnel." Rick motioned forward, and Rascal got down on his front paws and scrabbled his way in and through. "Good boy!" Rick said, handing him a treat and urging him forward to a set of three wooden steps back to back. Rascal climbed up the steps then down, got another treat, then pawed delicately up the teeter-totter.

I laughed at the display, but Rochester obviously didn't share my humor. I had to hold on to his collar to keep him from following.

"Now the weave poles." Rick urged Rascal forward to dart around a set of poles, in and out, and it made him look like he was following a very determined, agile squirrel.

A plane soared high overhead through the cloudless sky, and in the distance I heard someone firing up a lawnmower. A bee buzzed by in pursuit of pollen. It was the sort of glorious spring day which made me wonder why I'd ever left Pennsylvania, and glad I'd come back.

Rascal jumped up on a low, square table, and Rick counted off on his fingers as Rascal sat. At the count of three Rascal took off toward the limbo pole, but instead of going underneath he jumped over it. Then he raced back to the gate and sat down.

Rick loped after him. "Good boy." He patted the dog on the head and gave him another T-bone. "He should have stayed on the table for a count of five. We're working on that."

Rochester was still straining to follow in Rascal's paw-

5

prints, so I let him go. He ran right to the tunnel and squirmed inside. Then he stopped.

"You've got to run to the end," Rick said. "So he knows where to go."

"There's only one direction," I protested, but I hurried to the end of the tunnel and clapped for Rochester. "Come here, you goofball."

He rushed out of the tunnel and jumped up on me. "Up the steps next," Rick said. "No stopping."

"Come on, Rochester." I motioned him toward the steps, and he went right up and then down as he was supposed to. Then, with me urging him on, he did the teeter-totter again, and then I led him to the weave poles.

He was baffled, even after having watched Rascal. Instead of running between the poles, he ran around them a couple of times, barked, then jumped up on the table. "That's Rochester's way of saying those weave poles are dumb," I said.

I held up my fingers as Rick had, counting to five, then motioned Rochester down and toward the limbo pole, which he cleared gracefully.

"You should bring him to my training class." Rick handed Rochester a T-bone, which he gobbled greedily. "Tomorrow afternoon, out Scammell's Mill Road."

"You take him to a class to learn this?" I asked, as I followed him back inside, the dogs right behind us.

They collapsed on the kitchen floor, and Rick brought two bottles of beer out of the fridge. "This woman has a big farm out where Stewart's Crossing meets Newtown," he said. "She has a huge agility course set up, way more stuff than I have. She breeds Chihuahuas and dachshunds, but most of the course works for big dogs, too."

For the past few months, I'd been dating one of the professors at the college where I worked. As Rick and I sat down at the kitchen table, he asked, "How's Lili these days?"

Liliana Weinstock was an amazing photographer and the head of the fine arts department. She was beautiful and funky and talented, and she and Rochester got along well. But she had also been divorced twice, and we both agreed to take things slow. "She's doing well," I said. "It's the end of the semester, though, so she's swamped with all this department chair stuff, as well as finishing up her own classes."

"Then come with me to Rita's class tomorrow. Though I have to warn you she's a pain in the ass, and her little dogs can drive you crazy with their yapping."

"You make it sound so appealing." I tipped my beer bottle back. The brew was sharp but had a citrus aftertaste, and it made me think of summer.

"It's really fun. And you haven't laughed until you've seen a Chihuahua stuck on the teeter-totter when it's just about balanced, going back and forth like it's possessed." He smiled at the memory. "And Rita's got a mouth on her like a sailor when the dogs don't behave. It's a crack up."

We moved to the living room and Rick put a golf tournament on the big-screen TV. We played with the dogs, joked about the golfers on the screen, and downed another pair of beers. Then I looked at my watch. "Dinner with Lili tonight," I said. "What time is this class tomorrow?"

"Eleven. I'll pick you and Rochester up in my truck at ten-thirty."

I stood up. "All right. See you."

"Wouldn't want to be you," he shot back, the way we'd spoken back in high school.

All in all, though, I thought as I drove home in the old BMW sedan that was a relic of my past life in Silicon Valley, I had managed to rebuild pretty well. Sure, I still had to meet with my parole officer, and my finances were tenuous, if improving with every week of full-time work. I had started at Eastern as an adjunct instructor in the English department before I managed to score my current administrative gig, and I still taught occasionally when I could.

I had a great dog, a sweet townhouse and an even sweeter girlfriend. While I was still married and living in California, my dad sold our family house and moved into a townhouse in River Bend, a gated community of townhouses and single family homes tucked between the Delaware River and Stewart's Crossing's downtown, bordered on two sides by a nature preserve. He died while I was in prison, and left the townhouse to me, his only child. As I drove through the gates and waved at the security guard on duty, I thought again how lucky I was that to have had a place to come home to.

When we got home, I fed Rochester and took him for a quick walk around the neighborhood. It was especially beautiful in the springtime, and even though the sun was going down and the air getting nippy, I enjoyed walking with Rochester. He took so much pleasure in nature—sniffing every bush and tree for messages left by other dogs, chasing squirrels and ducks, rolling in the grass. Forsythia hedges were coming into bloom and all the maples and oaks budded with new growth. The air was sweet and floral, lights were coming on in houses around us, and I could hear the high sound of a child giggling mixed with car engines and someone's lawnmower.

We walked down the long access road to the neighborhood, bordered on both sides by the nature preserve, and passed the place where I had found Caroline Kelly's body. Rochester stopped to nose around, and I wondered if some scent of his former mistress still remained months later.

Was it her death that had set him on a life of crime detection? Was he happiest when he was nose to the ground in search of a villain, as he'd done twice before? Could he settle down to a happy life if I asserted myself as the alpha dog in our pack?

2 – They Call This Art?

I took a shower, got dressed, and left the door of Rochester's crate open in case he wanted to sleep inside it. Then I drove upriver to Leighville, where Lili rented a small house on the outskirts of town. It was only a half-hour drive, and I was able to do it on auto-pilot, since I'd been making that same drive to work at Eastern for over a year.

I thought about moving; Lili was in Leighville, and our work was, too. But Stewart's Crossing was the place where I'd felt loved and sheltered by my parents. Where we had my Mexican-themed fifth birthday party, complete with piñata, serapes, and pointy straw hats. Where memories lurked around street corners and behind buildings that were landmarks to no one but me and my friends. It felt like home, and I wasn't ready to give that up.

"Hey, sweetheart," I said, when Lili opened the door to me. I leaned forward and kissed her.

She was wearing a calf-length swirly dress in a red and blue pattern, and had a matching scarf knotted around her neck. "Hey, yourself," she said, when she backed away.

I liked kissing Lili. She always smelled and tasted so good, and I felt my hormones rise just being around her. I nibbled on her ear.

She laughed and backed away from me. "You're a meshuggeneh," she said.

Lili's use of the Yiddish word reminded me that despite her occasional Spanish expletive and her beautiful Hispanic looks, she was as Jewish as I was. Her Weinstock grandparents had left Poland in 1940, but they couldn't get visas for the US so they had gone to Cuba. Her father had been born in Havana, gone to college there, and married Lili's mother, a Sephardic woman whose roots were in

Spain.

Lili was born in 1965, two years before I was. Her father was an engineer, and in 1970 he was sent to Mexico to learn advanced hydraulics. While he was out from under Fidel's thumb he realized how repressive the Castro regime was, and he arranged to have his wife, Lili, and her younger brother smuggled out of the country to join him.

After a couple of years in Mexico, the family relocated to Kansas City, joining a small cluster of Cuban immigrants. From then on the Weinstocks moved every few years as her father got jobs. Lili never felt at home anywhere because her background was so odd. Either she was the only Hispanic, or the only Jew. Her parents had funny accents. She started using the camera as a way to frame and understand her existence.

Her language was a funny mix of Yiddish words, Sephardic expressions, and Midwest terms. She said, "Oy vey" and called soda "pop," and could sing lullabies she had learned from her mother in Ladino, the Spanish-based language of the Sephardim. Yet she was as far from my ex-wife Mary as a nice Jewish girl could be. Mary was a hard-charging executive who liked to be in control of everything. Lili was an artsy free spirit who didn't like to be tied down.

"Let's go. We don't want to be late." She grabbed her coat and locked the front door. We were going to a reception for an exhibit featuring her students' work, and then to dinner. I was hoping we could short-cut the exhibit and get to the food—and what was bound to come after.

* * *

We parked in the faculty lot and walked through the gathering dusk to the chapel, at the eastern end of the campus. It was a square stone building in the collegiate Gothic style, with ivy climbing the walls and an ecumenical-looking square spire. Being Jewish, I'd never been in the chapel myself until that evening, though I'd gone to college at Eastern back in the days when dinosaurs roamed the earth.

The main chapel was a large room with a vaulted ceiling and several rows of folding chairs in the middle. As we walked inside, Lili stopped and pointed up. "I love the pattern of that ceiling," she said. "I'm taking a series of photos of it at different times of day, with different filters. I don't know what I'll do with it but I'm interested in the way the light and shadow play against the woodwork."

I loved the way she looked at the world, always through the camera's eye. That was represented in the way she'd laid out the student work as well. Around the edges of the room her class had hung their paintings, photographs, drawings and watercolors on fabric-covered dividers. Several low pedestals held small clay sculptures.

"One of my students was having problems getting her work framed in time," Lili said. "I want to go over and check on her. And I need to make sure that all the students who are exhibiting are here to talk about their work."

I stopped to survey the first exhibit by the door, a series of photos taken by a senior named Len Scapon. I thought at first that the gorillas, zebras and giraffes in his pictures were from a nature park, but then I took a closer look at the captions. Len had received a grant from a nature foundation the previous summer and spent it hitchhiking through Equatorial Africa, taking pictures of animals out in the wild.

"I have to tell you, Len," I said to him, "I'm impressed not only by your art but by your chutzpah. If I had told my parents I wanted to do something like this when I was twenty, my mother would have taken my temperature and my father would have taken my passport."

He laughed. "My folks were real supportive. You need a ton of shots to go to Africa, and my mom's a nurse. She arranged all the vaccinations for me and even gave them to me herself."

"Well, it was worth the effort. The photographs are

11

amazing."

He scuffed his feet. "Thanks."

Next in line was a skinny, eager kid named Jeremy, whom I knew from a freshman comp class I had taught the year before. He stood nervously by his pictures in a navy blazer that his parents probably hoped he would grow into. He had taken some very atmospheric photos of the campus, focusing on architectural details—a gargoyle, a commemorative stone, a window frame and a huge oak door.

"I really like this one, Jeremy," I said, pointing at a shot of Fields Hall, the main administration building, shrouded in fog.

We were looking at it together when I heard a woman's shrill voice rise above the crowd. "They cawl this crap art?" she said, in a heavy accent, half *Jersey Shore* and half *Real Housewives.*

Jeremy and I turned in the direction of the voice. A short, slim woman in her mid-sixties, with close-cropped iron gray hair, was pointing at one of the paintings. I recognized the artist, who stood next to it. He was an Eastern European boy named Felae who had been in my mystery fiction class the year before.

The work in question was a gouache of a large, mixed-breed dog with black and brown fur, sprawled on his side on top of a large cross. His front paws were stretched out and bound to the left side of the cross, his back legs bound to the upright. In bright red lettering that reminded me of blood, Felae had scrawled "He died for our sins" at the bottom of the painting.

It was disturbing, to say the least. And the woman, who looked like she spent a whole lot of money on her clothes and purse, didn't like it one bit. She wore a form-fitting tan cashmere sweater and black pedal-pushers, with pointy-toed black high-heeled shoes that looked like they came from the Wicked Witch collection. "It's animal cruelty," she said, her voice carrying.

I saw Lili walk up to her. "It is a creepy painting," Jeremy said. "But Felae is a creepy guy."

"You know him?" I asked.

"From class. He's always mumbling to himself in Romanian or Bulgarian or whatever it is language he speaks."

I watched as Lili tried to placate the woman, leading her away from the disturbing painting to a series of cheerful watercolors of the Delaware River, painted by a chunky girl named Dezhanne, who I had taught in the same class as Felae. Calling the roll had always made me hungry—my students included Candy, Cinnamon, and Honey, as well as Dezhanne and Felae.

Dezhanne considered her body a work of art; she was constantly experimenting with piercings, henna tattoos, and strange haircuts. That evening she had huge black disks in her lobes, called ear gauges; matching black lipstick; and kohl ringed around her eyes.

She didn't look like the kind of girl who would paint light, airy impressionistic landscapes, but then, appearances are deceiving, after all.

I left Jeremy and picked up two glasses of white wine from the makeshift bar in the corner of the room and carried them to where Lili was still speaking with the loud woman. "Wine?" I offered them both.

"I don't drink alcohol," the woman said. "Only iced tea, with lots of sugar."

Lili took one of the glasses from me and said, "Ms. Gaines, this is Steve Levitan. He works in the alumni office here at Eastern."

"Margarita Stanville Gaines," the woman said. I thought I recognized the name, and then she said, "I'm on the Board of Trustees. I like to keep an eye on what's going on around the college."

That was it. I'd seen her name on fund-raising

materials at the office.

"And I have to tell you I don't like that boy's work," she continued. "It's sacrilegious and distasteful and it needs to come down."

Her elegant appearance was a real contrast to her uncultured voice. She pulled a cell phone from her pants pocket and flipped it open. "I'm calling President Babson right now."

"I'm sure you remember your own college days," I said, trying to stop the situation before it got worse. "It's a time for experimenting, figuring out who you are and what matters to you. I'm sure that's what Felae is doing."

"I knew exactly what I wanted to do when I came to Eastern," the woman said. "Make money. Lots of it. And I did." She turned away from us, but I heard her say, "John? Rita Gaines here."

I mouthed a word to Lili that rhymed with witch, and she smiled. As we stood there, I hoped we could get rid of the woman soon so Lili and I could do on to dinner.

Then Rita turned to Lili. "President Babson has authorized me to have that boy's painting taken down. Make it happen."

I was afraid Lili was going to explode, but she smiled tightly, then said, "May I speak to President Babson, please?"

Rita thrust the phone at her, and Lili introduced herself. "I'm concerned that the student could accuse the college of censorship," she said. "I'm Felae's professor and while I agree the painting is controversial, it's not gratuitously violent. It raises important questions about animal cruelty that I believe deserve to be discussed in an academic environment."

I watched as Rita's eyes widened. She was clearly a woman who expected to be obeyed without question.

Lili listened for a moment. "I understand," she said finally. "Yes, sir, I will."

She handed the phone back to Rita. "President Babson suggested that we isolate Felae's painting from the rest of the exhibit and post a content warning. I hope that satisfies your concerns."

I had seen Lili face down a lunatic with a gun, so I was already impressed with her—but my pride in her swelled as she smiled at Rita Gaines and without waiting for a response, said, "I'll talk to Felae and see that it happens."

Rita was fuming, so I tried to shift her attention. "What was Eastern like when you were here? Did we have a good business program?"

"It was terrible. I had to major in economics and half my teachers had no business experience at all. I couldn't wait to get out of here and get my MBA."

I smiled. Since I had started working at the college I'd come in contact with a lot of alums. Many of them had almost nothing positive to say about the current crop of students or the state of the college, and yet they were consistent donors and loved to talk about how great Eastern had been when they were younger. Rita was certainly different.

"Serving on the Board of Trustees is a big responsibility," I said. "I admire you for your commitment to the college."

"My accountants tell me I can either give money away or pay it to Uncle Sam." Her accent grated on me, reminding me of a couple of cousins on my father's side who grew up in the suburbs of Newark. My dad, who was from the same area but spoke without a hint of an accent, had always looked down on those cousins and I'd inherited his prejudice.

"With the state of the country today I'll be damned if I pay a penny in taxes," she continued. "And I don't have time to waste vetting a lot of different charities. I have a farm just down the river, so Eastern is convenient to me. Most of my donations come here, and I stay on the board so

15

I can make sure the money doesn't get wasted."

Across the room from us we could see Lili talking to Felae. From his defiant body language, the boy seemed to be arguing, but she stepped over to the wall and removed the painting. She carried it into an anteroom of the chapel, with Felae following.

The lights in the chapel dimmed a bit. "I understand that the Fine Arts department only has the room reserved until eight," I said.

"I've seen all I need to." Rita turned and strode toward the door.

"Pleasure meeting you," I said under my breath. I remembered what Rick had said to me earlier—see you, wouldn't want to be you.

Lili returned to me after Rita had left. "I had to make nice with Felae, and it wasn't easy," she said.

"You handled things well with Rita," I said. "Impressive. Was that Babson's idea, or was it yours?"

"Mine. He asked me to remove the picture as a personal favor. But I wasn't going to back down from that hyena in high heels."

She drained her white wine. "Now let's get some dinner. Something sweet to wash away the sour taste in my mouth."

3 – With Many Witnesses

I didn't stay over at Lili's that night, but I didn't get home early, either. I took Rochester out for a quick pee, and then went to bed, planning to sleep in. Sadly, at seven o'clock the big bossy dog was nosing me and licking my face. "Come on, Rochester," I said. "Let me sleep."

It was a losing battle, though, and soon I was up and walking him. It was shaping up to be another gorgeous spring day, and Rochester enjoyed snooping among all the new flowers, even trying to eat a yellow and white jonquil before I pulled him away.

The townhouses were all faced with fieldstone and had steeply-pitched roofs, with the occasional decoration reminiscent of Russian country dachas—gingerbread edging and modified onion-domes over the entranceways. The trees in the area reflected the relative newness of the development—they were pretty uniform, with maples and oaks alternating in the small front yards. The homeowner's association handled the landscaping, so everyone's grass was well-kept and only the occasional azalea or lilac marred the uniformity.

As we passed a bench overlooking a small lake in the center of River Bend, Rochester hopped up onto it and posed, as if he remembered the table in Rick's back yard. "You liked that agility stuff?" I asked.

He nodded his big golden head and woofed.

"All right, we'll go along with Rick today."

Rochester jumped down and took off in search of a good smell, and I laughed. "I guess I'm just as puppy whipped as Rick is."

Rick picked us up for the ride to the agility class, and we drove out Scammell's Mill Road in his truck, the dogs in the back. The sky was a robin's egg blue dotted with a few puffy white clouds like sheep in a field. Within a couple of miles the suburbs gave way to farmland, acres of peas, beans, corn, and asparagus in neat rows. A couple of dozen cows grazed in one field surrounded by split-rail fencing, and in another a guy rode a red tractor.

"I didn't realize the town limits of Stewart's Crossing extended this far inland," I said to Rick.

"Yeah, it's hell to patrol all the way out here. We only go about a mile past Rita's farm, though. Fortunately there isn't much crime—not like down in the suburbs."

A bell rang in my head. I remembered that the woman I met the night before had mentioned owning a farm downriver from Leighville. "Hold on. Is this trainer Rita Gaines?"

He turned to me. "You know her?"

"I met her last night. She's on the Board of Trustees for the college."

"Good luck with that. She's got a sharp tongue, that woman."

"Yeah, I heard her use it." I told him what she'd said about Felae's painting.

"He crucified a dog? That's nasty."

"He didn't actually crucify it. Just painted it that way. He was making a statement about animal cruelty."

Rick slowed down as we approached a sign that read "Good Dog Farm," and he turned in a long driveway. Ahead of us was an 18th-century stone farmhouse, the kind I'd daydreamed about living in when I was a kid and didn't know about low ceilings and antiquated plumbing. Next to the house was a big red barn, and beyond that a field full of the same doggy gym equipment I'd seen in Rick's back yard, but on a larger scale.

Rick pulled his truck in beside a row of BMWs, Jaguars, and other pricey cars. "This agility stuff attracts a wealthy crowd," I said, as we got out.

"Rita manages an investment fund. A lot of these

people are her clients."

I wasn't comfortable being around a lot of folks whose cars cost more than my house, but if a blue-collar cop like Rick could fit in, so could I. We put the dogs on leashes and they tugged us toward the ring, where it looked like a Ralph Lauren ad was being filmed—women in pastel pedal-pushers and men in plaid shirts romped with a mix of big and small dogs, from black and tan German shepherds to tiny brown Chihuahuas.

In contrast to the fancy cars and the elegant clothing Rita's customers wore, the yard smelled like a farm, a mix of manure, mulch and fresh growing things. As we got close to the ring, Rita approached, wearing skinny jeans and a light-blue chambray shirt with the sleeves rolled up. Her short, steel-gray hair seemed more appropriate with that outfit than with the fancy clothes from the night before.

Rick introduced us and said that Rochester was a novice at agility training. "But he learns fast."

"You work at Eastern, don't you?" she asked. "I saw you last night at that awful art exhibit."

Her accent was as strong and grating as it had been the night before.

I nodded, unwilling to engage her in a debate about art or morality. "You can take your dog into the training ring," she said, pointing to a circular area next to the main ring. "I've got to put King Otto through his paces." She whistled, and a long-haired dachshund came running toward her on tiny little legs, his reddish hair flowing behind him.

I couldn't help noticing that the way she pursed her lips together matched the look on the dachshund's face.

"She names all her dogs after German kings and queens," Rick whispered, as we followed her and the little dog over to the big ring. "Let's watch how she does it."

A half-dozen spectators stood at the split-rail fence around the ring. Rick introduced me to Matthew Durkheim, an older man with a shaved head, wearing a form-fitting white T-shirt with the Louis Vuitton logo and a pair of dark slacks. I noticed a tattoo of a rising sun on his right bicep, and it took me a minute to recognize it as the Eastern College logo. Calum, his black and white border collie, sat up at attention as Rochester sniffed him.

Then he turned to the other side and introduced me to Carissa Rodriguez, a Latin beauty, with a finely boned face and black hair, no older than thirty. She wore several gold necklaces, including one with a tear-drop diamond pendant that had to be at least a few carats; a woman's Rolex watch encrusted with diamonds; and a gold and diamond tennis bracelet. In her arms she held a sleek Chihuahua wearing a braided leather collar.

Rascal and Rochester nosed around the grass and then plopped down at our feet, and we all watched the show. Rita looked like a madwoman as she raced around the track with King Otto, snapping her fingers and waving her hands as the dachshund darted up and down and through the various obstacles. "At Rita's level it's about getting through the fastest, without making any mistakes," Rick said.

King Otto was graceful, though he caught his back foot as he jumped over the limbo pole, leaving it wobbling. "See, that's a fault," Rick said. "You lose points for that."

"I still think the whole thing is silly," I said.

"Don't let Rita hear you say that," Matthew said. "She's obsessive about her dogs."

"She is obsessive about everything," Carissa said, in a gentle Spanish accent.

"That's why she's such a good fund manager," Matthew said. "Wouldn't trust my investments to anyone else."

"Nor me," Carissa said.

When Rita finished her run, Rick said, "Come on, let's see how Rochester does in public."

He led us over to the training ring, and pointed out the

order of the stations. Rita had a lot more equipment than Rick did, including a big yellow hoop for the dog to leap through and several different limbo poles at different heights. The course was laid out with a couple of sharp turns and reverses as well.

"I'll take Rascal through once so Rochester can watch," Rick said.

Rick didn't look quite as crazy as Rita did, but I had to stifle a laugh a couple of times at how silly he looked, chasing around the course. Rascal seemed to love it, and Rochester was once again straining at his lead to follow him.

Rick was only slightly out of breath when he returned, though his hair was mussed and his cheeks were a bit flushed. "I get almost as good a workout as Rascal does," he said. "This'll be good for you, too." He poked me in the stomach.

I didn't deign to answer. "Come on, Rochester, let's show these rubes how it's done."

We walked out in the ring and I unhooked Rochester's leash. As soon as I did he took off for the first obstacle, a low-hung limbo pole.

"He's got to start from a sitting position," Rick said.

"Rochester! No!" I called. "Come back here!" He stopped and looked back at me. I pointed to the ground next to me and he ambled back. "Sit." I pointed down.

He stood there.

I pushed on his behind, and said, "Sit" again. This time he agreed.

Rick said, "I'll time you. Ready, set, go."

As soon as he said that, I ran toward the first pole, waving Rochester to accompany me. It took him a couple of seconds to follow, and I worried that he was going to stay there and make me look like a fool. But once he took off, we were running together and I was mimicking the hand motions I'd seen Rick make. I focused on trying to remember the right order of the obstacles, and on moving Rochester through his paces.

He zigzagged around the steps at first, finally climbing them when I patted the top level, and knocked over the second limbo pole. He still didn't get the idea of the weave poles, and when he went over one tall pile of fake rocks he landed in a big puddle of mud and splashed my jeans.

By the time the course was over I was panting for breath, and so was Rochester.

Rita stood next to Rick, arms folded across her chest, shaking her head. "That was terrible. Your dog is totally out of control."

"It's his first time," I said.

"It's not about that. I'll bet he doesn't obey a single one of your commands."

I was insulted. "He's a very smart dog."

She turned to Rochester. "Down," she said, pointing to the ground. He just looked at me.

"Down, boy," I said, mimicking her.

Instead of obeying, he jumped up and put his muddy paws on my thighs.

"See what I mean?" Rita barked. "You'll never be a success at agility unless you learn to control your dog."

She turned away, like we were wasting her time, and Rochester nuzzled against the back of her leg. Immediately she whirled on him and said, "NO!" in such a commanding voice that it startled the poor dog into plopping onto his butt, looking up.

I was torn, wanting to tell Rita Gaines off, but at the same time recognizing she was right—Rochester did exactly what he wanted and I let him.

"Come on, I want to watch some of the other dogs," Rick said, turning back toward the main ring. "There's a lot of strategy involved in handling."

"Something I seem to be lacking in."

"Rita says it's all about the relationship between you

and the dog. You have to show Rochester that you're the pack leader. I'll bet you feed him dinner before you eat yourself, don't you?"

"Sure. Why not?"

"And as soon as you walk in the door, you're all over him, right?"

"I guess so," I said.

"See, what you're telling Rochester is that he's in charge. Rita says that in a pack of dogs, the alpha eats first. So I make Rascal wait for his dinner until I'm done eating."

"That's mean. Doesn't he just sit and stare at you?"

"So? He does that even when I'm not eating."

We walked up to the split-rail fence again. Matthew and his border collie Calum were standing at the gate, waiting for a heavyset man with an unlit cigar in his mouth to finish his run with his German Shepherd.

Matthew said, "Don't mind what Rita said about your dog. She has no filter. You should have seen my dog Calum when we first started training here."

I nodded. "I noticed your Eastern tattoo. I went there too."

"I was on the crew team. Senior year we decided to get tattooed together. Stupid idea, but it's kept us close. We meet up at every reunion."

The German shepherd finished his run, and Matthew and Calum stepped into the ring. I was impressed with the rapport between them; all Matthew had to do was click his tongue and point, and the collie knew exactly what to do. Calum, like Rascal, didn't sit on the platform long enough, and Rita had some sharp words for him. Then Carissa took Tia Juana, her Chihuahua, out for a perfect run.

When they finished, Carissa walked over to where we were standing with Matthew, and Rita followed. Rita got down to the dog's level, scratching her behind her ears and purring. "Good breeding shows, doesn't it, my pretty?"

"Tia Juana was bred right here," Carissa said. "Her

dam and sire are both champions."

"How nice," I said. Rochester was a rescue dog, twice over. Caroline had brought him home from a shelter without knowledge of his parentage, and then he had come to live with me.

Carissa picked up Tia Juana and said, "We must go, Rita. Thank you so much. And I will talk to you this week about those mutual funds you suggested."

As she turned to go, a beat-up Japanese sedan pulled up in the driveway and a shaggy-haired young man got out. It took me a minute to recognize him as Felae, my former student, whose artwork Rita hadn't appreciated the night before.

"You are terrible woman!" he shouted, striding toward Rita. "You want to remove my scholarship? How dare you?"

Rita's mouth opened but she didn't say anything.

Rascal and Rochester both began barking, followed by at least a half-dozen other dogs from around the yard. I tugged on Rochester's leash and said, "Hush, dog." Then I looked up. "What's the matter, Felae?"

He turned from facing Rita to me. "Do I know you?"

It was hard talking over all the barking and yapping. I waited until Rick had Rascal quiet, and Carissa had petted Tia Juana into submission.

"Yes, Felae, you do," I said, my exasperation showing. How could he not remember me when I'd been his teacher for a whole semester? "My name is Steve Levitan, and I taught you in the mystery fiction class last spring. And I saw you last night at the art exhibit."

"Oh, yes. Then you know how awful this woman is!"

He turned and shook his fist at her. "I kill you! Right here! With many witnesses!"

Rita pulled a tiny stun gun from the pocket of her skinny jeans. "Come near me and I'll zap you into kingdom come, you little foreign bastard."

The dogs all started barking again. Rick handed me Rascal's leash and stepped forward. "Now, now. Nobody's killing or zapping anyone." He showed his badge to Felae. "I think you should leave, buddy. And forget about making any more crazy threats."

I kept yanking on both dogs' leashes and telling them to be quiet, without much success.

"She try to ruin my life!" Felae yelled. "I hear this morning from college president. She want to have my painting destroyed, my scholarship cancelled. What is next, horrible old woman? Send me back to my country to be killed?"

"Rick, you need to remove this individual from my property," Rita said. She put her stun gun back in her pocket and picked up King Otto. "I won't be harassed at my own home."

"You heard the lady." Rick was wearing a short-sleeved cotton shirt with the tails out, which I knew meant he had his gun in a waist holster. I hoped he didn't have to show it to Felae.

"Sergeant Stemper is right, Felae," I said. "You need to leave, right now."

"You are all toadies of the capitalist hierarchy!" Felae said. "In the new world order you will all suffer."

He turned and strode to his car, slamming the door behind him. Then he gunned the engine and dug a muddy rut through the manicured grass alongside Rita's driveway as he pulled away.

4 – A Happy Little Meeting

Rita stalked off toward her barn, and Carissa, looking shaken, carried Tia Juana toward the parking lot. Rochester and Rascal sat down and shut up as soon as Felae's car turned onto Scammell's Mill Road.

"Want to give the practice ring another go before we leave?" Rick asked.

"Sure." I handed him Rascal's leash, and the dogs jumped up, eager to keep going. They trotted forward, tugging us past the main ring, where Matthew was schooling Calum on the platform, making him remain seated for five beats before rewarding him with a treat.

"It's a good thing these dogs get a lot of exercise, considering all the treats they get," I said.

"You've got to get the miniature ones," Rick said. "If you keep giving Rochester those big ones he'll pork up no matter how often you run him."

"When did you get so smart about dog stuff? You've had Rascal what, four months, and now you're the dog whisperer?"

"I pay attention. Rascal and I watch Cesar Millan together, and all the dog shows on TV." He opened the gate to the training course. "And I read a couple of books."

I shook my head as he put Rascal in position. All I'd done when I got Rochester was ask the vet and the salesman at the pet store a couple of questions about toys and foods. Maybe that's why my dog was so headstrong.

Rick led his Australian shepherd through the training course, and I recognized the genes that had made that breed such a good herder. Rick made the Aussie shepherd stop when he didn't sit on the platform long enough, and do it again, three more times, until he was sure that the dog had the idea. Then they went back to the beginning and ran the course all the way through, and Rascal stayed on the platform the full five beats.

A cool breeze swept across the neighboring fields and raised goose bumps on my arms. Fortunately it also pushed aside the smells of dogs and dung.

I led Rochester into the ring, and this time he sat on command. Maybe Rita had scared him into obedience, or maybe he just knew what he was supposed to do. He still didn't like the weave poles, but I made him stop as soon as he'd run one circle around. I grabbed his collar and dragged him between the poles, in and out. He tried to sit down halfway through but I manhandled him. "I'm the alpha dog in this pack, buddy," I whispered to him. "Get that through your furry head."

He just looked at me with a goofy grin. But he did let me pull him through the poles. We went back to the start, as I'd seen Rick do when he schooled Rascal, and we started to run through again. When we came to the weave poles, Rochester tried to feint around them—but I gave my tongue a loud click, like I'd heard Matthew do.

And what do you know, the dog went right through the weave poles like a champ. He leapt right through the multi-colored plastic ring, and though he faulted over one of the limbo poles, his performance was a big improvement. I rewarded him with an extra treat and a lot of doggie love.

By then the rest of the owners had left, and Rita joined us at the practice ring. "Let me show you my barn. But you'll have to put those boys in your truck because of all the puppies."

Rick and I were as obedient as Rochester had been when Rita barked at him. Rick opened the tailgate to the truck and Rascal jumped right in. "Go on," I said to Rochester. "We won't be long."

He cocked his head, but when I waved my arm toward the truck bed he leapt up beside Rascal, and the two of them settled down next to each other.

Rita had renovated the old barn to serve as a state-of-the art kennel. She led us past the feeding troughs and the pens, which were half under cover and half open to the outside. She bragged about the bloodlines of her dogs, and every pen was lined with photographs of shows and awards. One dachshund bitch had recently given birth, and she was curled up in a big bed, her tiny blind puppies gathered around her.

The barn smelled like dog, but at the same time it was a clean, well-organized building, with rows of shelves of all kinds of products, from dog shampoo to flea control to a wide selection of leashes and collars.

Rita's cell phone rang and she answered, then walked away from us without even a goodbye. Rick and I walked back to his truck, where the dogs were sprawled in the back, both of them sleeping. We climbed in the front and Rick made a perfect K-turn, without touching a blade of Rita's manicured grass.

"I never did get the hang of the K-turn during driver ed," I said.

"Get Rochester to help you," Rick said, as we drove back down toward the river. "He learns fast. It took Rascal at least a week of trying to figure out the weave poles."

I sat back and watched the landscape go by for a while. "Rochester is spoiled, though," I said, as we approached River Bend. "You're right. I've let him think he's the boss."

Rick gave me a sidelong glance. "And he isn't?"

"Is there any reason why he shouldn't be?"

"According to what I've read, dogs misbehave when they don't know their place in the pack hierarchy. When they think they're in charge, they worry about you when you're gone, and that makes them act up. I want Rascal to relax and enjoy being a dog."

"You think Rochester doesn't?"

"If you let him think he's in charge, then he won't be

able to."

"Sometimes I think he's one step ahead of the rest of us," I said. "Look at the way he's been able to find clues."

Rick groaned. "Or he could just have a really good sense of smell." He pulled the truck into my driveway and pushed my shoulder. "Go on, get out. And take your dog. I've got to get home and get ready for a date. I'll email you Rita's training schedule, in case you decide you want to start taking Rochester."

That night I fixed dinner and ate, before I fed Rochester. He slumped on the kitchen floor dejectedly next to my chair, only perking up when I got up and poured out his kibble. "Get used to it," I said to him. "This is the new world order."

He didn't say anything, just scarfed down his food.

* * *

I spoke to Lili that night before I went to sleep. "How was your day?" I asked.

"After you left I slept in, then I worked on the computer for a while, manipulating some photographs I took a few years ago in India."

"India? Wow."

"I was on assignment, photographing children who live in the slums of Mumbai. But Felae's portrait of the dog reminded me of some photos I'd taken of dogs on that trip and I wanted to look at them again. At the time I was too busy to do anything with them, but now I might put something together – kind of as a response to his work."

"Interesting."

"I'm not sure anything will come of it. I often fiddle around for a while with images looking for something I can draw out of them. Anyway, after that I went over to the chapel for a while. Felae didn't show up to move his painting so I had to do it for him."

"I know where he was." I told her how he'd driven to Rita's farm and threatened her.

"Sometimes I wish I was a photojournalist again. Give me a good war, where the lines are drawn. I hate this kind of academic skirmishing."

"Wait til you come up for tenure. Then you'll see some casualties."

"I'll settle for making it through this semester. Thank God this is the last week of classes."

"You think you can break away for lunch one day?" I asked. "Maybe toward the end of the week?"

"We'll talk. Have a good night."

"You too, sweetie. Sleep well."

I looked over at Rochester. "You want to go for a walk before bed?"

He jumped up and nodded his big golden head. I wondered again if I had spoiled him too much, if I was stressing him out by making him think he was in charge. But he always seemed like such a happy dog, even if he was bossy.

We walked down Sarajevo Court, and he grabbed the flattened carcass of a frog in his mouth. I was right on him, prying open his jaws with one hand and grabbing the frog in the other. "That's disgusting, Rochester!" I wiped my hands on my jeans and reminded myself they had to go right into the wash.

* * *

The next morning before I left for work I checked my personal email, and found that Rick had forwarded an email from Rita Gaines with a list of the days and times she provided personal agility training for dogs, as well as when she opened her farm for people who wanted to practice on her courses. She used an online email provider, one that was notorious among the hacker community for shoddy security. Bad idea for someone who thought she was so smart, I thought.

I drove back up to Leighville on my way to work, with Rochester riding shotgun. So many people on the campus knew him that he was like a minor star. Students I didn't even recognize stopped to pet him, and one of the groundskeepers had a treat in his pocket for Rochester as we walked from the parking lot to my office in Fields Hall.

When Caroline was killed and Rochester came to stay with me, I was only working a few hours a week as an adjunct faculty member, and he got accustomed to having me around most of the time. I called him a Velcro dog.

When I accepted the administrative job, six months before, I made sure it was all right to bring Rochester with me to work, even though technically only service dogs were allowed on the Eastern campus. He did provide me a service after all; I was recovering from a bad series of events, and he made me feel more like a person who had a future.

Maybe that was why I had spoiled him so much. Was it time to change the nature of our relationship, making sure he knew that I was the boss? I'd have to convince myself first.

I led Rochester into Fields Hall, and then my office, and he relaxed in his usual position next to the tall french doors that led out to a garden on the side of the building. Then I sat down at my desk to get to work.

Eastern's graduation is always on a Friday, beginning a weekend of events for grads and alumni, and I had a lot of publicity to handle. I was proofreading a couple of posters to hang in the lobby of Fields Hall when Rick called.

"Bad news," he said. "Got called out to Rita Gaines's place this morning. She's dead."

In the background I heard the sound of a tractor, and realized he must still be out at the farm. "Wow. I didn't like her—but I wouldn't have wished her dead." I shivered, as I remembered the last person I'd seen just before his death, my college mentor Joe Dagorian. And then Rochester's former owner, my neighbor Caroline Kelly. I didn't like the idea of knowing so many people who had died while still

31

relatively young. I felt the goosebumps rising on my arms. I rubbed them as I recalled seeing Rita walk away from us the day before, talking on her cell phone.

"How did she die?" I asked. "And when? We saw her yesterday afternoon."

"Not sure yet. Waiting for the coroner's report to give us the means and the time of death, though I'm pretty sure it was at least a few hours after we left her. But I'm going to need the name of that student you talked to yesterday, the one who threatened Rita."

"Felae? You don't think he killed Rita, do you?"

"Right now I'm not thinking, just investigating. How do you spell that name?"

I had to check my archived class roster to get Felae's last name, which I reminded myself was Popescu. I spelled the first and last names for Rick.

"Jesus, whatever happened to names like Robert Smith?" he asked. "At least I shouldn't find too many matches in the system."

"You should call the registrar. They'll have his home address, phone number, email, that kind of thing. And they're the only ones who can give out personal data on students."

I hung up and turned to Rochester, who was lying sprawled on the wooden floor of my office. "You hear that, boy? That nasty woman we met yesterday is dead."

Rochester lifted his head, but didn't say anything.

"She was a bitch, but she loved dogs, so she couldn't be all bad. Don't you think so?"

Once again he declined to comment. Rochester seemed to have a nose for murder. He had helped me, and Rick, find Caroline's killer, and dug up some clues that helped solve a murder on campus, too.

I had to admit that I was a curious guy myself. I pulled out a copy of our college magazine in which I knew the Board of Trustees had been profiled, and read the article on

Rita Stanville Gaines.

She was an Army brat, born in 1946 at a military hospital in Bad Kreuznach, Germany. She had moved around the world with her family, until she was sent to a girls' boarding school in Washington, DC. After she graduated, she enrolled at Eastern College. Then she had gone on to get her MBA in finance at Columbia University.

She began her career on Wall Street as a trainee analyst (read glorified secretary), then worked her way up to a brokerage position, starting her own hedge fund in the glory days of the 1980s. She cashed out when Wall Street was on a high and retired to her farm to train dogs and run a private investment firm.

It was interesting that she and I shared two alma maters—I had my undergraduate degree from Eastern, and an MA in English from Columbia, though I was about twenty years younger than she was. I remembered how blasé she had been about her connection to Eastern when I met her at the art exhibition, and it made me wonder again why she was so involved with the college if she didn't care about it.

I realized that I should probably let President Babson know that Rita was dead, and that one of our students might be a suspect if her death was a homicide. That was going to be a happy little meeting. But I bucked up and stood. "Hold the fort while I'm gone," I said to Rochester. "Don't bother to take any messages, though."

I walked down the narrow hallway, lined with old pen and ink drawings of the campus in the 1880s, and into the executive suite.

"Do you think he'd have a minute for me?" I asked Babson's secretary, an older woman named Bernadette Bridge. She had unnaturally red hair in a sprayed bouffant.

"Mike MacCormac's in with him," she said. "I'll buzz."

That was good. Since Mike was my boss, the director

of alumni relations, I'd be able to kill two birds with one stone.

Oops. Bad cliché.

Bernadette hung up the phone and said, "You can go right in."

Babson was sitting behind his big oak desk when I walked in. He was a tall, rawboned man, with penetrating deep green eyes and dark, curly hair he styled with the greasy kid stuff I had abandoned when I reached puberty.

The office was filled with all the trappings of his presidency. On the walls hung lots of Eastern memorabilia, including old football programs and pennants, interspersed with photos of him with prominent alumni. I recognized Rita Gaines in a photo of Babson with the board.

Mike MacCormac was sitting across from Babson, in a spindle-backed chair with the Eastern logo. He typified the no-neck monster stereotype of college athletes. He was thick-set and muscular, with buzz-cut dark hair and a heavy five o'clock shadow, even early in the morning. At thirty-five, he was seven years younger than I was, shorter and stockier.

"Come in, Steve, sit down." Babson motioned me to the chair next to Mike.

"I got a call from a friend of mine on the Stewart's Crossing Police," I said as I sat down. "Rita Gaines's body was found at her farm this morning."

"Oh, my," Mike said. "I spoke to her last week." His face paled, and Babson's mouth opened in an "O" of shock.

"What a terrible loss," Babson said. "She was a real supporter of Eastern. And she was on our Board of Trustees. Oh, my. We'll have to put out a statement."

"The police don't know the details yet. But there's at least an outside possibility it was murder. I wanted you both to know as soon as possible." I explained about meeting Rita at the art exhibit on Saturday night, and how I had witnessed her complaint about Felae's painting.

"I remember that," Babson said. "I had to ask Dr. Weinstock to take the picture down, as a personal favor to me. When Rita got hold of something she was like a dog with a bone. She wouldn't let go."

"Well, the student in question wasn't happy," I said. "He showed up at her farm on Sunday afternoon and threatened her."

"The police told you that?" Mike asked.

"My friend on the police force has been training his dog at the agility track on Rita's farm, and he took me and Rochester to see the course. We were both there when Felae showed up."

Mike leaned forward. "You're telling me that a police officer witnessed one of our students threaten a member of the Board of Trustees. And then someone murdered her?"

I held up my hand in the universal gesture of *stop*. "We don't know yet that it's murder. The police don't have a cause of death. All I know is that Rick called me a few minutes ago to ask for the student's name and address."

"Who is he?" Babson asked.

"All I gave out was his name-- Felae Popescu. I told Rick that only the registrar is authorized to release personal data on students. I think he grew up somewhere in Eastern Europe, but I don't know if he came to the US with his parents, or on his own."

"This is a very tricky situation," Babson said. "We have to cooperate with the police, and of course we want them to find out who killed Rita, if indeed this turns out to be a murder case. But at the same time we are in *loco parentis* for these students—especially a young man from a foreign country."

The doctrine of loco parentis meant that college administrators had a legal responsibility to look after the students in their care—and that we had to be especially careful in protecting Felae until he was formally arrested and the police took over his custody.

"I'd better speak to Dot," Babson said. He picked up his phone and punched in a number, then drummed his fingers on his desk as he waited for Dorothy Sneiss, the college registrar, to come on the line.

"Dot?" Babson said into the phone. "What do you know about this student—Felix something? Yes, that's it. You did?" He listened. "All right. Keep me informed if the police come back to you for anything else."

He hung up. "She provided the police with the address and phone number she had on file. If they want any information on his academic or disciplinary records, though, they'll have to give us a subpoena."

Mike turned to me. "Can you ask this friend of yours to hold back the details of the investigation from the press? Until they know for sure if her death has any connection to the College?"

"I can ask," I said. "I don't think Rick would release any details of an active investigation anyway."

Babson drummed his fingers on his desk again. "Keep an eye on things, will you, Steve? Let us know if her death ends up having anything to do with Eastern? We had enough bad publicity over Joe Dagorian's death. And draft a statement for me—something about how much we appreciated Rita's support and we express our condolences."

"I'll get right on it." The statement would be easy; it was going to be tougher to convince Rick Stemper to keep me in the loop on his investigation.

5 – Schemes

It was already noon when I left Babson's office, so I detoured to the Cafette, an on-campus sandwich shop in an old carriage house behind Fields Hall. It was a worn, homey-looking place, decorated with Eastern pennants and faded T-shirts, with old wooden picnic tables and benches.

I got extra roast beef on my sandwich so I could share with Rochester. The goofy dog jumped up to greet me as soon as I walked in the door. It was either love, or the smell of the meat. I called Rick and left a message for him, then I peeled open my sandwich. I was about to hand off a piece of meat to Rochester but I remembered what Rick had said. I had to eat my own meal before I fed the dog.

I couldn't hold out, though. After I'd taken a couple of bites I gave into his mournful look and fed him a piece of beef, which he wolfed down greedily. At least he didn't like potato chips, so I had the whole bag to myself.

When I finished eating, I took Rochester out for a quick pee, then returned to my desk to focus on Rita Gaines. I had developed a standard press release for the death of benefactors and emeritus faculty, and I plugged in what I could find about Rita's background and her commitment to Eastern College, and how sad we all were about her death. By one-thirty I had a draft complete, which I emailed to Babson for his review. He emailed me back with the OK, and I sent out the statement to the local media.

I looked at the clock and realized it was time to teach. I jumped up and tossed Rochester a treat, which he gulped immediately. "Stay out of trouble while I'm gone, big guy."

When I returned to Bucks County, Lucas Roosevelt, the chair of the English department, had done me a huge favor and hired me to teach a couple of classes. So when he had called me a few weeks before and asked for a favor in return, I felt I had to oblige. He was in trouble because one of his elderly adjuncts had passed away halfway through the semester, and he had to scramble to find someone to fill in for her.

He asked me to take over her class in professional and technical writing. I'd already taught the class when I was adjuncting, and I had a strong background in tech writing anyway. Teaching made me feel involved in the real work of the college. But more than that, I enjoyed being in the classroom, and especially teaching tech writing. I focused on the concept of audience, and on how material could be presented in a bunch of different ways—in reports, flyers, presentations, and so on. I allowed the students to choose their subjects, as long as the I got to learn about new things every time I taught, from drifting to heart disease to the nutritional requirements for school lunches.

I walked across the campus to Blair Hall, mixing in with the restless tide of students moving between classes. I followed a bushy-haired kid whose T-shirt read "Don't tell anyone, but I'm in the witness protection program."

Most of Blair Hall was dark and gloomy, with tall, gothic-arched windows and dusty fluorescent lights hung on pendants. The classrooms had rich wooden wainscoting and scuffed floors, and I had fond memories of seminars in the small rooms on the third floor, a professor and a handful of students discussing the meaning of life and literature.

At least that's the way I remember it. My classmates and I were probably as uncommunicative as today's students, and our professors must have felt like brain surgeons, probing our heads for any spark of intelligence.

My class met in a first-floor computer lab in an addition at the back of the building that hadn't been there when I was a student. Tall windows looked out on a walkway between buildings, letting in a flood of spring sunshine. Computers lined the perimeter of the room. I walked up to the teaching podium and turned on the computer and projector.

About twenty students either sat at the terminals or at a couple of round tables in the middle of the room. "Hey, everybody," I said, as I waited for the equipment to warm up. "You all eager for the end of the semester?

There was general agreement. It was time for the students to present their PowerPoint presentations, so instead of teaching, I got to sit back and listen. I moved to one of the round tables and dropped my bag, then asked Lou Segusi, one of the stronger students, to close all the blinds.

"Who wants to go first?" I asked.

Barbara Seville, a petite blonde, raised her hand, then teetered up to the podium on very high heels. When I began teaching the class, right after the midterm break, she had been a bubbly girl, a member of the Booster Club who was always willing to raise her hand with a comment. Because of the death of the woman I'd replaced, Barbara had gone through a lot of emotional upset during the term, and for the last few weeks she'd been very quiet, just keeping her head down and doing her work. I felt bad for her and tried to cut her a break when I could.

Her presentation was on schizophrenia, and it was marked how her demeanor had changed from earlier in the term. She kept her head down as she spoke, so that we all had to strain to hear her. At least her slides were colorful and filled with information.

Yudame (pronounced you-dummy), a skinny boy with a wild bush of hair that varied in shade from blond to brown, followed her with a business presentation. With his tie-dyed T-shirt and Birkenstock sandals, he looked more like an escapee from the 1960s than the kind of kid who'd be leaving Eastern on a direct path to an Ivy League MBA, but you never know these days.

That reminded me of Rita Gaines. As Yudame fumbled with his jump drive, and then getting the presentation going, I wondered what kind of a student Rita had been. Her abrasive personality made me think she'd been talkative in class, even argumentative.

Yudame's presentation began with an animation of angels flapping their wings and strumming harps while flying over Wall Street, which got the class's attention. "I'm going to talk today about people called angel investors," he began.

His next slide popped up, a mockup of a stock certificate for Facebook. "Angel investors aren't creatures from the Bible; they're rich people who provide startup capital for small businesses, in the hopes that they will get big payoffs."

He went on to explain the way an individual or small group might come up with an idea for a product or service, but need money to get it off the ground. "Usually an inventor starts with money from the three F's: friends, family and fools." He paused for a laugh.

"Once the business has shown it has some potential, the inventor turns to outside sources of capital. But venture capital companies like the big Wall Street firms like to see a real product and a record of earnings before they pour millions of dollars in. That gap is filled by angel investors."

I was surprised to see Rita Gaines's photo pop up on the screen. "One of the most prominent local angel investors was an Eastern College alumnus named Rita Gaines. She passed away recently but she made a lot of investments in high-tech companies."

I had read a bit about Rita's investments in her obituaries, and I was pleased that Yudame had done enough research to discover her, and that he was savvy enough to include her in his presentation. And sensitive enough not to add angel wings to her photo.

We made it through half the presentations that day,

with the rest scheduled for Wednesday. As I was walking out, Lou Segusi said, "Hey, Prof, can I talk to you?"

I picked up my bag. "I need to get back to my office. Can you talk on the way to Fields Hall?"

"Sure." He hesitated, then jumped in. "So, I've been doing this tutoring gig at the Writing Lab, like I'm supposed to."

He had been pressured into writing papers for a couple of other students, and while they had been expelled I had argued on his behalf, and he had agreed to volunteer for tutoring in the lab, which helped students improve their writing.

"How's that going?" I asked, as we walked outside.

"Real good, real good. But there is this problem."

"Hey! Lou!"

We both turned at the sound of a young woman's voice. She was a voluptuous brunette with skin the color of very light coffee. "Oh, hey, Des," he said.

He turned to me. "This is Desiree."

I nodded. Lou had been sneaking around with Desiree earlier in the term, and when her boyfriend found out, he'd broken Lou's arm. All part of the drama of undergraduate life; I remembered a number of similar incidents when I was a student.

"This is Professor Levitan," Lou said to Desiree. "The one I told you about."

Desiree came up to Lou and snuggled under his arm. I noticed it was the one that hadn't been broken. "Listen, I'll talk to you about that later, Prof," Lou said. "Thanks."

"Sure. You know where my office is."

They turned away from me, and I wondered what Lou's problem was. I hoped it wasn't going to involve police action—as his previous problems had. I'd had enough of that.

When I got back to my office I still hadn't heard from Rick, so I called and left another message. I spent the rest of the afternoon coordinating details for an alumni reception during graduation weekend. Mike was hoping to put together a group he wanted to solicit for major gifts for the capital campaign, and I knew everything had to be perfect.

As I was shutting down my computer for the day, Rick finally called. "Got your messages but I've been swamped all day. You up for a beer tonight? We can talk about whatever you want then."

"Sure. Let me take Rochester home, and I'll meet you at the Drunken Hessian around six. We can get a couple of burgers."

Spring was bursting out all over campus as Rochester and I walked back to my car, and I could see that the Building and Grounds department had been busy prettying up the place in advance of graduation. Tulips, daffodils and hyacinths bloomed in big clay pots, the grass was neatly trimmed, and new, darker asphalt covered the winter's potholes.

Rochester stopped several times to sniff and pee, and I enjoyed the fresh evening air. Around us, students hurried from dorms to libraries lugging rolling suitcases full of textbooks. The palpable sense of urgency and desperation around us probably had to do with final exams coming up.

A pair of students passed us as we were entering the parking lot. "I can't believe he's going to fail me," a girl in a Burberry skirt cried. "I went to every class. Just because I didn't write the papers."

"These professors are assholes," her friend said. "They have no sense of priorities. I tried to explain to my organic chemistry professor about James getting tickets for the Squashed Mushrooms concert on Monday night in Philadelphia, and asked if I could take the final exam some other day. He stared at me like I was crazy."

I'd heard many similar stories from my own students, and I had probably said the same kind of thing when I was an undergrad. I refrained from commenting to either girl.

That reminded me of Lou Segusi, and I wondered again what his problem was. I hoped he hadn't gone farther than he was supposed to with his tutoring, writing the papers for students he was supposed to be helping with grammar and structure.

Then Rochester strained ahead, and reminded me what my real priority was. Taking care of one very bossy golden retriever.

6 – The Drunken Hessian

Once Rochester had been emptied and refilled, I left to meet Rick at the Drunken Hessian, a bar in the center of Stewart's Crossing. It had the oldest continuous liquor license in the county, and looked like it hadn't been redecorated since Lucius Stewart started his ferry crossing business in the late 1700s. At least they kept up to date with their beer selection; they had the best range of microbrews in Bucks County.

"Did you get hold of Felae?" I asked when we were seated at a booth in the back.

Rick shook his head. "College has an address for him in an old house at the far end of Leighville, but the housemates say he moved out a year ago. Nobody liked him, so no one kept in touch with him. He doesn't have an account with PECO for gas or electric, he doesn't own property, and the address listed with Verizon for his cell phone service is a post office box."

I picked up my Dogfish Head Midas Touch ale and sampled it. I knew that it was made from ingredients found in King Midas's tomb, and had a sweet, yet dry flavor that was halfway between beer and mead. "Students move around a lot."

"Especially students with an FBI file." Rick was drinking the 90 Minute IPA, and I had to wait until he'd taken a healthy swig to hear more. "Seems like Mr. Popescu has been very active with animal rights groups. He's been arrested for protesting outside animal shelters, and he's a suspect in a break-in at a pharmaceutical lab that tests products on rabbits."

"And the FBI is involved in that?"

"They consider it domestic terrorism," Rick said. "They've got a whole task force keeping tabs on people just like your student."

"Former student. Hey, you know, he used to work at the Hungry Horse in Leighville as a server, but I haven't seen him there in a while. Maybe they have an address for him."

He pulled out a spiral notepad and wrote the restaurant's name down. "Remember when that was?"

"Sometime during the winter. Not that long ago."

I drank some more beer. "What's going to happen to all Rita's dogs?"

"She had an arrangement with another breeder," he said. "Guy from the horse country in North Jersey. He's coming down to pack up the dogs. In the meantime her neighbor is taking care of them."

I sat back and looked around me. The ceiling lights advertising various beers glowed dimly, and the wooden booths were scarred with centuries of names, hearts and epithets. I wouldn't have been surprised to see a George ♥ Martha somewhere.

Our burgers arrived. I got mine with ham and cheese, accompanied by curly fries. Rick was a purist; he ordered the quarter-pound burger with no garnish at all, and a trough of onion rings. "You can't taste the beef if you cover it up with all that crap," he said.

"Who says I want to taste the beef here?"

"Hey, I've been eating these burgers since high school and I'm still here."

"You used to come here in high school?" I asked. "Even though the drinking age was twenty-one?"

"With my parents. My dad loved the burgers. And when my mom wasn't looking he'd let me have some of his beer."

Rick looked over at my burger. "How can you eat it so bloody?"

"It's medium," I said. "Pink. Not bloody. Yours is burned beyond recognition."

"At least I know it's dead. And speaking of blood, we got the autopsy results back on Rita Gaines late this afternoon," he said. "Very strange."

"That's gross. You talk about my burger and then you go right into autopsy results."

He laughed. "You know you want to hear all about it. Your junior investigator badge is glowing right now."

Rick had teased me in the past about my interest in investigating murders. But honestly, I grew up reading mystery novels, from *Freddy the Detective* to the Hardy Boys to the classic British authors like Agatha Christie and Dorothy L. Sayers.

I feigned nonchalance. He could tease me if he wanted—but I'd wait him out until he couldn't resist telling me what I wanted to hear. I ate a hunk of burger, listened the jukebox play a Springsteen song, and then asked, "How's Rascal?"

"He's okay. You'd think all that running around yesterday would have tired him out. But no such luck."

"You need get him some sheep to herd. They could keep your grass cut for you."

"Can't raise livestock on less than two acres," he said. "You need a farm like Rita's."

I put my burger down. "All right, I give up. I do want to know about what you found out. What was weird about her autopsy?"

"She had a high level of flunitrazepam in her blood. You know what that is?"

"Am I wearing a white coat? Do I have an MD after my name?"

"Don't get snotty." He picked up a couple of french fries and nibbled on them. One of the waitresses passed by carrying a platter of cheesesteaks oozing sautéed onions and spray cheese, curly fries spiraling off the plates.

"Are we playing twenty questions? Is it some kind of sleeping pill? Did she commit suicide?"

He swallowed the fries and leaned closer to me across the scarred wooden tabletop. "It wasn't suicide. The brand name is Rohypnol, but on the street they're called roofies."

"The date rape drug? Somebody raped her?"

"Keep your voice down," Rick said. "There was no evidence of rape. It looks like someone slipped her a couple of roofies to knock her out. But that's not what killed her."

Rick picked up his bottle and drained it.

I wanted to kick him under the table. "Come on, don't keep me in suspense. What did her in?"

"You won't believe this. Cobra venom."

"Are you kidding? Do we have poisonous snakes in Bucks County? Cobras? I thought they were only in India."

"Join the club. I asked the medical examiner if he was sure. Got my ear reamed out, including a list of where he had gone to school and every certification he has in pathology."

"You think a cobra was out at her farm? Underfoot when we were there?"

I shivered. What if Rochester had stumbled on a poisonous snake while he was running around the farm?

He shook his head. "She wasn't bitten. Doc found a puncture wound in her wrist. Looks like the killer injected the venom directly into her vein with a hypodermic needle."

"So it was murder?"

"Looks like it."

"Then it should be easy to figure out who did it," I said, sitting back against the hard wood of the booth. They probably don't sell cobra venom at your ordinary drugstore. Or even veterinary supply place. Can't you trace who bought it?"

"It's not legal to sell, though you can buy a cobra and milk it if you want the stuff. And if you know someone who has a cobra…"

"Why would you? As an antidote for snake bites?"

"Beats me."

"Any idea who could have killed her?" I asked. "Strictly off the record, of course."

He shook his head. "You're not a journalist, Steve, so there's no record in the first place. And in the second place, it's way too early. I need to find Mr. Popescu, and I need to look some more into Rita's life and her business and see if anyone else has a motive. I won't even start speculating until I have all that under my belt."

"Party pooper," I said.

"Hey, remember, we're talking about a dead woman here. A woman you talked to yesterday. This isn't some murder mystery novel or TV detective program."

"I remember. I still think of Caroline sometimes. And reminders of Joe Dagorian are all over Fields Hall." Both of them had been killed in the past, and in both cases Rochester and I had been involved in the investigation.

We both passed on dessert. Cake, pie and ice cream had become the latest casualties in my war against a creeping paunch. Crossing over forty had been a kind of Rubicon for me. I was in prison in California for that birthday, and I made a lot of extravagant promises to myself then, most of which I hadn't kept. I was going to exercise more, eat better, color between the lines and keep my nose clean. I'd danced close to the edge a few times but I was still free, and that was what mattered most.

I met regularly with my parole officer, Santiago Santos, and he did his best to help me avoid cyber temptation and the lure of snooping in online places I didn't belong. And having a best friend who was a cop was a definite help.

We split the check and threaded our way between the wooden booths and the packed tables to the back door, then out into the spring air, that much fresher for the contrast to the fustiness and spilled-beer smell of the bar.

"See you," Rick said, as we reached our cars.

"Remember, don't burn your bridges—there might be crocodiles in the river."

"Words to live by," I said.

7 – Preventer of Information Technology

The *New York Times* dedicated a couple of inches to Rita Gaines' obituary—with no mention of murder, just that she had been found dead at her farm. I was impressed at the Fortune 500 CEOs who knew her and contributed reminiscences. I was pleased to see a mention that she had graduated from Eastern and served on the Board of Trustees.

I tried to keep track of every time Eastern came up in the media. I had a Google alert set up to tell me whenever we were mentioned online, but most of those were useless, simply directions to student blogs. But that morning the list was long, as many different papers and websites picked up the obit from wire services. I copied the obits and put them into a file I labeled with Rita's name.

When I finished, I started work on the first of a series of profiles of graduating students, part of my promotional efforts tied to graduation. Mike hoped to use them as an incentive to get alumni to fund more scholarships.

Faye Tallity had spent the summer between her junior and senior year volunteering with a group that searched for unexploded land mines in Cambodia. In her spare time, she sang lead with an all-girl band called The Thin Mints, which played a lot of campus events. Their music was heavily based in punk, and they dressed in Girl Scout uniforms pierced with safety pins, with their hair dyed bright colors. Faye wrote most of the band's music, which tended toward the nihilistic, at least based on what I saw of them on YouTube. They had also put out a self-published album on iTunes, which was selling well in the punk category.

I opened a video clip of The Thin Mints playing, "Just Shoot Me" and Rochester sat up and barked. "It's only a song, boy," I said. "Go back to sleep."

He slumped to the floor, and a reminder popped up on my computer. I was due at a meeting to discuss graduation. I left Rochester snoozing and walked around to the registrar's office at the front of the building.

Dot Sneiss, whom President Babson had spoken to about Felae's records, was the college official in charge of registration, student records, and matriculation requirements. She chaired the committee, which was composed of a half-dozen members of the faculty and staff. She was a plump, motherly woman with fading brown hair, wearing a pink cardigan over her white blouse.

Her staff worked in an office suite on the first floor of Fields Hall, down the hall and around the corner from mine. When I walked into the conference room there, she was wiping down the white board. "I understand the Stewart's Crossing police called you for Felae Popescu's address," I said.

"I gave him what I had," she said, turning to face me. "Unfortunately about ten to fifteen percent of our records are out of date at any one time. Students are supposed to update address, phone and email when they register each term, but some of them don't."

"So it's not necessarily suspicious that his info is out of date?"

She shook her head. "If every student who didn't keep up with us was dangerous we'd be overwhelmed with crime in Leighville."

The next to arrive was Dr. Jim Shelton from the History Department. As Commencement Marshal, he kept the students in line, organized the faculty procession and carried the mace, a ceremonial staff topped with the Eastern logo, a rising sun. He was about five years older than I was, a genial heavyset man with a salt-and-pepper beard. It was hard to get faculty members to serve on a committee whose responsibilities ran into final exam week; most were busy grading papers then.

But Jim was chair of his department, which meant he only taught one class. He was also chair of the Faculty Senate, and he preferred college politics to academic research and publication. His kids were in their early twenties, and he had no grandchildren to spoil.

Right behind him was Dr. Fred Searcy from the biology department. In the sciences, at least at Eastern, most exams are multiple choice, slid through a machine that grades them automatically, leaving Fred free for committee service if he chose.

He was a slim sixty-something guy in a white lab coat, totally bald, with a friendly smile. I'd seen him working with students and been impressed with the passion he had for his subject and the ease he had in communicating it. He had helped me out a few months before when I was looking for information on a rare plant. I walked over to him. "Hey, Fred, I'm trying to find out some information about cobra venom."

"You'd need Dr. Conrad," he said. "She teaches Anatomy and Physiology, and our one course in Zoology. If anybody can help you, she can."

"Her office in Green Hall?" It was the oldest classroom building on campus and the least "green" of any of our buildings. One of the main targets of the capital campaign was a new building for the physical sciences, with up-to-date computer-equipped labs.

"Down the hall from mine. You can't miss it. Diagrams of the body systems on the wall around her door."

"Thanks. I'll have to check out her office hours."

"I can do that for you," he said, as we sat down at the big conference table. He pulled out a smart phone and typed with amazing speed. "Her office hours are from two to five this afternoon," he said.

I shook my head. "That's cool."

"Gotta keep up with the times."

The rest of the committee was made up of administrative types like me, including a couple of staffers from student advising, a guy from Eastern's Investment Office, and Verri M. Parshall, a woman I liked to call The Preventer of Information Technology, though her official title was Associate Dean for Technology and Information Systems. She was a classic example of the Peter Principle; she had worked her way up from a data entry operator back when the college kept its records on punch cards, and in my opinion she was scared of any new technology. It was funny that Fred was more comfortable with high-tech than she was.

Dot Sneiss stepped up and called the meeting to order then. "Verri, there seems to be a bug with the program that audits student graduation requests," she said. "Students are complaining that they need the most recent version of Internet Explorer to access it."

Verri was in her mid-fifties, and everything about her was brisk and no-nonsense, from her short, gray-brown hair to her man-tailored pants suits. "Then they need to download it. It's free."

"But that version is still very shaky on the Mac," Jim Shelton said. "I had a student show me the problem he was having."

"The Macintosh is not part of the college's supported hardware package," Verri said. "We've installed computers all over campus for students who don't have their own PCs."

"The ones in the lobby outside our office are always breaking down," one of the staffers from student services said. I was pretty sure her name was Shireen, but her long dark hair blocked her name tag, so it could have been Shirley, too. "Students keep complaining to our office staff."

"Then your staff needs to put in a service request."

"We do that, almost every day," Shir-something said. "But you need to manage your equipment better."

"I'm happy to remove the computers from your lobby if you prefer," Verri said, pointing outside. She wore no jewelry beyond a plain watch, and no polish on her fingernails. She probably used a DOS-based computer, too. No fancy icon-based systems for her. "Frankly I'd be happiest if we restricted on-campus computer use to as few people as possible."

"You can take that up separately," Dot said. "Let's get back on track here."

She explained the process of degree audits; apparently the online system wasn't working properly, so each student who wanted to graduate would have to schedule an appointment with an advisor.

"There's no way we can meet with every graduating student in the next two weeks," Shir-something protested. "Verri, can't you make the system work properly?"

"I don't appreciate your personal attacks," Verri said. "If you have a problem, you need to call the help desk and put in a ticket."

"The help desk phone number is always busy," Jim Shelton said. "I call at least once a week with a problem in my office or in a classroom. All I get is a recorded message telling me to send an email."

Verri looked at him like he was stupid. "If you and the rest of the faculty didn't make so many requests, we wouldn't be so overwhelmed."

"They aren't requests, Verri," he said. "If you maintained the computers on campus better, or you let faculty download programs they need, we wouldn't be calling you all the time."

"I have more productive things to do than listen to your gripes." Verri stood up. "Dot, you can email me meeting notes with anything you need from my department."

"My email address is corrupted," Dot said. "I've been waiting three days for a tech to come to my office and fix it."

"Put in another request," Verri said. "I can't do anything for you unless you go through the proper channels."

She turned and strode out of the conference room. The foam rubber soles of her orthopedic shoes squeaked on the hardwood floors. "Well," Dot said, sighing. "Where were we?"

It was Phil Berry's turn next. He was an African-American guy in his mid-thirties with close-cropped black hair and skin the color of milk chocolate, a financial geek who had worked at one of the big Wall Street firms and escaped before it imploded. Now he managed the college's investments. Most of the time I could barely follow him because of all the financial jargon.

He pulled out his BlackBerry and punched a couple of keys.

Okay, Phil Berry was black, and he had a BlackBerry. I suppressed a giggle as he started to speak. Dot had given him the responsibility for coordinating our commencement speakers, and for once I understood everything he said.

The meeting dragged on all morning and I started to wonder if we were ever going to finish. A few minutes before noon, Fred Searcy said, "Sorry, folks, I have a class."

He stood up. Dot Sneiss said, "I think we've covered everything. I'll send out the meeting notes and then we'll reconvene in a week."

I walked out with Fred. "I don't really have a class," he said. "But Dot will go on all day if you let her. I need my lunch."

I laughed, and continued down the hall to my own office. As soon as I walked in the door, Rochester jumped up and nuzzled me. "You want to go for a quick walk?"

He went into the downward-facing dog yoga position, always an indication that he was ready to play, and I hooked up his leash. I opened the french doors and we walked out into the chilly sunshine.

We strolled around the azaleas, blossoming in shades of red and purple. A bee buzzed around the blossoms of a honeysuckle that grew on a wooden trellis. While Rochester sniffed the fresh mulch laid around the newly trimmed boxwood hedges, I sat on a wrought iron bench.

Despite the aggravation of working in a complex organization, I liked my job, and I thrived on the energy and enthusiasm of a college campus. Sure, I worked with some difficult people—like Verri Parshall; the idiot in the payroll department who screwed up the direct deposit of my paycheck; and a bunch of the faculty, who sometimes seemed to forget that the students were our whole reason for being at Eastern.

Which reminded me of Rita Gaines, and made me wonder again what she was doing on the Board of Trustees. Why was she wasting her time with us, if she didn't care about students or have fond memories of Eastern? Was there something good underneath the hard surface she showed to the world?

Rochester circled back and hopped up on the bench. He rested his head in my lap. "What do you think, boy?" I asked. "Was Rita Gaines a good person because she liked dogs?"

Suddenly he sat bolt upright, then lunged off the bench. I grabbed his extendable leash just in time to keep him from chasing a squirrel with a death wish all through the campus, though it felt like my arm had been jerked out of its socket in the process.

Maybe he wasn't so focused on crime-solving as I thought.

8 – Anatomy and Physiology

I picked up a sandwich from one of the food trucks at the bottom of the hill, then spent my lunch hour at my desk transferring "To do" list items from my pad into my office computer and my iPhone. Sadly, the two can't talk to each other because I'd have to get the Preventer of Information Technology to allow a tech to come to my office and install the relevant software. She told me she didn't "see the necessity as reflected in the college's priority statements for informational technology." That's bureaucrat speak for "leave me alone, jerkwad."

I know that language well, because I spent close to ten years, right up to my unfortunate incarceration, in the corporate world myself. If I wanted, I probably could have hacked into my desktop computer and installed the software myself—but I had promised Santiago Santos and Mike MacCormac that I'd keep my nose clean.

Rochester was bored by my concentration on the computer, and he got up and nosed against my leg. I had gotten to know his moods, so I knew this was a "play with me" moment, rather than a "take me outside" one. What the hell, I couldn't do anything on the computer until the sync process was finished.

I grabbed a blue plastic ball from my top drawer and squeezed it. It let out a couple of little shrieks that drove Rochester wild, and I tossed it across the room. He scampered after it, his toenails clicking on the wood floor. He grabbed the ball in his mouth and made it squeak again. "Bring me the ball," I said.

He ignored me. Every couple of seconds the ball would slip out of his mouth, and he'd grab it again. "Fine, be that way," I said. "I have work to do."

I looked at my to-do list. Next up was another

graduating student profile, this one of Boris Oxhoff, a business major who had done an independent study project during his junior year on microfinance, the practice of loaning small amounts of money to entrepreneurs in the developing world and other economically deprived locations.

During the summer break between his junior and senior year, Boris had run his own microfinance project in North Philadelphia. He began raising money with a series of yard sales, asking Eastern students for their castoffs. Then he caught the attention of a wealthy alumnus who staked him to ten grand.

Boris loaned $250 to an immigrant from Senegal who wanted to start her own tailoring business. He advanced $500 to a guy who did yard maintenance in the Northeast and who needed a new lawn mower. Boris had his own website, with a whole list of those whom he had helped, accompanied by their testimonials. According to the spreadsheet he posted there, 95% of his loans were being paid off regularly; the remaining five percent had been written off due to serious illness or death of the recipient.

I admired him, as I did all the other graduates I was profiling. When I was an Eastern senior on the verge of leaving Leighville, I was like a blind puppy newly weaned, with no real sense of the world or where I would fit in it. I had contributed nothing to the world and had no idea where my true talents were.

What were they, anyway? Like Rochester, I had a nose for crime—only mine was usually on the wrong side of the law. I could follow the logic of code until I found a place where I could slip past a host computer's defenses, where I could assume a user's identity, access passwords or other forbidden information. I had never used that ability for malicious purposes, but I knew that I could.

Fortunately, I hadn't discovered that ability until I had the maturity to handle the knowledge. Perhaps my ex-wife and my parole officer might dispute that—but if I'd been a teenager in today's environment, and figured out how to hack, I know I'd have gotten into much more trouble. I seriously doubt I'd have had the maturity or insight to have turned out like Faye Tallity or Boris Oxhoff.

I finished the profile on Boris, then caught up on my email inbox. By then Rochester had given up on the squeaky ball and gone back to sleep. I retrieved the plastic ball, wiped the saliva off it, and put it back in my desk drawer.

Around three o'clock I walked back over to Green Hall to talk to Dr. Jackie Conrad about cobra venom. The last time I took biology was in high school, so I could barely make sense of the posters outside her office.

She was talking to a student about the way the blood pumped through the heart, so I waited out in the hall until she was finished. When the young woman left, I stuck my head in her door. "Dr. Conrad? Dr. Searcy suggested I talk to you. My name is Steve Levitan."

"Have a seat." She motioned me to the chair across from her desk. Her office was littered with textbooks, piles of papers, and small furry hand puppets in strange shapes. She was fifty-something, with an open, friendly face, framed with blonde curls, and I hoped she wouldn't close up when I asked her about a poison.

"You look too old to be a student and too young to be a parent. What can I do for you?"

"I work in the alumni relations office, but my question has nothing to do with the college." I explained about Rita Gaines' murder and the use of the cobra venom.

"I met her," Dr. Conrad said. "About a year ago. The science faculty did a meet and greet with the Board of Trustees. She was a dog breeder, wasn't she? And if I can say it without speaking too ill of the dead, wasn't she something of a bitch herself?"

"You've got that. Any idea where somebody could get

cobra venom? And how common it would be?"

"Cobra venom." She thought for a minute. "Of course, she was a dog breeder."

That connection made no sense to me, but it seemed to turn a light bulb on over Dr. Conrad's head. She turned back to her computer and started typing. "I used to be a vet," she said. "Long ago, when we were still treating woolly mammoths for broken legs and tooth decay. We used cobra venom for something... I just can't remember what."

While she typed, I looked more closely at her furry hand puppets. They weren't little teddy bears or pigs or even any animal I recognized. The closest to anything I knew was a fuzzy tan oval with brown tentacles—it looked like a mutant jellyfish.

She kept typing, muttering to herself, opening and closing windows. "There it is!" she said in triumph. "Acral lick granuloma."

Once again I thanked my lucky stars I had never had an interest in science. "Excuse me?"

She turned back toward me, and the breeze created by her chair moving rattled the bones of the plastic skeleton hanging behind her. "Cobra venom is a powerful neurotoxin that acts as a painkiller when administered in small quantities. We used to use it to treat something called an acral lick granuloma. You have a dog, don't you? Collie or golden retriever?"

"A golden. How did you know?"

"The fine hairs on your slacks. At a glance it looked like one of those two breeds." She looked up. "Imagine your dog gets a tiny sore, say on his paw, and he licks it. Putting medication doesn't help, and it starts to spread, and the skin around the area gets thick, scarred and irritated. That's an acral lick granuloma."

"Yuck."

"It's very tough to handle. You end up with little

pockets of bacteria, broken hair follicles, plugged and scarred oil glands and dilated and inflamed capillaries. If you surgically remove them, the dog just licks at the sutures or incision line after the surgery heals and creates a brand new granuloma right where the original one was."

"Sounds terrible."

"It is. Some theories say that the dog's focus on licking it is psychological, and today vets prescribe anti-anxiety drugs to stop the licking, and antibiotics to clear up the sores. But back in the day, we used cobra venom to numb the nerves and shut out the pain."

I shivered, thinking what would happen if poor Rochester ever had one of those. I was sure it would drive both of us crazy.

I picked up one of the puppets. It looked like a plush gray crab with a starfish attached on a long, nobby cord. I thought Rochester would destroy it in about sixty seconds.

"I keep those around in case I need an extra brain cell," she said, holding another of them up to her head and wiggling it so the starfish part bobbed up and down. She turned the label toward me. "See? It's a brain cell."

"I could use a few of those myself."

"I use it in class. This is e-coli," she said, holding up the fuzzy oval with the tentacles. "And these? They're gonorrhea microbes." She showed me a handful of little fuzzy blobs with eyes. "You don't want to have these hanging around your system."

"Certainly not."

"Where were we? Oh, cobra venom. Your victim might have used cobra venom in the past for a problem, and still had some around her kennel."

"Not *my* victim," I said. "Just a kind of – victim."

I thanked Dr. Conrad. "I'll bet if you were teaching here when I was a student I'd have liked science."

"Back when you were a student the kids came to college better prepared," she said. "But thank you for the compliment."

On my way back to my office I called Rick. "Did you find any cobra venom at Rita's farm?"

"When we did the search we didn't know the cause of death. I need to get back up to the farm later."

I told him what I'd learned from Jackie Conrad. "Rita probably had some of the venom in her kennel. Want Rochester and me to meet you there?"

Rick groaned. "Come on, Steve, you're not a detective."

"But you know Rochester has a unique talent for this kind of thing. And don't you want to get this case solved?"

I waited. It was almost like I could hear him thinking through the phone. Finally he said, "Nobody else can know about me taking you out there."

"Of course not. And it's not an active crime scene any more, right? You've already been through the place."

"I'll meet you at five-thirty. We should still have enough light."

I started to say something else, but he said, "You should hang up before I realize what a dumb idea this is and change my mind."

I did what he suggested.

Green Hall was at the far side of the campus, near the football stadium, and since it was such a nice afternoon I took a detour in that direction. I felt guilty that I didn't have Rochester with me; I rarely took a walk without him. But this once I'd let myself get away with it.

One of the guys in my dorm freshman year was a football recruit, and many of from that dorm I maintained a friendship through all four years, which meant I saw a lot of football games as an undergraduate. I remembered those fall Saturdays well—the crisp autumn afternoons, the cheers I knew by heart, the camaraderie of my fellow students.

A soccer field stood next to the stadium, bracketed on

two sides by bleachers like the ones at my high school. Beyond it was a big grassy lot where students played pickup games of football, baseball and volleyball, and right next to that was one of the big student parking lots.

I wandered around for a while, then returned to my office, where I sent an email to President Babson updating him on the status of the investigation into Rita Gaines's death—I didn't have much to report, but at least the papers hadn't figured out it was a murder, or that Felae Popescu was a suspect. I was considering what else I had to do that day when Lou Segusi rapped on the door jamb of my office. Rochester woofed once in greeting, but didn't get up.

"Hey, Prof, got a minute?"

"Sure, Lou, come on in."

He wore an Eastern hoodie and jeans, and slouched in the spindle-backed chair across from my desk. "What's the problem you wanted to talk about yesterday?" I asked.

"Well, it's not my problem, really. It's this other guy's."

"Uh-huh."

"No, really, it's his. He works for the help desk."

"Oh, God. Not with Verri M. Parshall. That must be a nightmare."

"Yeah, that's kind of his problem."

I remembered dealing with Lou earlier in the term, when he was having his own troubles, and how difficult it was to pull information out of him. "And?"

"It's really stressing him out, and he's falling behind in his assignments, which is why he came to the Writing Lab," Lou said. "It's not that he can't write, he just can't focus with all this crap going on."

"I'm not following you, Lou. And it's getting late, and I've got a meeting tonight."

"Oh, like AA or something?"

I cocked my head and looked at him. "Are you

completely nuts? Whatever meeting I have is none of your business." I flashed on big-mouthed Lou telling all his friends that his Prof was in Alcoholics Anonymous and hurried to add, "Although to be clear I don't belong to any twelve-step program."

"Sorry, my bad. Anyway, this guy Dustin. He doesn't know what to do. But I told him you were cool and totally tuned in to the administration, and you had helped me."

"Lou, I still don't understand what Dustin's problem is."

"I'll let him explain it. Can I have him come by here tomorrow?"

I looked at my watch. It was time for me to leave for Rita's farm so I had to get Lou out of my office. "Sure. I'll be here."

"Very cool. Thanks, Prof!"

He jumped up and hurried out, showing more animation than I'd seen in a while. I shook my head. I had no idea what Dustin's problem was, but hopefully he'd be easier to talk to than Lou.

I loaded Rochester into my old BMW sedan, but instead of driving down to the Delaware and taking River Road south, I headed out a long, winding road I knew would take us close to Rita's farm. He leaned out the window, sniffing the fresh air and occasionally woofing at something we passed.

When I was in high school, I was active in a lot of clubs—the newspaper, the literary magazine, and the miniature golf team. At least a couple of days a week I had to take the late bus home.

Our regular school bus made the trip from Stewart's Crossing to the high school in about twenty minutes. Our driver picked up kids from our neighborhood, The Lakes, then got on the highway that went to Levittown. But the late bus ranged a lot farther, taking curving country lanes lined with farms and fields. By the time I got my driver's license I knew most of the back roads and where they went.

When I returned to Stewart's Crossing after nearly twenty years away, I found the landscape had changed a lot. New developments had taken the place of farms, and wooded fields had been replaced by shopping centers. The 18th-century stone farmhouses had been renovated and locked behind high, wrought-iron gates, and many of the stop signs had been replaced by traffic lights.

But the old country roads still existed, though many had been upgraded and expanded, and I found my way to Rita's farm with only a single wrong turn. Rochester and I arrived a few minutes early, and instead of seeing Rick's cruiser I noted that a beat-up pickup was pulled up next to the barn.

As I stepped out of the car, I heard a cacophony of barking. Then a grizzled older man with a smashed-in nose stepped out of the barn with a rifle over his shoulder.

"This is private property," he said. "Get out now before I shoot your ass."

9 – Roofing

Rochester started jumping around and barking inside the car. I held my hands up in front of me. "Hold on. I'm meeting Sergeant Stemper from the Stewart's Crossing police. He should be here any minute."

"For what purpose?"

"He's investigating Rita Gaines' death. I brought up my dog to help him look around."

I pointed to the car, where Rochester had stopped barking, but had his front paws up on the dashboard and was watching us closely.

"That's all right then," the old man said. "Don Kashane."

For a minute I thought he had switched to German, but then I realized that was his name.

"I live down the road. I stopped by to make sure the dogs were all fed and exercised, and hose down the barn."

He looked like he'd stepped out of *Green Acres* or some other parody of farm life, wearing a pair of denim overalls and a plaid, long-sleeved shirt, with a white undershirt poking out at the neck.

"Steve Levitan." I shook his hand, then nodded toward the car. "Mind if I let my dog off his leash to run around?"

"Go right ahead. Long as he won't run down the driveway to the street."

"No, he's pretty smart about cars." I unhooked Rochester's leash and he took off toward a tall maple next to Rita's garage.

"I've still got to feed the older pups," Don said. "You can come with me if you want."

No wonder the dogs were barking; they were hungry. I hoped Rochester wouldn't decide to chow down on whatever Don was putting out.

Don started toward the barn and I followed. "You known Rita a long time?"

"Ten years. When she bought this place it was a real shit hole. She fixed it up nice. Hope the next people take as good care of the land."

"She get along with most of the neighbors?"

He laughed hoarsely as we reached the barn door. Rochester was nosing around under the big maple, intent on some scent. "Rita pissed off most everybody she ever met," he said. "I have the same effect on people, so we hit it off fine."

I wondered who he'd pissed off to smash his nose in but didn't ask.

"Neighbors over that way are city people," he said, motioning down a slight rise to an impressive stone mansion a few hundred yards away. "Always complaining about the smell and the noise from the dogs."

The yipping and yelping from the tiny dogs reached a new crescendo as Don and I walked into the barn. I could only imagine how it would be to live nearby. I'd have a perpetual migraine.

I was struck once again by the strong doggy smell, even though I could see the place was clean. In the first of the converted horse stalls, four tiny dachshund puppies, who couldn't have been more than a week or two old, sucked at their mother's teats. Their eyes were squeezed shut and they looked like little piglets.

"Then there's Hugo Furst," Don said, pulling a big bag of dog chow down from a shelf. He carried it to a double-wide stall where the older and more independent puppies had been placed. "He's got the property between me and Rita. A little bitty stream runs between them, and he says she polluted it with runoff from the dog shit she hoses down."

He leaned over the gate and poured the chow into a trough. It was comical to watch the puppies climb over each other to get to the food, yelping and pushing and nipping with their tiny teeth.

"You tell Sergeant Stemper about these folks?"

He shrugged. "Ain't met no sergeant yet. Just ordinary cops." He shouldered the half-empty bag and led me back up toward the front door.

I heard a car pull up outside the barn. "That's gotta be him. I'm sure he'll want to hear what you've got to say."

I went outside, where I saw Rick step out of a patrol car. Rochester launched himself toward him and Rick braced himself against the vehicle.

The Stewart's Crossing police department is pretty large for a town of our size, but Rick still went out on patrol sometimes in addition to his detective duties. He was wearing a patrol uniform, too, which was surprising, since he usually worked in plain clothes.

"What's with the Offissa Pupp outfit?" I asked. Rick was a fan of the Krazy Kat cartoons, I knew, and had a framed strip with the cat and his canine nemesis hanging in his kitchen.

"Wicked flu going around the station." Rick turned his head and coughed. "Hope I'm not getting it, too. We've got four officers puking their guts out, so I had to take a shift."

"Stay away from me," I said, holding my fingers up in the shape of a cross. "I don't need to catch it too." I nodded toward the barn. "One of Rita's neighbors is feeding the dogs. He told me about some people who don't like her."

Rick dug in his back pocket for his notebook, struggling to pull it out when his duty belt was loaded with a radio, baton, flashlight, pepper spray and handcuffs. His gun was in a thumb-break holster over his right pocket.

We had gone to the shooting range a couple of times, and I was impressed at how quickly he could draw and shoot; I had to stand quietly, focusing and steadying my breathing, before I could get off a decent shot.

"I'll talk to him. You'd better rein in your crazy dog."

Rick nodded to where Rochester was chasing a squirrel across the grass.

As I watched, the fuzzy-tailed rodent scampered up the trunk of the big maple. Rochester skidded to a halt by the tree's base, then got up on his hind legs, his front paws gripping the bark. He woofed a couple of times, and the squirrel hopped out on a branch above him and chittered madly.

Rochester sat back down on his haunches and stared up at the squirrel. I walked over and grabbed his collar. "Come on, boy, time to get to work." I clipped his leash and dragged him away from the tree. When he figured out we were heading toward the barn, he scampered ahead of me.

When we walked inside, I saw Rick at the far end of the big, high-ceilinged room, talking to Don Kashane. I kneeled down and spoke to Rochester. "We're looking for cobra venom, all right? See what you can find."

He looked at me and licked my chin. I laughed and pulled away, then stood. "All right, dog, do your thing."

Instinctively, he knew what I was asking, and he tugged his way across the concrete flooring. I stumbled behind him as he went into sled-dog mode, sure he was on the trail that would lead us to Rita's killer. Just in time, though, I realized all he was doing was making a beeline for the double-wide stall where Don had poured the dog food. The wall around the pen, tall enough to keep the little dogs inside, was no match for a seventy-pound golden, and he stepped right over it. I tugged back on his leash as his big nose was pushing past yapping and snarling Chihuahuas, no more than six or eight weeks old.

"Get back here, you big goof," I said, pulling on the leash. My foot slipped on what I realized was dog poop, and I lost my balance and fell backwards on my ass.

Rick saw me and burst out laughing. "Great detective," he said. "Found his way right to the food."

Don Kashane shook his head and mumbled something

69

about city folk, which irritated me because I'd grown up no more than a couple of miles away and I thought I was far from a city slicker.

I scrambled up to my feet. "Bad dog!" I said to Rochester. "You're supposed to be looking for cobra venom, not puppy chow!" I reached over to a roll of paper towels on the wall and started to clean my shoe.

"Cobra venom?" Don asked. "What do you need that for?"

"You know anything about it?" Rick asked.

Don shrugged. "Rita kept a batch of it somewhere. She was old school. She said nothing beat it for taking the pain away from a dog."

Rochester decided my shoe-cleaning was a game, and got one end of the paper towel in his mouth. I was balanced on one leg playing tug of war, trying not to fall again, but not willing to let Rochester chow down on the poop-covered paper.

Having finished their meal, the older dachshunds and Chihuahuas began yelping again. I got the paper out of Rochester's mouth and pushed my hand against his snout. "Sit!" I yelled.

Rick was still talking to Don Kashane, but he had to raise his voice. "You know where she kept the cobra venom?"

"Don't know. She told me she had it once, but that she kept it put away so nobody could use it by accident." He looked at his watch. "I've got to get back to my own farm. Nobody else gonna to take care of my livestock while I'm farting around over here."

"Thanks for your help," Rick said. "Steve, why don't you take Rochester outside while I look around in here." He pulled a pair of rubber gloves out of a back pocket.

His frown said it wasn't worth arguing with him, so I followed Don, dragging a protesting Rochester behind me. At least the air was fresh outside. I closed the barn door and once Don climbed into his pickup and drove away, I let Rochester off his leash to go chase squirrels again.

I paced around the front of the barn. I was disappointed in Rochester. I expected him to head right into the barn and pick up the appropriate clue, even though I knew that was dumb and completely un-doglike. Of course he'd gone for the food. That was his natural instinct.

Perhaps he didn't have a nose for crime at all, and the things he'd done to help solve the two previous murders had been pure coincidence. That was what Rick believed.

Rochester began to get bored, and when that happens he gets in trouble. I walked him over to Rita's practice ring, and ran him through a couple of exercises. He didn't like the weave poles, which made me even more determined to force him to master them. "Damn it, Rochester, you know what you're supposed to do," I said, dragging him by the collar back to the start. "Just do it."

He sat on his butt and stared at me.

If he wanted a showdown, he was going to get one. I glared at him with my hands on my hips. He slumped to the ground and rested his head on his paws.

Wait a minute, I thought. I was smarter than he was. I knew what motivated him, and I knew how to get it. I remembered seeing a jar of training treats on a shelf in Rita's barn. I turned slowly and strolled out of the training ring. Rochester remained on the ground, watching me.

I shut the gate to the ring behind me. That wouldn't stop him; if he got up a head of steam, he could jump over it. I walked across the grass to the barn, picked up the jar of treats, and walked back outside. Rochester was sitting up by the fence, looking in my direction. Fine. Let him wait for me.

I took my time returning to the practice ring. When I opened the gate he tried to jump on me, but I said, "Rochester, sit," and pointed at the ground. When he obeyed, I praised him lavishly and gave him a treat. Then I led him over to the weave poles and carefully led him through, giving him one of the tiny bits every time he did something right.

By the time Rick finally walked out of the barn, holding a sandwich-sized baggie in his right hand, Rochester was going through the weave poles correctly all at once, for a single treat.

"Found it," Rick said, as he approached us. Rochester slumped to the ground, his work complete. "No thanks to you or your dog."

Inside the plastic bag I could see a small vial. "Where was it?"

"Hidden inside a canister in the shape of a sleeping Mexican," he said. "Sombrero tipped over his knees and everything. Very non-PC, but very Rita."

"I can see that. You need anything else here?"

"I'm going into the house to look for any glass that might have residue of the sedative."

"She was drinking her iced tea out of a big plastic tumbler on Sunday," I said. "I'll come inside with you. I want to see where she lived."

"You can come in but leave the dog out here. Preferably tied up somewhere so he can't get into trouble." He pulled a pair of rubber gloves from his back pocket. "Put these on before you come inside."

I led Rochester over to Rita's small practice ring. "Go to town, dog," I said, letting him in the gate, then closing it behind him.

He cocked his head and looked at me. "Go on. Practice."

He woofed once, and took off for the teeter board. I turned around and walked over to the front door of Rita's house, then put the gloves on and walked inside.

Her living room looked like she had simply walked into a Ralph Lauren Home store and bought everything— leather armchairs and sofas, ribbons from dog shows, silver picture frames, and a rustic stone fireplace with a stack of rough-cut logs beside it.

I snooped around myself, looking for evidence of Rita's connection to Eastern. Her office was adjacent to the living room, a modern space with an ergonomic chair and sleek metal shelves full of legal and accounting reference books. No sign of her college diploma, artfully framed in Eastern's blue and white colors, as I'd seen in so many alumni homes. No photos of her with John William Babson or other college dignitaries. Not even an Eastern coffee mug.

I was itching to get my hands on her computer. It was like a sickness, this nosiness of mine when it came to electronics and databases. I liked to know things. It was incredibly satisfying to snoop in places where I wasn't supposed to be, whether they were in a company's online archives, or buried somewhere on a public website. But even when I was arrested for hacking into my then-wife's credit records, it was for a good cause—to keep her from bankrupting us in her depression over her second miscarriage.

My unfortunate incarceration had done a lot to tamp down those illicit impulses, but they still bubbled up from time to time. I felt a physical yearning to walk over to Rita's laptop, turn it on, and let my fingers loose. But that was foolish, as well as illegal. I didn't know what to look for, or enough about her to guess at her passwords.

Oh, and a cop was snooping down the hall, too, one who knew my temptations very well.

If Rita Gaines had secrets in her computers then they were safe from me. Resolutely, I walked to the kitchen, where Rick had found the big iced tea mug Rita had been drinking from on Sunday, and placed it into an evidence bag.

"Rita lived well," I said, nodding toward the high-end appliances, the marble counters and the rack of gleaming copper pots hanging over the prep island.

"The rich are different from you and me," Rick said.

"Yeah, they have more money. And since when are you quoting F. Scott Fitzgerald?"

"Hey, I read. And I know the Hemingway quote you parroted back, too."

Rick and I paced back through the house one more time, but nothing struck either of us as evidence. By the time we stepped out the front door, Rochester had escaped from the practice ring and was jumping against a big metal trash can next to it, as if trying to knock it over.

"Here, boy. Come on, let's hit the road." I patted my thigh a couple of times.

Rochester jumped against the can again, and this time it tipped over. "Rochester! What are you doing?" I hurried to the can, where he had begun nosing through the garbage.

"Is there something in the trash can?" I said, as I reached him. "Did you find a clue, boy?"

"Steve," Rick said from behind me.

I grabbed Rochester's collar and pulled him away. "No, maybe he did find something after all." He sat on his haunches next to me with a woeful look on his face.

"It's probably just a food wrapper," Rick said.

"No, that's his 'I found something' look." I still wore the blue plastic gloves Rick had given me.

Rick shook his head as Rochester slid down onto his haunches beside me. "Go for it," he said.

"You're not helping?"

"I'm just sitting here with Rochester, watching you work."

He plopped down on the grass next to the dog, and Rochester stuck his big head in Rick's lap. I got down on my knees and started pawing through the garbage. Rita hadn't emptied it after the training class on Sunday, and it was a mess of dirty paper towels, treat wrappers and soda cans. Toward the bottom, I found a half-empty bag of doggie treats, a gourmet brand that was way out of my budget. I shook my head at the idea of people so rich they could throw away something I couldn't even afford.

Rochester stuck his head toward me and sniffed. "So you found some treats," I said. "Fine. Have one."

I handed it to him and he sucked it down greedily, then looked eagerly at the bag. "You can have more later," I said. I crumpled the bag and stuffed in my back pocket.

As I began putting the trash back in the can I spotted an empty blister pack of the kind used for round tablets. All six pills had been popped out, leaving only a few tiny shreds of foil on the back. A faint trace of white powder remained on the plastic.

"You see this?" I asked. "Think it held dog medication?"

Rick shrugged. "No idea. I used my last evidence bag inside, so let me get another one from the car, just in case."

While he was gone, I pulled out my phone and took a couple of close up shots of the packaging. By the time Rick returned I was innocently feeding Rochester more of the meaty-smelling expensive treats.

"You want to get some dinner?" I asked, as I piled the rest of the garbage back in the can.

"You kinda smell like trash," he said. "You should go home and take a shower. Wash those clothes, too. Whatever you do, don't go see Lili smelling like that or you'll be single faster than you can say loser."

10 – Freezer Burn

I followed Rick's advice. I drove Rochester home with the windows down and took him for a quick walk. I tossed a frozen pizza in the oven, then began running water in the big Roman tub in the master bathroom. I threw my clothes in the washing machine, and once the bath was ready, I turned the washer on and climbed upstairs.

I grabbed a whole stack of towels and left them on the counter, then stepped into the tub. Rochester came over and stood next to me. "How about it, boy? You want a bath, too?"

He looked at me with his soulful deep brown eyes. "Come on in, then." I grabbed him by the scruff of his neck and lifted him up, and then he clambered into the tub with me. I had to give his hind legs a boost.

The tub was plenty big for one person, but not so comfy for a person and a big dog. I sat up on the low ledge and picked up a big plastic pitcher I kept on the windowsill above the tub, filled it, and dumped it on Rochester.

He wasn't the type of dog to go splashing in a pool or lake, but he submitted to bathing pretty well. He stood patiently as I rinsed him down, then massaged shampoo into his fur. I had to hold him to stop him from shaking, though, and then keep one hand on his back while I rinsed him down. I accompanied the bathing with lots of reassuring noises, telling him what a good boy he was, and how soon he would be a lean, clean puppy machine.

I released my grip on him to reach for the towels, he shook his whole body, spraying the walls around the tub, the bathroom floor, and me. I yelped, "Rochester! Bad dog!"

At least it was clean water.

Golden retrievers have a soft, water-repellent coat, and

then a heavy undercoat that's hell to get dry. He was as slippery as an eel, struggling to get away from me and go shaking water over the whole house, but I manhandled him into submission. I went through five towels before Rochester was merely damp, instead of soaking wet. Then I let him go, and he scampered away.

I let the dirty water out of the tub, and refilled with clean water. Then I relaxed and leaned back. Rochester returned, slumping on the tile floor next to me as I scrubbed myself down. When I felt clean enough, I grabbed the last clean towel and dried myself.

I ate my pizza, giving Rochester some crusts, and then washed up. I dialed Lili's cell to check in, but the call went direct to voice mail, so I left a message. Rochester was snoozing on the tile floor in the kitchen as I turned on my laptop.

Since my problems with the California penal system had arisen based on my computer hacking, the conditions of my parole restricted me to owning only one computer. It was a decent laptop, though already over a year old. I thought I might lean on Santiago Santos to relax that condition and let me get another electronic device, maybe a tablet or a netbook. Just for fun, of course. For the most part, I had turned my back on my hacking past.

The first thing I wanted to know was more about cobra venom, so I did a quick search. The scientific name for the nerve blocking agent was Alpha-Cobratoxin, and as Dr. Conrad had said, it was used to numb the pain when a dog kept chewing away at a bite.

It was a powerful neurotoxin that acted as a painkiller when administered in small quantities. I wondered how much of it would have been necessary to kill Rita Gaines, but I couldn't find anything online to tell me. I did discover that the possession of cobra venom wasn't a crime, although the substance had been banned in horse racing.

Rita might have mentioned the cobra venom in the

sleeping Mexican to anyone who'd come to her barn. That would let out Felae. She would never have shared a glass of iced tea with him or talked about dogs and their treatment with him. I doubted he would have known about cobra venom on his own, known where she kept it, or even known that she drank iced tea with lots of sugar that would disguise the taste.

Who else could have known that Rita had cobra venom in her barn? Don Kashane had known. And he'd been nosing around her property right after her death, carrying a shotgun. Did he have a motive to kill her?

Rochester got up and moved behind my chair, where he settled down again.

Perhaps it was someone who brought a dog to Rita's agility training sessions, or someone she'd sold a puppy to. I made a note to ask Rick if he had found anyone with a dog who had a grudge against Rita.

I remembered the rude way Rita had spoken about Rochester. A lot of people are very possessive about their dogs. Had she insulted someone badly enough to get herself killed?

That didn't seem very reasonable, despite all the rabid dog-lovers I had met since Rochester came into my life.

What about the flunitrazepam the coroner found in her system? She probably didn't have that lying around her barn, so the killer must have brought it with him – or her. I remembered the photo I had taken of the blister pack Rochester found in the trash, and I transferred it from my phone to the laptop. Then I opened up Photoshop and enhanced the image. I didn't want to say anything to Rick, because I knew he'd tell me I was jumping the gun, but I thought Rochester might have discovered the packaging for the drug the killer had used.

Rochester curled around the back of my chair, as if he was keeping me at the computer until I figured out what I had.

Once I had a decent image, I searched for pictures of Rohypnol packaging, and found a good one for comparison. I could make out the left part of the capital R on the left side of the open circle, and what looked like the top of the L on the right.

The giveaway, though, was the remainder of the black hexagon at the bottom of the package. The manufacturer of Rohypnol was Roche Labs, and the bottom part of the Roche logo was clearly visible in the bottom part of the hexagon.

"Good boy," I said, leaning down to scratch behind Rochester's ears. He was still damp, and I knew he would be for a while. "Even though Rick laughed, you found a clue after all."

Rochester yawned deeply and sprawled on to his side. He knew his work was done.

I called Rick in triumph. "That blister pack I found in the garbage? It's for Rohypnol."

"How do you know that?"

I told him about taking the picture, enhancing it and matching it.

"You can't leave things alone, can you?" he said.

"Hey, I'm not calling up your chief and telling him I'm doing your job. Just you."

"You're not doing my job, Steve. Most of the time, you're getting in the way."

"Don't be a dick, Rick. Hey, that rhymes."

He sighed. "Email me your picture and the match. Now go watch TV or something."

Of course I couldn't do that. Instead I started surfing the internet trying to figure out how easy it was to get your hands on Rohypnol. Not that I was actually going to buy it, you understand. I wanted to know where the killer could have gotten it, and if I could find a purchase trail for Rick to follow.

I was able to order it from a dozen online

pharmacies—no prescription needed, as long as I was willing to fill out an online questionnaire that would evaluate whether the medication was right for me. If I passed, then their "on-call physician" would write the script so they could fill it.

I made a list for Rick of all the online pharmacies. It was a long shot, but maybe he could get a subpoena for client records and match them to someone who knew Rita and had a motive to kill her.

That reminded me of Felae, who was in danger of losing his scholarship, and perhaps even being sent back to his country, wherever that was. I did a quick search for Felae Popescu, but all I could find was his involvement with an animal rights group called Don't Operate on Animals, or DOA. He had been involved in a couple of protests at medical research facilities and had written numerous blog posts about treating animals properly. I couldn't argue with any of that.

It was almost eleven o'clock by then, so I took Rochester out for a quick walk. A cold front had swept in, and the air was chilly, but the sky was so clear I could see dozens of constellations. Orion the hunter loomed right overhead, and I wondered who had been hunting Rita Gaines—and why.

* * *

When I woke up the next morning, Rochester was on the floor next to my bed, lying on his back and waving all his legs in the air like a dying cockroach. I looked over at him and laughed, and he immediately rolled over and jumped up to lick my face. We carried out our usual morning routine. We went outside, and Rochester chased a couple of dead leaves fluttering past in the light breeze as if they were prey he was going to capture and return to me in exchange for a treat. Then we drove up to Eastern.

I was in my office working on another of the many press releases I had to complete for graduation when

Rochester sat up and barked a couple of times. I looked up to see a tall, rangy kid with crooked teeth and acne standing in the door. "The dog doesn't bite, does he?" he asked.

"No, he's sweet." I turned to the dog, who was still barking. "Rochester, hush."

Then I looked back at the kid in the doorway. "Can I help you?"

"Lou from the writing lab told me to come talk to you. I'm Dustin De Bree."

"Oh, yeah. Come on in, have a seat. Lou said you were having a problem?"

"Can I close the door?" he asked.

"Sure."

He closed it, then sat down across from me. He wore a light blue Eastern ball cap turned backwards on his head.

"So what's going on?"

"Can this, like, be in total confidence? I'm really freaked and I don't know what to do." He picked nervously at a zit on his neck.

"I can't promise you anything until I hear what your problem is. But I can tell you I have a friend on the Leighville Police, so if you're in trouble with them..."

"Oh, no, it's not illegal. I mean, I'm not in trouble. But I saw something I wasn't supposed to. And that might be illegal."

I blew a breath out through my pursed lips. "Let's start from the beginning. You're a student here, right?"

He nodded. "I'm a sophomore, majoring in computer science. I've always been really good with computers. I have a work-study job in the IT department. My job is to go around to people's offices and stuff and fix their computers when things break."

"We really have people who do that? I thought you just put a help desk ticket in and they ignore it."

"Lots of stuff we can't actually do anything about. There's this weird control program installed on all the computers on campus, called Freezer Burn. No matter what you do to the computer when it's on, as soon as you reboot, Freezer Burn brings it back to the original configuration." We'd had a similar program at the place where I worked in California. "But can't you customize Freezer Burn to accept changes if an administrator makes them?" He shook his head. "It's a really crappy program, but Mrs. Parshall won't let us use anything else."

That sounded like Verri M. Parshall to me.

He took a deep breath. "That's where the trouble is."

"Go on."

He sat up. "See, I kept wondering why we use such a crappy program. It's constantly screwing up all kinds of systems because it wasn't designed for such a large installation like we have here."

That made sense. I remembered hearing the problems the registrar was having with graduation audits, and Verri's unwillingness to do anything about them.

Dustin gave up picking at his zit, but began rubbing his hands against each other.

"So why are you here, Dustin? Sounds like a problem within your department. And you're only a work-study student, aren't you? It's almost the end of the semester. Your job's going to be over in a week or two."

He nodded. "But see, the other day I saw something I wasn't supposed to, and I feel weird about it, like I should report it to someone. It's really messing with my head, you know? Like we had to sign the Eastern Pledge, right?"

The Pledge was something all freshmen had to sign. Students agreed not to cheat on exams, to plagiarize papers, to steal from the College or from each other, and so on. I'd signed it myself, long ago.

I nodded, though I didn't know what the Pledge had to do with anything.

"Mrs. Parshall had left this folder open on her desk, and I saw a check inside," Dustin continued. "From this company called MDC."

"So?"

"So that's the company that makes the Freezer Burn software."

I was starting to get impatient with Dustin. I had to get back to my press release and get it finished before some other crisis came up. "Was it some kind of refund?" I asked.

He shook his head. "No. It was payable to her personally. For like twenty thousand dollars."

I turned my head a few degrees and pressed my lips shut. Why would Verri M. Parshall be getting a personal check from a vendor?

"You get it, right?" Dustin asked. "It must be some kind of payoff, for using this crappy software. And I'm afraid she knows I saw the check. What if she has me killed or something?"

"I think you've been watching too many movies, Dustin," I said. "Mrs. Parshall isn't a mob boss. You're not going to wake up one morning with a horse's head in bed next to you."

Dustin recoiled in horror. "A horse's head? What would that be for? Does she keep horses or something?"

"It's a scene from a movie. *The Godfather*. But don't watch it. It'll only give you horrible ideas."

"I've got enough of those." He was wearing one of those evolution T-shirts, the kind with a progression from left to right, starting with a monkey, then a Neanderthal, and so on. At the far right was a guy sitting at a computer terminal, with the slogan "Something went terribly wrong" underneath it.

"What should I do, Mr. Levitan? What she's doing is wrong, and it's screwing up the college computers. But I'm afraid that if she knows I reported her, she'll fire me, or even get me expelled or something."

"Let me think about it." I had been puzzled over

Freezer Burn's obvious flaws, and yet Verri's unwillingness to take action. If she had accepted a bribe to install inferior software, that explained her behavior. It was also a very serious charge to make against someone, especially a college employee with such a long tenure and so many friends in high places.

I had no idea what I could do, but my words seemed to have a good effect on Dustin De Bree. For the first time since he'd walked into my office he relaxed.

"Leave me your phone number and your email address," I said. "I'll get back to you."

He scrawled it on the top page of an Eastern College logo pad, and pushed it across to me. "I feel so much better. You're like, really cool. Lou was totally right about you."

"Thanks."

He left, and I went back to my press release, which was sounding wooden and boring. I couldn't focus on it when I had Rita Gaines and now Dustin De Bree taking up space in my brain.

So I took Rochester out for a walk. Instead of traipsing down the hill, like we usually did, we circled around the back of the campus, where the hillside sloped down sharply to a wooded ravine. A burbling creek marked the edge of the college property. Beyond it lay a series of fields burgeoning with new growth. I let Rochester off his leash and he took off down the slope toward the darkness, his golden flanks shimmering as he ran.

It was so peaceful back there—and yet my brain was filled with murder and corruption. Just like that thicket, dark places could be found around the campus, both literal and metaphorical. The college newspaper regularly reported break-ins and the occasional assault. Students had been arrested on and off campus for drug possession, and at least once a year a depressed young man or woman committed suicide.

I shook those gloomy thoughts off as Rochester dashed

around, stopping to sniff and pee, then galloping again. Every time I saw him going toward the thicket I called him back, but he couldn't resist stepping in to the dense underbrush. I had to scrabble down the slope myself and step between the trees, pushing aside fiddlehead ferns and something prickly.

It was much cooler inside. I could barely hear the noises of the campus—the whirr of the generators, the beep of a truck backing up, rap music from a car passing. It smelled musty and primeval.

Rochester had stopped to sniff some flat-topped mushrooms, and I was able to hook his collar and jerk his head back before he could eat any. Holding him tight, I backed out of the thicket, scratching my arm on the tree bark. Once we were outside I turned and dragged him back up the slope behind me.

We stopped at one of the lunch trucks on the way back and I got a couple of slices of pepperoni pizza. We sat on a bench and I fed him the meat circles as I ate. By the time we were finished I felt refreshed enough to tackle the graduation press release again. I had it ready to go by the time I had to leave for the last day of my tech writing class.

Lou was standing at the teaching podium when I walked in. He'd smartened up for his presentation, wearing a collared shirt and neatly pressed jeans. As the rest of the class filtered in, he said, "I can't get my presentation to start. I don't know what's wrong."

I groaned. It drove me wild when I was teaching and the computer systems weren't up to date, and there was nothing I could do about it. Every time I wanted to show a class a Flash movie, I had to fill out a licensing form. Each time I wanted to open a PDF file, I had to accept the conditions of the software. I couldn't download and install anything myself, even freeware to help students edit pictures or sound clips for their presentations. And when a student used a personal address to email me a paper and I tried to download it, the system took it for a virus and forced my system to reboot.

Lou turned the computer off and then on again, and we waited for it to cycle through its seemingly endless start-up menu. But once it did, whatever had hung it up before was fixed, and he was able to get his PowerPoint running.

The first screen had a picture of a bunch of students sitting at computers, with his name and the title of his presentation: WRITTING BETTER WITH THE HELP OF THE LAB. I chose not to point out the typo in the headline.

"The Writing Lab is located at the rear of Blair Hall, around the corner from this room," he said to us. "You may never have been there, but it can be a valuable resource for you. I'd like to explain why."

He clicked forward to a list of all the help a student could get at the Writing Lab. "Most students think the Lab is only for remedial help, but anybody can go in for paper reviews, too," he said.

He showed a short video clip of himself working with a female student I recognized as his girlfriend Desiree. He was explaining how important structure was in an academic paper.

When the video ended he flipped forward. "Need help with your research or citation?" he asked the class. "You can come to the Writing Lab for help." He showed a second clip, of him helping Dustin De Bree with MLA-style citations for an English paper.

As the second clip was finishing, the computer froze. "Shit," Lou said. Then he looked up at the class. "Sorry."

"Reboot," I said. I took a deep breath. It never paid to get irritated when things went wrong in class; the students could sense your fear and uncertainty and would pounce on you like wolves, asking if they could leave early, get extensions on deadlines, or skip taking exams. "While you're waiting for the computer to come back, why don't you take some questions from the class?"

Barbara Seville asked if professors minded if students got help from the Lab. "Isn't that like cheating?"

"We get lots of students who come in with referrals from their professors," Lou said. "What do you think, Prof? Is it OK with you?"

"I think it's great, as long as the tutor only helps you recognize your problems and gives you advice on how to fix them."

The computer came back up, and Lou was able to finish his presentation. But it crashed again on the student who followed him, and then on another, and I considered us very lucky to finish the last presentation just before the class was over.

I felt a great sense of relief when I stood up. "Thanks for being a great class," I said. "Remember, you get an extra twenty points added to your final score if you fill out the online course evaluation by next Monday. If you have missed any assignments, you have until Saturday at midnight to submit them through the online system. I'll be calculating your grades and I'll post them sometime next week."

The class applauded, which was always nice. Especially since I was a fill-in; they had started the semester with Perpetua Kaufman, who had died during the winter break. It was my first time teaching that class in years, so I was lucky she had left behind detailed lecture notes, assignments and links to online exercises.

As the class was filing out, Lou stopped next to me. "Did Dustin talk to you?"

"Yeah. I'm not sure what I can do to help him but I'll try."

"Thanks, Prof. He's a good guy. I know you can help him."

I wasn't sure Lou's optimism was warranted, and as I walked back to Fields Hall I kept thinking about what I could do to help Dustin. I was so preoccupied with his problems I'd forgotten all about Felae Popescu—until I found him in the hallway outside in my office, accompanied by Lili Weinstock.

11 – Bender

As I opened the door to my office, Rochester jumped up from his place by the french doors and rushed over to Lili, who scratched him behind the ears. Her masses of auburn curls were tamed by a series of butterfly-shaped barrettes, and she wore a blue chambray shirt and skinny black jeans. She had her messenger bag over her shoulder. After all the drama I'd been going through between Rita Gaines' death and Dustin De Bree's problems, I was delighted to see her, even if she was accompanied by the dour Felae.

"Felae called me this morning and I convinced him to come in," she said. "I thought maybe you could talk to Rick Stemper for him."

Felae stood beside her sullenly. "I am Felae," he said, extending his hand to me. "Dr. Weinstock tells me I must come to you for help."

"Sit down, Felae, and cut the act, all right? You know exactly who I am, and I'm tired of this stupid pretense you have. If you don't remember that I was your teacher last year for the mystery fiction class, and that you've seen me around campus at least a half dozen times since then, then you're probably dumb enough to have killed Rita Gaines."

"Steve!" Lili said, as Felae sunk into one of the two visitor's chairs across from my desk.

Felae sighed deeply. "Is true. Americans are too friendly, so I am often pretending not to know people. I remember Mr. Levitan's class. Was a good one."

Lili looked from him to me, then shook her head and sat down. I sat behind my desk, and Rochester sprawled protectively around Lili, between her and Felae.

"Let's back up," I said. "Why were you so angry at Mrs. Gaines?"

"I am getting call from president on Sunday morning," he said. "He tell me that I must destroy my painting or I will lose my scholarship."

I looked to Lili. "Can Babson do that?"

She shrugged. "You've seen the way he runs this college. I'd say he can do just about anything he wants."

"So you drove up to Rita's farm and confronted her?" I asked Felae. "How'd you know where she lived?"

"I recognize her from Don't Operate on Animals rally, and know she contribute to group. I find her name and address in book they keep."

"And what did you think you were going to accomplish? You think she was going to say, 'Sorry, Felae, my mistake'?"

His shoulders sagged, and although he looked older, I realized he was barely out of his teens, just a kid. "It is wrong, I know. But I did not kill her!"

Rochester reacted to the anger and desperation in his voice, looking up at him and then sitting up. He rested his head in Lili's lap and she stroked the soft fur atop his skull.

"The police may have a different opinion," I said to Felae. "Where did you go after you left Rita's house?"

"I get lost on back roads. I am driving around for a long time. I end up in Levittown." He said the city name like it was a bad word, and for a lot of people I guess it was. Built in the late 1940s to house returning vets from World War II, the city had a reputation for cookie-cutter housing, endless cul-de-sacs, and a repetitive naming convention for streets. Every street in Twin Oaks, for example, began with a T; every one in Orangewood with an O. Even if you knew where you were going, it was easy to get lost.

"What time did you get home?"

"Maybe midnight."

"Midnight! But you left Rita's late in the afternoon. You were driving all that time?"

Rochester slumped back to the floor and began gnawing on a rawhide bone. I figured he'd make about as much progress with it as I was making with Felae.

"I find this bar, and I am served beer. I drink for a while."

Great. "You're not twenty-one, are you?"

"Not for six months yet."

With Felae's brooding face, dark hair and heavy five o'clock shadow, I could see a bartender not bothering to card him. But it might be hard to verify his alibi if the bartender knew he was being exposed to a charge of serving a minor. And the police could easily argue that Felae had killed Rita, and then gotten drunk in remorse or anger.

"You live with anyone?" I asked.

He nodded. "Four roommates in house. Two of them see me when I get home."

"The police will need to know where you were from the time you left Rita's until your roommates saw you," I said. "You'd better have an answer for them."

"No police!" he said.

"Felae. You're a suspect in a murder investigation. If you don't talk to the police willingly, they'll hunt you down and bring you in."

He shivered, and I felt sorry for him. Rochester must have felt the same, because he pushed aside his rawhide and sat up, this time pushing his head into Felae's lap. Reflexively, he stroked Rochester's neck.

"Have you called your parents?" I asked.

"My father, he is dead. My mother is back in my country."

"What country is that?"

"Moldova. Is former part of Soviet Union, between Romania and Ukraine. I am from town of Bender, outside capital. I want very much to study in United States, and Eastern give me scholarship."

Wow. My trip to Eastern had been more of a commute than a pilgrimage, having grown up in Stewart's Crossing. I couldn't imagine how hard it must have been for Felae to leave behind his family, his country, even his language, to get an education.

"I'm calling my friend," I said, picking up the phone. "He's a good guy. He'll treat you right."

He turned to Lili. "You will go with me? You are only one I trust."

"Steve and I will both go with you," she said.

Great. Escorting a student and murder suspect down to the Stewart's Crossing police station. Add that item to my datebook.

"I have Felae Popescu in my office," I said, when Rick answered his cell. "Can I bring him down to your station?"

"Where'd you find him?"

I looked over at Felae, who was still stroking Rochester's head. "He found me. Or rather, he found Lili and she brought him over to me."

"How soon can you be here?"

It was only three o'clock, but Babson had asked me to keep an eye on the investigation into Rita's death, so taking two hours off qualified as a PR emergency. "Half an hour? I'll have to drop Rochester off at home first."

"Bring the dog," Rick said. "We can park him with the desk sergeant. I want Mr. Popescu here as soon as possible."

We took separate cars, Lili and Felae in hers, Rochester with me. The quiet in the car was oppressive as I pulled out of the college parking lot, so I turned on the radio and pressed the CD button. A moment later Amadou and Mariam began singing about fast food in Senegal. I thought the upbeat tempo would be a good balance to Felae's infectious dourness. By the time we got to Stewart's Crossing they were singing "Je Pense a Toi" and I felt better. I couldn't speak for Rochester, but then he's generally pretty easy-going.

The police station was a squat, one-story building from the 1970s in the poorer neighborhood of town, at the corner of Canal Street and Quarry Road, at the edge of downtown. Canal Street was a block off Main, a mostly residential street whose houses backed on the old Delaware Canal. The towpath on the other side of the canal was now a state park.

Quarry Road was one of the main east-west streets in town, running from the flat plain along the river's edge, over the canal on a two-lane bridge, across Main Street and up the hill toward Newtown and Lumberville. Main Street was our central business district, or what there was of one; mostly doctors, real estate brokers, gift shops and so on. Small older homes lined Quarry Road as it climbed the hill, until the sprawling suburbs began. Cops could get almost anywhere in town within minutes.

I parked in the lot behind the station, and Lili pulled in next to me. Rochester had a quick pee next to a scraggly boxwood hedge, and then the four of us walked in the station's front door. Ahead of us I saw Rick sitting at a scuffed wooden desk in a big bullpen area; three desks around him were shared by other detectives, behind the gated front area where the desk sergeant sat.

"No dogs in the building," the sergeant said.

"They're with me," Rick said, standing up from his desk. "Steve, why don't you and Lili take Rochester for a walk while I talk to Mr. Popescu."

"You cannot stay with me?" Felae said, turning to Lili.

"I promise I won't bite," Rick said. "You'll be fine."

Felae turned to me. "I am needing a lawyer?"

That was a tricky question. An attorney would surely caution Felae not to speak to the cops on his own. That would hold up Rick's investigation and leave Lili and me stuck in Stewart's Crossing waiting.

Lili made the decision for me. "Felae is innocent," she said. "So he doesn't need a lawyer."

Felae looked at me. Were we throwing him under the bus, leaving him on his own at the police station? I took a deep breath. I knew that Rick was a good guy and an honest cop, and that he wouldn't do anything to railroad Felae. I nodded. "What the lady said. If you are innocent, that is."

"In my country is enough to just be suspected. If you are suspect, you are guilty."

"You're not in Moldova, Felae. The rules are different here." I put my hand on his shoulder. "And Detective Stemper is a good cop. He won't hurt you and he won't try to show you're guilty of anything you didn't do."

That must have convinced him. He stepped forward, and Rick opened the gate to usher him through to the interview room I knew was at the back of the station. I'd been there a few times myself in other situations.

"We'll be at The Chocolate Ear," I said to Rick. "Call me when we can come back for Felae."

"Will do."

Rochester, Lili and I walked back outside. "You think he'll be all right?" Lili asked.

"I believe what I said about Rick." And I did. But if he couldn't verify Felae's alibi, and the sullen kid was uncooperative, then I could see a lot more trouble brewing for him.

12 – Santiago Santos

Rochester seemed to know where we were going, leading Lili and me up toward Main Street and The Chocolate Ear. When I was adjuncting at Eastern, I had become friendly with the owner, Gail Dukowski, and often graded papers at her café. She made delicious sandwiches and killer desserts, and brewed specialty coffees out of a small stone building on Main Street, a couple of blocks from the police station. I still often stopped by for coffee and pastries, and a biscuit for Rochester.

It was a gorgeous afternoon, perfect for sitting outside at one of Gail's wrought iron tables. I left Lili and Rochester at a table and went inside. The room had been painted a cheerful yellow and decorated with art deco-style posters advertising French foods, from wines to olive oils to chocolates. Gail's grandmother Irene was behind the counter. She was a short, spry woman with iron gray hair and she exuded cheerfulness.

"Steve! It's so good to see you. Where's Rochester?"

"Outside." I nodded to where Lili sat, with the big golden retriever by her side. I was relieved that he liked Lili as much as I did, and she'd taken to him as well.

"Now, who is that? She's lovely."

"My girlfriend, Lili."

"I'll have to call Gail out from the kitchen. I'm sure she'd love to see you. But what can I get started for you?"

"How about a pair of raspberry mochas, with whipped cream and a mocha drizzle? And a couple of pastries." While Irene started the cappuccino machine, I browsed the case. Gail had been a gourmet pastry chef in New York before coming back to Bucks County to start her café, and her desserts were delectable. "We'll have one of those chocolate dome things, and a Napoleon, and an éclair. And a plain croissant for Rochester."

"You go sit down and I'll bring everything out, or Gail will," Irene said.

I went back outside. "Stewart's Crossing is such a pretty little town," Lili said. "Much more charming than Leighville."

"You think so?" I sat down beside her, both of us facing out toward Main Street. Rochester sprawled on the pavement next to Lili, and I remembered all the times I had come to the café with him, grading papers with him by my side.

"I do. What was it like growing up here?"

"Ordinary. Your basic small town. We were lucky to be close to New York and Philadelphia, so we didn't feel quite so isolated as we might have."

Most of the buildings in the downtown area were gingerbread Victorians, many converted to stores or doctors' offices. A couple of uglier buildings were from the sixties and seventies, but a few years before, the town had put in ornamental street lights and flower beds outside the businesses. Daffodils, crocuses, tulips and hyacinths were blooming, and an array of colorful flags flapped in the breeze across the street at the Hair-Due Salon.

Gail came outside with our coffee and pastry on a tray. Rochester sat up on his haunches; he knew food when he smelled it, and he knew Gail, a pretty blonde in her late twenties, was a soft touch, too. "Haven't seen you here in a long time, Steve," she said.

"I'm working full-time now. Don't have as much chance to hang out in cafés as I used to." I introduced her to Lili and said, "Gail kept me caffeinated last year when I was adjuncting a couple of courses."

Gail handed Rochester a dog biscuit; I knew that she baked a batch every now and then and kept them on hand for her favorite canines. He greedily wolfed it down. We chatted for a couple of minutes, then Gail went back inside.

"What if Felae really is guilty?" Lili said when she had left. "And we sent him in there without an attorney to protect him?"

"If he's guilty of murder, he deserves to be punished," I said. "But let's assume that he's not, all right? That means he's going to tell Rick what he was doing after he left Rita's on Sunday. Rick will check out his alibi, and then he'll be free to go."

"What if his alibi doesn't check out?"

I ripped a piece of croissant and fed it to Rochester. "Lili. Either he's guilty or he's not. If he didn't do it, then eventually that'll be clear, and he'll be all right."

She drummed her fingers nervously on the table. "I don't know what to do. I'm worried about Felae. But at the same time I know I should be back at the office. I have so many papers yet to grade. I like being a professor, but this time of year is hell. I don't have a chance to work on any of my own projects and I'm starting to get itchy to have a camera in my hands." She dug in her messenger bag and extracted her iPad. "You don't mind if I check my emails, do you?"

"I should do the same thing." I pulled out my phone and hit a couple of keys to draw in my college emails and started answering them. Lili and I sat outside the café, drinking coffee and eating pastries, both of us doing our work while we waited for Rick to call me.

Just before five, my cell rang. "You can pick up Mr. Popescu," Rick said. "For now, his alibi checks out, and I know how to get hold of him if I need him."

I thanked Rick and hung up. "Should we drive Felae back up to Leighville and then get some dinner?" I asked Lili. At the mention of the d-word Rochester's head popped up.

She shook her head. "I have so much work to do. I'll drop him off on my way home. And you're already almost home. There's no reason for you to shlep up to Leighville."

97

The three of us walked back to the police station, Rochester once more in the lead. Felae was standing in the parking lot beside Lili's Mini Cooper, looking only a bit more cheerful than he had before. I felt pretty cranky myself, since I had expected to have dinner with Lili, and perhaps reap some reward for helping her out with Felae.

Instead I took my dog home and made myself a big pot of shell macaroni with butter and grated parmesan cheese, my childhood comfort food. Rochester got his regular bowl of kibble. I guess that was his comfort food.

I was washing the dishes when my doorbell rang and Rochester launched into a paroxysm of barking. I dried my hands and looked out the peephole to see my parole officer, Santiago Santos, in the courtyard.

He was Puerto Rican, with a bachelor's degree in sociology from Drexel, and looked like an amateur boxer, about 5-8, stocky, with muscular forearms. "I was in the neighborhood and thought I'd drop in," he said. "This a good time?"

I stepped back to usher him in. "Sure."

In the Pennsylvania state parole system, officers visit parolees at their homes. I'd been to his office in Bensalem, for my first visit and to fill out paperwork, and he'd been out to my townhouse in Stewart's Crossing on an average of once a month since then. They were almost always unannounced visits like this one, as if he was trying to catch me doing something I wasn't supposed to.

Well, I guess that was his job, after all.

I brought him my laptop, and he sat down at my kitchen table with it as I made us both mugs of tea. One of the conditions of my computer use while on parole was the installation of keystroke software, which tells Santos which keys have been pressed, and which windows they were pressed in. It captures emails, usernames, passwords and chat conversations, and only he has the password to see what's been recorded.

I wasn't particularly nervous. I'd been a good boy,

keeping my nose clean and resisting the urge to hack into websites.

Rochester was sprawled behind Santos's chair, and I had to step over him as I brought the pair of mugs to the kitchen table. Santos swung my laptop sideways so I could see what he was looking at. "Rohypnol, Steve?" he asked. "I'm disappointed in you. You know the conditions of your parole. No hacking, no drugs. No illegal activity of any kind."

My mouth dropped open. Sure, I'd been searching for information on Rohypnol, but it was in a good cause. And if I wanted to trick him, I could—but I'd never even considered that Santos would find anything unusual on my computer.

"You have a reason for this?" Santos asked, looking at me. "Or am I going to have to write you up for a violation?"

My blood pressure zoomed, but I forced myself to stay calm. "Just some research for Rick Stemper," I said. "We found this blister pack up at a murder scene, and I wanted to see if I could figure out what it was."

He looked skeptical.

"Honestly, Santiago. You think I'd do that? I committed computer fraud, not a sex crime. And I have a girlfriend. I don't need date rape drugs."

"You don't understand, Steve. Criminal activity isn't about the actual violation—it's about a mindset. The idea that you're someone special, that the ordinary rules don't apply to you. That you can take what you want, or do what you want."

His sociology background popped up like that. His analysis did sound like my personality, especially when I was on the trail of some piece of information. But I remembered the mantra I had repeated often when I was in prison. I had committed a criminal act, but I wasn't a criminal.

"Let me show you what I was doing." I sat down next to him and pulled up the photo I had enhanced, and matched it to the sites I'd been searching. "If you don't mind, I'll give Detective Stemper a call," he said when I was finished.

"Go right ahead."

He stood up and walked toward the doorway so I couldn't overhear his conversation. I sat there petting Rochester and fuming. How had I been so stupid? I knew Rohypnol wasn't legal in the United States, but I'd still left an audit trail on my laptop looking for it. It wasn't fair. I hadn't tried to buy the stuff. Any other Joe could have done what I did without penalty. But I was still paying for one stupid thing I had done in California, three years before.

Scratching behind Rochester's ears calmed me down. Then Santos returned to the kitchen. "Rick confirms you were looking into the Rohypnol for him. But Steve, you have to remember you can't do anything you want. You're a convicted felon, on parole. Everything you do has to go through that filter."

"For another six months," I said.

"And if you don't learn to change your habits you'll do something stupid and end up in prison again. I see a lot of guys like you, Steve. You think you're smarter than the system. But the system always wins."

We talked for a while about my job, and how I was using computers there, but I was still simmering with resentment and couldn't get him out of the house fast enough.

I was determined not to let Santiago Santos interfere with what I thought was right. Of course, I was going to report as required, and let him know every time I changed residence or job. I had surrendered the handgun my father left me to Rick, to hold until my parole was over, because simple possession of a gun was enough to violate me.

But ordinary online searching was allowed under the

terms of my parole. So I wasn't going to let Santiago Santos threaten me. If I wanted to help Rick investigate Rita's murder I damned well would.

It looked like Felae hadn't killed her—but who else might have? What new information could I discover that could be useful to Rick?

13 – Country Homes

I got up and started pacing around the house. I didn't have far to go; the downstairs of my townhouse is compact, with a living room, dining room, kitchen and breakfast nook. I didn't count the laundry alcove, where I had a washer-dryer, or the guest bathroom.

Rochester hauled himself up from the tile floor and began following me. "Go lay down, dog," I said, pointing at a round, fluffy bed I had bought for him. He stood there and looked at me.

I slid open the glass door that led to the walled courtyard that protected my house from the street. I had planted a row of lilac bushes when I moved in, and tiny purple clusters of buds had begun to appear. I was eager for them to open and fill the air with perfume. Rochester crowded up against my legs, sniffing the fresh air.

From down the street, I heard my neighbor Thad Hertz blasting Bill Halley's "Rock Around the Clock." He liked to sit in his driveway in the evening, sharing his taste in music with the whole neighborhood. At least it wasn't rap.

Neighbors. Don Kashane said that several of Rita's neighbors had complained about her. Who were they? Would any of them have had a motive to kill her?

I returned to the laptop and called up the property appraiser's records for Bucks County. I entered Rita's name—but got no results.

Huh? Didn't she own the property?

I scrabbled around for the paper Rick had written her name and address on, and once I found it I entered the address, on a street called Berkey Farm Road. The property was owned by an entity called StanVest LLC. Well, that made sense; I remembered her full name was Margarita Stanville Gaines.

From the record, I saw that she had paid a half-million dollars for a home, a barn, and four acres, some ten years before. I stepped back a level and entered "Berkey Farm Road" in the search box. While the system searched for the records for all her neighbors, I opened a new window and pulled up a map program. I wanted to see a visual of her property and how it abutted her neighbors.

Berkey Farm Road was a north-south dead-end off Scammell's Mill Road, which led east to Stewart's Crossing. I went back to the main window and noted that there were only three addresses on the road. By going back and forth between screens, I figured out that as you turned from Scammell's Mill Road toward Rita's, Don Kashane's farm was on the left. A property belonging to Mark and Selena Hubbard was on the right; Rita's was next to it.

The road dead-ended into a thirty-acre farm owned by Hugo and Marjory Furst. A tiny stream ran from the Tohickon Creek along the north side of Rita's property, forming the border between her farm and the Fursts'.

Rochester got up from his place behind me, walked over to his water bowl, and slurped for a minute. Then he came back to me and rubbed his wet face on my leg. "I'm not your towel, dog," I said, but my mind was on what Don Kashane had said. The Fursts were angry that dog waste from Rita's property was polluting the stream, and the Hubbards hated the noise and smell from Rita's kennels.

Which one to start with? I flipped a mental coin and landed on the Hubbards. It was such a common last name, though, that I came up with over six million hits. Finally using a combination of words and quotation marks, I landed at the site for *Country House Journal*, a glossy magazine that featured custom homes in rural settings.

I discovered a photo-heavy feature on the Hubbards' home, written by Naomi Schechter, who had once been an assistant professor in the English department at Eastern. When she was denied tenure, she had turned to a freelance career, though she still taught a course or two as an adjunct. We had a nodding acquaintance; during the past year, we had shared space in a narrow room full of computers and semi-private cubicles where part-time faculty could meet with students.

The sprawling, two-story house had a living room as big as my whole downstairs, with rustic, exposed-beam ceilings, flagstone floor and walls hung with modern art. The rest of the rooms pictured were equally lavish.

I could imagine that the Hubbards, whose property was valued at over a million bucks, wouldn't be happy about a bunch of yapping, smelly dogs next door. From the article I could tell Naomi had interviewed the Hubbards, and I opened another new window onto the Eastern College website, where I was able to find out that Naomi had office hours the next day from ten to twelve. I made a note of it.

A motorcycle zoomed down Sarajevo Court, and Rochester jumped into guard-dog mode, his toenails scrabbling on the tile floor as he rushed toward the door, his bark deep and throaty.

"Quiet, Rochester!" He kept barking, until he was sure that the motorcycle was long past. "You really are not in charge around here, you know."

He looked at me and smiled a big doggy grin, then slumped back to the floor.

The article mentioned that Mark Hubbard was the CEO of a computer software company, and with that information I was able to pull up his corporate bio and a picture of him and his wife. He was a tall, slim man with salt and pepper hair, while Selena was a buxom dark-haired brunette at least twenty years younger.

They also owned a penthouse overlooking Central Park and a vacation getaway on St. Bart's. Well, if Rita's dogs got on their nerves at least they had someplace else to go.

The Furst property was appraised at only a hundred grand, which was surprising considering how much bigger

it was than Rita's or the Hubbards'. But an asterisk noted
that it had an agricultural exemption, hence the lower
value. I opened a new window with Google Earth, and
looked at the satellite photos of the area. I could pick out
Rita's house and barn, the Hubbards' sprawling mansion,
and the Furst farmhouse and a big barn. The area around
the house showed evidence of constant cultivation. Cows
grazed in a field beside the barn, and I wondered if Furst
had a dairy operation as well.

It was bedtime by then, so I took Rochester for a walk
around River Bend. Thad had gone in, shutting down his
music, and the neighborhood sang with crickets, frogs and
the distant hum of a car engine. Rochester chased a squirrel
and tried to clamber under a forsythia hedge, abundant with
yellow blooms, but I pulled him back. I heard the
Philadelphia train approach the crossing at Scammell's Mill
Road, a couple of miles away, the long whistle that always
reminded me of faraway places.

I used to hear that whistle all the time as a kid, and
because I knew you could hop on the train in Stewart's
Crossing and get to Philadelphia, and from there to
anywhere, it resonated with me and how I wanted to travel
far away from Bucks County, see those places I could only
read about in *National Geographic*. I remembered lying in
our back yard on summer afternoons, watching planes fly
high overhead, wondering where those people were going.

Now I was content to be back home. I hadn't seen the
world, but I'd lived in Manhattan and Silicon Valley,
vacationed in Europe and Mexico and the Caribbean. With
luck, I'd hold on to my job at Eastern, and Lili and I might
go somewhere together. As a photojournalist, she had
traveled a lot more than I had, but I hoped she still had
places she wanted to see—with me.

14 – Problems Cascade

The next morning I dropped Rochester off at my office with a fresh rawhide bone, and hung around the cubicles and round tables of the adjunct area for a half hour, waiting for Naomi Schecter to come in, but with no luck. I ended up leaving a note in her mailbox asking her to call or come by my office.

On my way back to Fields Hall, I detoured past Harrison Hall, the dimly lit stone building where the history department was located. Jim Shelton, who was on the graduation committee with me, was the chair of the department. His office was on the ground floor, across from the secretarial area where students got their closed class cards and asked random questions they could have answered by checking the college website.

Jim's office was lined with bookshelves, and a miscellaneous collection of texts and reference books crowded together with piles of handouts and student papers. His large desk was so covered with file folders and post-it notes there was little room for his keyboard and mouse.

I rapped on the doorframe, and he looked up from his paperwork. "Hey, Steve. Come on in. I was looking over this graduation fiasco."

"What's wrong now?"

"The same stuff we were talking about in the meeting. The program that vets student transcripts for graduation keeps breaking down. I'm worried we'll have to let anyone who applies march in the procession and then clean up the mess afterward."

"That's why I stopped by." I told him what Dustin De Bree had told me, about seeing the check from Freezer

Burn to Verri M. Parshall.

He sat back in his big wooden chair. "That's a serious accusation. But I can't say it sounds unfounded. I've fielded more complaints about computers in offices and classrooms this semester than ever before, and Verri doesn't seem to care."

"What do you think we should do?" I asked. "Tell Babson?"

"Not without some proof," he said. "Verri's been around forever and she has a lot of support around the campus. Plus she's a special pet of John Babson's. Not to mention the fact that she's got a stranglehold on IT around here."

"We should talk to Dot Sneiss," I said. "Maybe we can go at this from a different direction. If this Freezer Burn program is screwing up registration as well as classrooms and offices, then Babson will have to get involved."

Jim picked up his phone. "Dot? Jim Shelton here. You have a few minutes this afternoon to talk? Four o'clock?" He looked at me and I nodded. "Steve Levitan and I will come over to your office then."

I stood up. "Thanks, Jim. I didn't know what do when this kid came in to me. At least now we have a plan."

I was curious to know more about Freezer Burn. But I didn't want to go right back to my office and start searching in a way that might be tied back to me. So I walked to the library instead.

When I was an Eastern student, the library was a run-down repository of books older than the statue of old man Fields that stood in front of it. I had once asked one of the librarians where the contemporary novels were and she told me, in very frosty tones, that the library was intended for serious research, not pleasure reading.

As an English major, I had spent many hours in the dusty stacks, searching for research material. Once I returned to Eastern, though, I discovered that the electronic revolution had finally reached Leighville, and the bulk of the collection had been digitized. The old wooden card catalogs had been replaced by sleek metal tables lined with desktop computers, and most of the rows of study carrels now had computers as well. I found one in a back corner and slid into the chair.

All the public computers are automatically logged into the Eastern network under a Guest ID. So short of dusting the keyboard for my fingerprints, there was no way Verri could tie what I was doing in to me personally.

I did a quick Internet search for Freezer Burn, and came up with thousands of hits. The most interesting was a blog called "ihatefreezerburn" which had attracted a lot of comments, mostly from students at colleges that had instituted the software. As an English teacher, it was almost painful for me to read through their ungrammatical, misspelled rants, but one thing was clear: students detested the software.

Not for the obvious reasons—that it might block their access to social networks or personal email. No, they hated it because it caused campus computers to freeze on a regular basis, often in the middle of exams or while a student was trying to research and write a paper. It seemed that no matter how powerful the computer or stable the network, Freezer Burn managed to do something to screw things up.

Why use it, then? I navigated my way to the corporate website. Freezer Burn was an independent start-up company, run by a couple of IT wizards who had cut their teeth at Microsoft and Apple. The video explaining the software had high production values, and I could see how someone might be seduced. It looked like they were preying on fear, promising system administrators that Freezer Burn would reduce vulnerability to hackers and viruses, protecting student data and network integrity.

One warning flag to me was that they were only on

release 2.02. I knew that meant it was only the second patch, or revision, to the second version of the software. I couldn't imagine how anything so new could manage to negotiate with the wide variety of hardware and software you'd find on a college campus—everything from the homemade programs the math department used to format equations to the sophisticated databases that managed registration and grade processing. I knew from experience that the computers on the Eastern campus were a patchwork of older and newer models, both PC and Mac, with a range of operating software and peripheral equipment. Every time Microsoft comes out with a new edition of Windows, people complain that their older printers and other equipment are left behind because the developers didn't bother to build in the capability to work with those older, nearly obsolete pieces of equipment. I had the feeling that problem would be even worse with a new company like Freezer Burn, which wouldn't have the resources to devote to tracking down every old piece of software and hardware and creating drivers to accommodate them.

I rebooted before I left the library. One good thing about Freezer Burn was that it would erase my browsing history on that computer. It was almost lunchtime, so on my way back to Fields Hall I picked up a roast beef hoagie. I had missed those big, beefy sandwiches when I lived in New York and California; nobody makes them the way they do in Philly and its suburbs. I liked my hoagies on a fresh-baked crusty Italian-style roll, layered with Russian dressing, shredded lettuce, sliced tomatoes, and thin sheets of rare roast beef. Heaven on a bun.

I took it back to my office to eat, where Rochester was delighted to see me. Or maybe it was the hoagie. He sat up right next to my desk, and I fed the fatty bits of beef to him. I had just crumpled the wrapper and tossed it in the trash when he woofed once and I looked up to see Naomi. She was a short, compact woman wearing a man's blue and white striped shirt over black pedal-pushers, with a ruby starburst pin over her right breast.

"Oh, Steve, it's you," she said. "I wasn't sure when I saw your note. You're an administrator now?"

I stood up. "Yeah. You know what a sucker's game adjuncting is. Had to find a better way to pay the bills."

"Tell me about it. Freelancing is only marginally better."

We both sat. "Thanks for coming by. I know this must be a busy time for you."

"I'm only teaching two courses this term, so I'm almost finished grading." Rochester shuffled over to Naomi and sniffed her outstretched hand.

"Do you remember interviewing Mark and Selena Hubbard about their house?"

"Oh, God, them," she said. "Don't tell me he graduated from Eastern?"

I was puzzled for a moment, then realized she'd made a connection to my job. "No, but he and his wife live next door to Rita Gaines, who was on the Board of Trustees. She was murdered this past Sunday, and President Babson asked me to keep tabs on the police investigation to manage any PR fallout."

I sat back in my chair. "The police detective investigating the crime is a friend of mine, and I was out at Rita's house with him the other day. One of her other neighbors said the Hubbards and Rita had squabbled, and when I saw you'd interviewed them I thought I'd ask you about it."

"If you've been out there, you know how the place smelled." She looked down at Rochester. "No offense to you, doggie, but when a bunch of you get together you can make a real stink. Not to mention all that yapping."

"Yeah, I know. That bothered the Hubbards?"

"You bet. Apparently Rita only had a few dogs when

they moved in, but over the years she developed a real breeding operation and things got worse and worse."

She fished in her bag for a tissue and blew her nose. "It's a beautiful home, but they can't keep the windows open in the spring or the fall. They can't go outside in the summer and swim in the pool or have a barbecue. The noise and smell of Rita's dogs was a real sore point for them."

"They complained?"

"Especially Selena. She's a former beauty queen from Venezuela and Mark spoils her rotten. Second marriage, you know."

"I guessed."

"He does everything he can to please her. Fortunately he's got the money to do it."

"You think he'd go so far as to kill Rita?"

She shuddered. "I wouldn't put it past either of them. One day when I was at their house a couple of petals had fallen off the roses in the living room and the maid didn't clean them up fast enough. Selena let loose on her in Spanish. And you know how Mark made his money, right?"

I shook my head. "I thought he owned a company."

"Yeah. He started out in business with a partner who was some kind of genius programmer. Within a year he had screwed the partner out of his ownership. He leveraged the business to buy a competitor, and then he took off. Buying companies, gutting them and then dumping them. He's not a nice man."

She looked at her watch, a Swatch with gaudy designs along the plastic band. "Gotta run. I'm actually on my way out to the Hubbards' now. I'm ghost-writing a business book with Mark."

"After all you know about him?"

"That's how I know it all. And he's paying through the nose because this is a big vanity project for him. When you're a freelancer, you've got to go where the money is."

"I know that. I worked my butt off trying to start a tech writing business when I first moved back here." I stood up and shook her hand. "Thanks for coming by. And good luck with the book."

"It doesn't have to sell," she said. "I just have to finish it. Right now I'm half writer, half therapist. Fortunately I have a high tolerance for nuts with money."

After she left I sat back at my computer. So Mark Hubbard was a corporate raider with a spoiled wife and no conscience. Would he have gone so far as to kill Rita Gaines to please his wife and protect his country idyll?

I spent the next couple of hours researching details of our honorary degree recipients and then knitting them into a press release that didn't bore the pants off the reader.

Just before four o'clock, I took Rochester out for a quick pee. Students stood, sat and lounged in an endless line that snaked out of the front door of Fields Hall and along a flagstone path that led to the Cafette. I overheard a girl say, "I am so glad to be getting out of this place. I have this friend who's a junior, who says her father has gotten three tuition bills for the fall, all with different amounts. He's going crazy."

I saw Yudame from my tech writing class halfway along the line. He was wearing a T-shirt with the psychedelic logo for the movie *Taking Woodstock*, along with artfully torn jeans, which had either come from the Goodwill store in Leighville or a fancy Manhattan boutique. I couldn't tell the difference. "Looks like you're camped out for tickets for a rock concert or something," I said.

He shook his head. "Yo, my Prof," he said. "I wish. Just these skeezy graduation audits."

Like many other students, in class Yudame spoke well – excellent grammar, enunciating the last letters of words, never using slang. But outside? It was another language.

Level of discourse was one of the things we talked about in tech writing—targeting your speech and writing to your audience.

"Audits?" I asked. "Like to make sure your bills are all paid up?"

"Nah. There's some kind of epic fail with the big brother computer system. So you got to make sure you ain't got probs with your classes – you gots all the ones you need, or the haters be making sure you ain't getting no diploma. So we all gots to wait in this line and talk to a dude in meat space."

He looked like that prospect didn't thrill him. But that was the net generation; most of my students would rather interact with computers than people, and they'd rather text a friend than meet up in person.

He leaned down to pet Rochester, who reared up and put his paws on Yudame's jeans. The kid just laughed and scratched behind his ears. Maybe they were from the thrift store. Or Yudame's parents were so rich it didn't matter. At Eastern you never know.

I returned Rochester to my office, then walked back around the corner to the registrar's to meet with Jim Shelton and Dot Sneiss. Fields Hall was an old fieldstone house that had been retrofitted a hundred years ago as an office building, and many of the spaces inside were unusual in shape. The registrar's lobby was an odd half-hexagon, with three teller-like windows and a rope to organize those waiting in line. But so many students had crammed into every corner of the room that I had to excuse myself and squeeze past to get to the door that led to Dot's office.

I tried the door handle, and since it was locked I knocked lightly. No answer. I looked around but couldn't get the attention of anyone behind the window to buzz me in. I waited, uncomfortably squeezed between a guy in a ball cap and football jersey and a heavyset young woman wearing stiletto heels that were too high to keep her balanced.

Jim Shelton shouldered his way through the crowd a couple of minutes later, after I'd knocked three more times. "This is chaos," he said. He dug his cell phone out of his jacket pocket, apologizing to the teetering girl for elbowing her, and called Dot.

The line moved forward, the guy in the jersey squeezing past us so he didn't lose his place in line. Finally the door opened, and Jim and I were able to slip inside.

I took a deep breath. "That's a mess out there."

"I'm going to kill Verri Parshall one of these days," Dot said. "I'm extending hours til eight o'clock tonight, and even then we won't get through everyone waiting."

She led us into the conference room. "What's up?"

We sat down at the big oval table and I explained what Dustin De Bree had told me. "That explains a lot," Dot said. "I couldn't imagine why we were still using that product when it was so crappy."

"Have you spoken to John Babson about these computer problems?" Jim asked Dot.

"Just in the most general way. He's been traveling a lot lately and I haven't had the chance to sit down with him one on one."

"I think you're going to have to," Jim said. "We don't want to accuse Verri of anything based on one student's sour grapes, but Babson needs to know that we're in danger of a massive screw up with graduation."

Dot sighed. "I know. I've been here twenty years and things have never been this chaotic. I'll try and get a meeting with him as soon as possible."

"This has gone beyond the level of an inconvenience," Jim said. "Very soon, you're going to have the entire faculty trying to access the mainframe computer to enter our final grades. At least one third of our classes are taught by adjunct faculty who go off the payroll, and in many cases disappear, as soon as the semester is over. If they can't get their grades in, students can't graduate."

"You don't have to tell me, Jim," Dot said. "Transfers get screwed up, too. And don't even think about Federal financial aid. If we can't demonstrate that students successfully completed their courses, we'll lose our funding. The whole damn college will grind to a halt."

"All from a software malfunction," Jim said.

"Welcome to the world of computers," I said.

15 – Itchy Fingers

Dot let Jim and me out a back door into the garden so we didn't have to fight the crowds. "See if you can talk to that student again," Jim said, as we walked back around to the front of the building. "We're going to need every piece of ammunition we can find against Verri if this comes to a fight."

"I'll try."

I also wondered if I could dig up any evidence myself. Eastern wasn't only my employer, it was my alma mater. I couldn't stand by and let someone sabotage it, if that's what was going on. Even if it was only massive incompetence, I had to do what I could to head off disaster.

I could already feel my fingers itching. Instead of going back to my office I headed for that secluded carrel in the library. I felt like some kind of undercover agent as I looked all around me before I slipped into it.

I sat down at my computer and flexed my fingers. I was going to enjoy this. Verri's team had locked down the college system, but I'd gotten around such safeguards in the past.

I got myself a DOS prompt and started trying to figure out how I could get around Freezer Burn. If it was as crappy a program as I thought, I knew I could find a back door into it. At my last job I had gotten a lot of experience trying to break into software, helping the engineers figure out where the bugs were and how to fix them. I'd learned that hitting a random mix of keyboard keys and function keys together often confused a program. I'd run password generating programs that tried endless combinations of letters, numbers and symbols until they hit one that would give me high-level access, enabling me to actually edit the code that ran things. I had a lot of ideas and I was willing to use them all.

I was right; Freezer Burn was a crappy program. It took me only a half hour to figure out that if I arrested my computer's boot-up before it hit the Freezer Burn code, I could bypass that section of the routine. Once I'd done that, I could also bypass the software that restricted what could be done on any campus computer based on its location and internet protocol address. The computers open to students for their use, for example, couldn't access the employee database, even if you logged into one with an employee ID.

Without Freezer Burn blocking my access to the college's mainframe computer, I was able to start figuring out why our systems seemed to be constantly failing. One routine asked for an employee password before granting access to the college network. It looked to a particular database to validate the credentials. However, the path to that database required the employee to already have logged in to another database on a different server.

That server was supposed to be first on the path to log in—but if you were logging in from an off-campus computer, or a computer the network didn't recognize, the path didn't lead you in the right direction.

Freezer Burn was clearly a lousy program, and one that the college was wasting money on. But what should I do with the information? I couldn't go to President Babson with the evidence I'd discovered without admitting that I'd broken the law myself. And no matter how valuable the information was, I couldn't see how he could justify keeping an unreformed hacker on his staff.

It was after five o'clock by then, so I gave up hacking for a different kind of investigation. I shut the computer down, looked around to make sure the coast was clear, and then left the carrel, and the library.

When I unlocked the door to my office, Rochester rolled over onto his back and waved his paws in the air. "What, you don't want to go home?" I sat down on the floor next to him and rubbed his belly. "Who's a good boy?"

"You do love that dog, don't you?"

I looked up to see Mike MacCormac at my office door.

"Yeah. A friend of mine has a term for it. Puppy whipped."

Mike laughed. "I guess I belong in that crowd, too. Anyway, I came by to ask if talked to Mariana at the News Bureau about helping her with press releases."

The News Bureau handled all the general public relations work for the College, while I handled everything related to fund-raising. "Yeah, I'm splitting the workload with her. I've finished one for each recipient of an honorary degree and sent them out, along with bios and photos. Next up I'm working on a couple of releases about the valedictorian, the salutatorian, and the students who won the honor awards."

Like any old-line college, Eastern had a range of legacy awards given to exceptional students—all related to our logo, the rising sun. The Ray award was for school spirit, the Corona for volunteerism, and so on. "I'll be sending them to all their hometown papers, too. I figure any mention of Eastern is good for us."

"Great. Why don't you cross-reference our donor database and email them to any alums in the area, too? It'll be nice for them to hear something from us that isn't asking for money."

I stood up. "Will do."

Mike left, and Rochester scrambled to his feet. "Feel like a ride, boy?" I asked, as I hooked up his leash. I wanted to go back out to Berkey Farm Road and take a look at Rita's neighbors. When I'd been to her farm in the past I hadn't noticed them at all.

I rolled down the windows, and Rochester sat on the passenger seat with his big golden head streaming in the breeze as we navigated those country roads once again. As we got close on Scammell's Mill Road, I slowed down to note my surroundings.

One new development was under construction, a series of sprawling faux-Colonial homes on wide lots, and I wondered who had the money for such properties in the current economy. I passed a couple of farmsteads, and then approached Don Kashane's property. He kept a couple of horses in a field by the road, protected by a white split-rail fence. Beyond them I could see his house, and a series of newly planted fields. I smelled dirt and fresh grass as I signaled my right onto Berkey Farm Road.

As soon as I made the turn, though, the breeze shifted and I smelled dogs, and dog shit. Rochester sniffed it too. I could also hear the cacophony of barking, even far from Rita's driveway. I could only imagine how irritating it would be to have every evening ruined by that kind of sound and smell.

I pulled next to Don's fence and stopped the car. A big Jeep Grand Cherokee sat in the Hubbards' driveway, and from the Eastern parking decal on the back window I assumed that meant Naomi was still there. The house was faced with fieldstone, and floor-to-ceiling windows looked out from what was probably the living room. A flagstone path led up to the front door, which sat slightly back, protected by the two-story right wing of the house. The yard was immaculately groomed, with fresh-blooming tulips in beds around the maple trees.

Could I be living in a house like that, I wondered, if Mary hadn't miscarried, if I hadn't hacked into the credit bureaus, if I hadn't gone to prison and we hadn't divorced? Was this my road not taken? Mary had been a high-earning business executive, and though I hadn't matched her income, I'd done well for myself.

Suppose she hadn't miscarried, and we'd moved back to the East Coast. We could have had a house like that— maybe not quite so fancy or expensive, but we probably

119

could have bought in that development I had passed. Would I be a stay-at-home dad, freelancing or doing computer consulting?

Rochester leaned over and put his head in my lap. "Yes, boy, that's not a road we want to go down, is it? My life has led me here, to you, and we're going to make the best of it, aren't we?"

He snuffled my crotch and I laughed. "Come on, let's go." I put the car in gear and we cruised down the road, past the driveway that led to Rita's property. Berkey Farm Road dead ended at Hugo Furst's drive, and I noticed a farm stand in the Fursts' front yard.

Jars of strawberry and rhubarb preserves shared space on a splintered plywood table with bundles of fresh asparagus and spinach, heads of green leaf lettuce, and a tray of other mixed vegetables. An older man sat behind the table and looked up as I got out of the car and walked over. He wore a pair of overalls and a white T-shirt.

"Evening," I said. "Wow, those asparagus look great."

"First of the season. I'm Furst, and I raise 'em."

For a minute I misheard him and thought he was talking about poker. But then I made the connection. I picked up a bunch of asparagus. The spears were crisp and straight, and the heads were compact. "I'll take two of those," I said.

As if on cue, Rita's dogs erupted in a new round of barking as Furst flipped open a brown paper bag.

"How many dogs do they have? Sounds like a hundred." I knew the number was closer to fifty, but I thought asking the question might be a good conversation opener.

"Too many," Furst said. "But not for much longer. Woman who lived there got herself killed, so all them little Chihuahuas and dachshunds will be moving on."

I picked up a head of lettuce and sniffed it. It smelled fresh and earthy. "Bet it won't come soon enough for you."

"You got that. I got nothing against dogs, you know." He looked beyond me to where Rochester had his front paws on the windowsill of the passenger door. "Got two of 'em myself. But that witch Rita, she had forty or fifty at a time. And it's not just the noise, either. She hosed down the kennels and the dog shit ran right down into my land."

"Isn't manure good fertilizer?" I asked innocently.

"Not dog shit, with all the chemicals in their food. But you can be sure, my produce is one hundred percent pure and organic."

I picked out some ripe Jersey tomatoes, a couple of zucchini, and a few other vegetables and then pulled out my wallet. "I'll take two heads of lettuce, too. So the woman was killed? Run over or something?"

He shook his head as he took the bills from me. "Nope. Somebody poisoned the old bitch. If I knew who, I'd shake his hand. You have a nice night, now."

"Thanks. You, too."

I could see Hugo First was glad that Rita was dead. But had he hated her enough to kill her? I couldn't say.

As I drove back toward Stewart's Crossing, I realized that I didn't have a main course for dinner—just the asparagus and the lettuce. I could have stopped at the McCaffrey's grocery and picked something up, but it was on the other side of town and I didn't feel like going all the way over there. Instead I called Rick. "You want to grab a burger at the Drunken Hessian?" I asked.

"I'm wrapping up here. I have to head home and feed Rascal. Why don't you come over to my house and we'll order a pizza?"

"Sounds good to me. You can spare a bowl of chow for Rochester, can't you?"

"I can, but I'm not sure Rascal will share."

"Rochester will see to that, don't you worry."

I pulled up in Rick's driveway as he was getting out of his truck, and Rochester bounded out of the car and rushed up to him. As I got out I could hear Rascal going wild inside his crate in Rick's living room. Rochester and I followed Rick inside, where Rascal was up on his hind legs shaking the metal bars of the crate as if he was Jimmy Cagney in some old prison movie.

Rick opened the crate and Rochester and Rascal went wild together. Rick opened the door to his back yard and said, "Go pee!"

Rascal took off, Rochester right behind. Rick opened the fridge and pulled out Sam Adams beers for himself and me. His kitchen hadn't been changed much since the house was built in the fifties; he'd put in a new fridge, oven and dishwasher, but the Formica cabinets were original, as was the big stainless steel sink and the brown and tan patterned linoleum floor.

By the time Rick had the beers opened the dogs were back inside, and while I distracted them with some squeaky toys he put two bowls of food out on his kitchen floor. They both chewed noisily as he called in the pizza order to Giovanni's, in the shopping center in downtown Stewart's Crossing. Luckily we both liked the same kind—a thick crust with spicy Italian sausage crumbled and scattered over a base of homemade tomato sauce, freshly sautéed mushrooms and shredded mozzarella from an artisan cheese maker in New Hope.

"I drove out past Rita's on my way home from Eastern," I said, after I'd taken my first swig of beer. "I wanted to check out the neighbors."

"Why? You're not going Nancy Drew on me again, are you?"

"Hey, I've been able to help you before. And I told you, I prefer the Hardy Boys as a reference, not Nancy Drew."

"So what did you find? Anybody confess?"

"Not yet. I leave the waterboarding to the cops. Have you looked into any of them? I know that the Hubbards have been complaining about the noise and the smell of her dogs."

"Already checked their alibis. They were at some fancy soiree on Sunday night in Manhattan, and they stayed over at their Fifth Avenue penthouse. Doormen on both the evening and day shifts verified."

"They could have hired someone. People that rich don't do their own dirty work."

"And you know about that how? From reading?"

"I know a few things."

The doorbell rang and the dogs exploded in barking. I pulled a twenty from my wallet and handed it to Rick, then grabbed both dogs by their collars.

"Rochester, this isn't even your house," I said to him. "Shut up."

He took his cue from Rascal, though, and neither dog would stop barking until Rick had closed the door on the scared-looking delivery boy.

The pizza smelled great, and both dogs sat on their haunches next to us as we began to eat. "You know I'm not giving you any," I said to Rochester. "So you can give it up."

"A little crust won't hurt him." Rick pulled two pieces off and tossed them into the air, one after the other. Rascal jumped up and wolfed his down, and Rochester followed his lead.

"Your dog is teaching mine bad habits," I said.

"Your dog is smart enough to figure it out without mine to teach him. You took him up to Rita's with you this afternoon?"

"Yup. But he didn't discover any new clues."

Rick nearly choked on his pizza. "Gee, imagine that."

"I did talk to Hugo Furst, too. The guy on the north side of Rita's. He's awful glad she's dead."

"Yeah. But that doesn't mean he killed her."

"You check his alibi?" I finished my slice and took

another swig of beer.

"His wife says he was home all night."

"Not much of an alibi," I said.

"Good enough for now. Besides, I'm thinking I need to look more into her dog breeding and training business. You know as well as I do how crazy dog people can be. And I've started hearing some rumors about the way Rita treated people she sold dogs to."

"Well, we saw how bitchy she was on Sunday."

"I've got a list of all the people whose dogs she trained, including the ones who only came over for agility practice, like me, and another list of everyone who bought a dog from her for the past five years. Tomorrow morning, first thing, I start calling them all. And then there's an agility show this Saturday at Northampton Community College in Bethlehem. You remember those people we met on Sunday-- Matthew and Carissa? They're both scheduled to show their dogs. I was thinking we could take Rochester and Rascal up for the show, talk to people." He looked at me. "Since you're so eager to be Joe Hardy to my Frank."

"Hey, isn't Frank the older brother? I want to be Frank."

"Tough shit. I'm older than you are, so I get to be Frank."

It was true; Rick was about three months older than I was. I groused for a while, and complained when he threw more crust to Rochester, but we both knew I wouldn't turn down the chance to go to the dog show with him and nose around. I guess it was Joe Hardy for me.

Better that than Fred Jones or Shaggy Rogers from *Scooby-Doo*. Though like Scooby, Rochester was goofy and prone to get into trouble.

16 – Unauthorized Snooping

Friday morning I dropped off a head of lettuce and a bunch of asparagus at Lili's office. "How's the grading coming?" I asked, as Rochester walked around her office, sniffing the art books on a low shelf next to her window.

Her office was a large, well-lit room in Harrow Hall, the fine arts building, and the walls were hung with student drawings, paintings and charcoal sketches. She had her auburn curls pulled up to the top of her head in a Pebbles ponytail, and she wore a T-shirt from an exhibition at the Brooklyn Museum.

"Only a dozen portfolios left to look over," she said. "You have it easy in the English department, you know. Papers are so simple. You can email them, print them, carry them around if you need. Try grading a refrigerator-sized oil painting sometime."

"Rochester, stop sniffing," I said. "You're not an art critic." He came over to me and I rubbed behind his ears. "Think you'll be free for dinner tonight?"

She shook her head. "Sunday. Brunch?"

"It's a date." I leaned down and kissed her. "I'll let you get back to your appliances."

Rochester and I left Harrow Hall and walked up the hill toward Fields Hall, past the library. I looked at my watch. Nothing much on my agenda, so I had time for some more sleuthing. I took Rochester back to my office, closed the door, and put up a note that I was in a meeting.

Then I returned to the library and found my way back to that same secluded carrel where I'd been the day before. I turned the computer off then on again, hitting the same key sequence so I could disengage Freezer Burn. Then I let my fingers do some walking.

One of the things I learned during my years as a tech

writer and web developer was that often computer people get so cocky they ignore basic safeguards. I found a list of all the techs who worked for Verri M. Parshall and played around with breaking into their email accounts. And what do you know? Her assistant director, Oscar Lavista, used 1-2-3-4 as his password. It's like he was almost begging me to break in and read his mail.

Once again, my adrenaline was racing and my fingers tingled. But then my hacking instincts kicked in. It seemed almost ludicrous that he'd make it so easy—perhaps he was setting up a honey pot, a trap to detect hackers. We'd had one of those where I worked, a false entry into the website with some decoy files. I opened the computer's task manager and made sure no security-oriented programs had opened and were writing anything to remote directories.

While I gave the system a minute to be certain nothing was going to kick in, I looked around. The other computers were occupied by students, and I was conspicuously older than they were. What would I say if someone I knew came by and spotted me?

Of course. I'd say that my office computer was acting up and I was waiting for tech support. Given all the problems we'd been having with Freezer Burn, anyone on the college staff would believe me.

When I was pretty sure no alarms had been triggered, I opened Oscar's email account. It didn't look like a decoy; I had access to hundreds of emails he had sent and received.

I shook my head. Not only was his security shoddy, his mail folders were poorly organized. I was trained to manage my inbox; every time I dealt with a message I either deleted it or placed it in a relevant folder for archiving. But Oscar didn't believe in that. He had a mix of opened and unopened messages in his in-box. He didn't even bother to delete those campus-wide spam messages we get about toner cartridges, union votes, and farewell parties for staffers most people didn't even know.

Was he incompetent, though, or just overworked? As I read through the messages he had sent, I saw that he understood the issues involving not only Freezer Burn, but the other software and hardware he dealt with. The time stamps on his messages indicated he was often responding to questions late at night.

He had clearly tried to communicate to Verri the problems that the techs were having with Freezer Burn, and every time she shut him down. I wondered if he'd be a good informant. Perhaps he'd be willing to go on record about problems in a way that Dustin De Bree couldn't afford to.

I couldn't get into Verri's account; she was smart enough to use a complicated password that was hackproof, at least without the advanced tools I had hidden away at home.

I looked up Oscar's profile on the campus Intranet. He was a moon-faced guy with dark hair and a mole on his chin. I didn't think I'd ever seen him. He held an associate's degree as a computer tech specialist from Broward College in Florida, and had been with Eastern for two years.

Should I suggest that Jim Shelton or Dot Sneiss talk to him about the problems with Freezer Burn? Or approach him myself? I pushed away from the computer, stood up and stretched.

"Hey, Prof, what are you doing over here?"

Once again, my adrenaline zoomed. I looked behind me and saw Lou Segusi holding hands with Desiree in front of a display of illuminated manuscripts from the college's collection. I didn't even need the excuse I'd prepared—a simpler lie came right to my tongue. "Just needed to use a computer for a couple of minutes and I didn't want to go all the way back to my office. How are you doing, Lou?"

"Two final exams, and I'm done," he said. "And I heard from Penn State—I got accepted into their Master's of English Ed program."

"Congratulations. How about you, Desiree? You graduating this term?"

"If I can. My degree audit's all screwed up, and the lines at the registrar's office are out of control."

"Desi's moving to State College, too," Lou said. "She's getting her master's in environmental science."

"Cool. Well, good luck to you both."

I gave them a brief wave and left the library, relieved that no one had caught me with Oscar Lavista's email account on my screen.

When I walked back into my office, Rochester hopped up from his place by the french doors. But instead of coming over to greet me, he jumped up on the low table by the window and posed, his head up. He looked at me as if I was supposed to understand what he was doing.

But I was baffled. He held his right paw up to me, as if he wanted me to shake. I took it and said, "Yes, pleased to meet you."

As soon as I let his paw go, he jumped down and ran in a couple of circles around me. "I get it," I said. "You're practicing for the next dog show." I motioned him back up to the table, and he jumped up. Then I held out my hand the way I'd seen Rick do, counting down the five seconds, and when I finished, Rochester jumped down.

I laughed, gave him a treat, and sat down at my computer, only to discover that the entire college's email system was down. I experienced a momentary pang of guilt, worrying that I'd done something to trigger the catastrophe. But that wasn't possible; all I'd done was disable Freezer Burn on a single computer.

It was a pleasure to be able to get some work done without the constant interruption of incoming messages, though. I had a boss once who called it "being in the zone," when you got so wrapped up in your work that you were most efficient and didn't even notice time passing. I spent the morning finishing all the press releases on the student award winners, and then wrote a quick program to search through the databases for alumni who lived near a winner and also had given us an email address. When email access was restored just before noon, I sent the press releases out in small batches to avoid getting caught in some alum's spam detector.

I'd made myself a big salad that morning using the fresh lettuce from Hugo Furst's farm stand, and I sat at my desk and thought about Rita Gaines as I ate. Her killer must have brought the Rohypnol to her farm. But had he or she known about the cobra venom, or found it once Rita had been knocked out?

Rochester wasn't happy with my vegetarian lunch; he'd eat the occasional chunk of carrot or zucchini slice, but for the most part he was a carnivore. He had to be happy with a couple of treats from my desk.

Either way, it seemed, the killer had to be someone who was familiar with Rita's farm. I remembered Rick saying that he had a list of the people who had trained their dogs with Rita, as well as those who had bought dogs from her, and I called him.

"How are you doing with that list of dog people?" I asked.

"Haven't even looked at it," Rick said. "Break in at the Crossing Florist last night—somebody stole about a hundred expensive orchids. I've been swamped with that. Turns out the florist is best friends with the mayor's wife."

"You want me to look at the list for you?"

He groaned. "Steve."

"Hey, we're going to that dog show tomorrow. You should be prepared in case we run into anyone who might be a suspect."

"I really hate you, you know that?"

"Oh, come on. You know you don't mean that. Just send me the list. You know you want to."

"If I didn't have this other case that the chief was hot for…"

"I know, I know. I'll do some quick research for you, just to help you focus."

"Fine. I'm emailing you the list now."

"See you tomorrow morning. I'll call you if I find anything before then."

The email popped into my inbox a minute later, with three Excel spreadsheets attached. I saved them all to my jump drive and then opened the first one up.

It covered the casual clients who, like Rick, brought their dogs up to Rita's occasionally for help with agility training. I was interested to note that Rick had been paying Rita twenty bucks a week for her help in preparing Rascal.

I opened the other two spreadsheets. One included a worksheet for every dog Rita had sold for the last five years, including the dog's parentage, current owners, and any medals won at dog shows. The other was similar, but these were dogs Rita trained for both obedience and agility.

The sheer number of people was overwhelming, and I started to think that Rick had played me the way Tom Sawyer did when he got his friends to paint that fence for him.

I decided to begin with Rita's training clients, because I'd seen the way she behaved, and it was easy to imagine her pissing someone off. There were a dozen embedded worksheets, one dog per sheet. Eight were current clients, and four were people who had trained with Rita in the past. I opened up the worksheet for the first of the ones who were no longer Rita's clients.

The sheet for a dachshund named Lady's Luscious Lover, aka Lush, indicated he was nowhere near a champion. He had been entered in eight shows, and only won a third-place ribbon once. Rita's notes were scathing—Lush's owner, a woman named Paula Madden, was unable to control him; the dog was slow, lazy and a disgrace to his pedigree. And those were the G-rated comments. I was surprised that Rita would use words like easy and brain-dead to describe Paula. I wondered if she'd said those things out loud, too.

I did a quick search on Paula Madden and discovered she owned a shoe store at the Oxford Valley Mall. When I pulled up one of her online ads, I saw that little Lush figured prominently. He was photographed resting his head on a pair of pumps, sniffing high heels, and with one paw delicately placed in a jeweled sandal. The rhinestones on his collar matched the ones on the shoe's straps.

Okay, another crazy dog lover. I couldn't throw stones, though. The big goofy golden dog snoozing on the floor next to me was proof of that.

The next sheet was curiously brief. Baby Blue Eyes had a similar pedigree, but had never entered a show. A brief note at the bottom of the page read: "Deaf. Offered replacement, but idiot refused."

The owner's name was Sal Piedramonte. His address was on Samarkand Court in Stewart's Crossing, and I recognized it was one of the short cul-de-sacs in River Bend, at the other end of the neighborhood from my townhouse.

I lived on Sarajevo Court, which ran into Minsk Lane. The complex had been built by émigrés from the former Soviet Union, who had brought a bit of home to Stewart's Crossing. My two-bedroom townhouse, with an attached garage, was a Latvia, and models were named for Serbia, Lithuania, Estonia and Croatia. The largest was the Montenegro, which I'd heard one of my neighbors call the Mount Negro.

I tried to remember if Rochester and I had ever met a deaf dachshund on our walks, but little dogs barked aggressively at Rochester, so we usually walked quickly past them.

Nothing jumped out at me about the dog on the next sheet, Puffball, other than that he had only one name, and I couldn't find out anything about his owner, Pippin Forrest. Puffball had entered a few shows but Pippin's handling was sloppy and according to Rita's notes the dog hadn't medaled.

The last owner to have left training with Rita was Mark Figueroa, and I knew him. He was an antique dealer in Stewart's Crossing and he often stopped in at Gail's café for coffee when I was grading papers. He was an avid reader, and we talked about mystery novels and travel memoirs sometimes. I didn't realize he had a dog.

Rochester turned on his side and scratched his toenails against the wooden floor. "Rochester! No!" I didn't want to end up getting stuck with a bill for refinishing the floors.

His feathery tail thumped against the floor, but he didn't lift his head. "What's up, boy? You need to go out?"

He jumped up as if he'd stuck his paw in an electric socket and began dancing around. I wanted to open the french doors and let him out into the garden, but I knew he couldn't be trusted. He'd tackle some sandwich-eating student, intercept someone's frisbee, or terrorize the squirrels.

Of course, because I had a lot on my plate, Rochester was maddeningly slow about doing his business. By the time I got back to the office a slew of new email messages waited for me, and I had to put aside sleuthing to work at the job that paid my bills. I kept hoping I could come up with some way to delegate some of the work to Rochester, because there had to be some way to channel all his intelligence and energy.

Instead, I did all the work myself, and he slept. Before I closed my computer down for the day, I printed out all the worksheets Rick had sent me so I could study them at home the next morning.

As usual, though, Rochester had other ideas.

17 – Defective Merchandise

I meant to make myself a quick dinner and then sit down with those printouts. But Rochester was antsy, even after our regular walk and his bowl food. He kept rocketing around the living room and the only thing I could do was take him for a long walk, and use the opportunity to check out my newly-discovered neighbor, Sal Piedramonte.

It was still early evening, the sky a violet blue, as we circled through the Eastern European-named streets of River Bend. We walked slowly, heading toward the other end of the neighborhood. I wasn't sure where Samarkand Court was but I had a general idea, and after continuing past the big lake at the center of the community, we approached it. I noted Sal Piedramonte's house, the same model as my own, and continued walking. When we turned the corner onto Vilna Vista, we stumbled into the middle of a doggy play date.

A dachshund and a Shih Tzu rolled around together in the grass. A golden we knew named Hopi dashed around them. Hopi's dad, a white-haired retiree named Dave, motioned us to join in. I let my dog off his leash and he went chasing after Hopi, and I walked up to Dave.

He introduced me to the twenty-something dark-haired guy with him. "This is Sal. "That's his doxy, Blue. The Shih Tzu's my son's. I'm taking care of him while they're on vacation."

"I've never seen a dachshund with a white ear before," I said to Sal, happy to run into the guy I'd been looking for. "Gives her character."

"There's a reason for that," he said. "One white ear, plus blue eyes, are markers for congenital deafness."

I remembered the note on Rita's spreadsheet. "She can't hear at all?"

He shook his head. "The first couple of months I had her, I thought she was just stubborn, the way she ignored all my commands and couldn't be housebroken. Finally one day a friend of mine was over and he figured out she wasn't stubborn. She was deaf."

"Wow. You didn't know that when you got her?"

"The breeder should have known, but she pretended she didn't." The big dogs continued to run circles around us, but Blue and the Shih Tzu came over and sprawled on the ground at our feet. "I went back to her and complained, and you know what she said?"

I shook my head.

"She said she didn't sell defective merchandise. So she would take back Blue and put her to sleep, and give me a choice of another dog."

"That's harsh," I said. "I'd never consider a dog merchandise."

"Me either. I told her what she could do with her merchandise and I walked out."

"This was a local breeder?" I said, playing along.

He nodded. "Her name is Rita Gaines. Stay away from her."

Dave agreed. "I've heard bad things about that woman, and not just from Sal."

"Rita Gaines," I said. "Isn't that the name of the woman who was killed last week?"

"Really? You mean somebody beat me to it?" Sal said. "Good job, whoever did."

"Now, Sal, you shouldn't say things like that," Dave said.

"Why not? She was a bitch, and I'm glad she's dead." He leaned down and picked up Blue, cuddling the dachshund in his arms, and I could see how bright her blue eyes were.

"How is it, having a deaf dog?" I asked. "I mean, you can't call her or scold her or anything, can you?"

"We have a series of hand signals. Once I made sure she was always looking at me when I wanted her to do something, we started to get along fine."

He raised the dog up and kissed her on her snout. "Isn't that true, Baby Blue?"

Rochester hopped up and put his paws on my groin. I reached down and scratched behind his ears, and then we said goodbye to Dave and Sal and their dogs. Walking home, I wondered if Sal had been faking his surprise at Rita's death.

Could he have killed her? What if he'd gone back to her to complain about something, and she'd made disparaging comments about his baby. Could he have gotten so angry that he'd have killed her? He was a young guy; he probably knew, at least a bit, about roofies and the effect they had. He could have slipped the roofie into her iced tea, then injected her with the cobra venom.

I shook my head. Rita hadn't been killed in the heat of an angry passion—someone had thought the crime through carefully, noting the cobra venom at the barn and then figuring out how to inject Rita with it. That didn't sound like a guy who was pissed off because his dog had been called defective.

Darkness fell quickly as we walked back home, and by the time we got there Rochester was worn out, and I'd spent too much time thinking about Rita Gaines without any result. I tabled those thoughts and turned to my laptop. I logged into the online course management software Eastern used, and navigated to the drop box where my tech writing students had submitted their final research papers.

Most of the students were decent writers, and we'd done enough exercises through the term that they had their research and citations pretty close to correct. I marked them on a couple of other criteria—including an appropriate, and correctly sized, picture or photograph; using a table to lay out the picture and the accompanying text; using different fonts as appropriate for headings and captions.

I looked up from grading the last paper to see Rochester over by the coffee table where I had piled the printouts of Rita's customers. He had his nose up to them, and as I watched, he reared up and used his paw to swipe them to the ground.

"Rochester!" I yelped, jumping up. "Don't do that."

He began pushing the pages around with his nose. He had an unfortunate taste for paper, and I was worried that the next morning I'd be pulling the ropy, barely digested pulp out of his butt—not something I particularly enjoyed.

I remembered I had carried the sheets home in my briefcase—where I often had a couple of dog treats as well. Had the smell of the treats attached themselves to the pages?

He was sniffing at one sheet in particular as I leaned down and cleaned them up. I snatched it out from under his paws and saw it was the one for Mark Figueroa, my antique dealer friend, and his dog, Judy's Last Song, a Chihuahua. Doing a bit of quick cross-referencing, I saw that Judy and Carissa's dog, Tia Juana, had been littermates. But Mark had only attended a few training sessions with Rita before dropping out.

Did he have some kind of grudge against Rita? Perhaps she had criticized his dog, too. Mark and Gail, from the Chocolate Ear, were close friends, and I could ask her about him. But her café had closed by then, and Mark's antique store in downtown Stewart's Crossing would be closed, too.

I picked up all the spreadsheets and put them on top of a counter Rochester couldn't reach, then went back to my laptop to finish grading the last paper. Then I exported the grade book to another Excel spreadsheet, where I calculated the semester totals. The last step was to enter them into the college mainframe. But since a couple of students might still submit their work late, I decided to wait. It was a lot of trouble to change a grade once it was in the mainframe.

After I shut down the laptop, I dug around on the kitchen counter until I could find Rochester's brush. "Come here, puppy," I called, and sat down on the tile floor. "We have to make you handsome for the show tomorrow."

He scampered over and put his head in my lap. I started brushing his coat, pulling out strands of soft golden hair. "I could make a sweater out of you," I said, as the hair piled up. He kept trying to go under the kitchen table, leaving me only his back end to brush, then turning around on me.

By the time I was finished hair was everywhere, and I had to get the vacuum cleaner out to pick it all up. Rochester clambered upstairs and hid from the noise under my bed. When I came upstairs myself, he came out and jumped up on the bed to watch TV with me.

As I scanned through the channels with one hand and scratched behind Rochester's ears with the other, I felt very righteous about completing my grades, since they weren't even due for a few more days. That freed me up for investigating over the weekend with Rick. I thought about entering them into the college's mainframe computer, but that's always more of a pain to do from home than from school, even without the interference of Freezer Burn, so I thought I'd wait until Monday.

18 – Show Time

Saturday morning, Rick picked Rochester and me up in his truck, and we drove up route 611 through Doylestown and Quakertown to get to Bethlehem. Dogwoods were blooming in pink and white and maples were rich with green buds. We passed at least three spring-cleaning yard sales, rickety card tables piled with chipped dishes, out-of-date textbooks, and other useless junk its owners hoped would put a few bucks in their pockets.

We parked in front of the college's Technology Center, in view of a series of white tents where the show was being held. Around us were dozens of cars, trucks and RVs, and almost every one sported some sort of dog bumper sticker, from "My Labrador Retriever is smarter than your honor student" to "It's the Golden Rule: Goldens Rule" to "Proud Parent of a Bichon Frise."

"Dog people," Rick said, shaking his head.

"And what are we? You spoil Rascal more than I do Rochester."

"Don't remind me."

From the parking lot, we heard the loudspeaker announcing the walk-through for the standard class for novices. "Shit, that's us," Rick said. "We've got to hustle."

"What do you mean? Are you competing?"

Rick tugged Rascal's leash and hurried forward. "It's Rascal's first time," he said over his shoulder.

I shook my head and followed with Rochester. He had already prepaid his admission and Rascal's entry fees, so he sailed past the elderly woman at the registration table. By the time I had paid our admission and picked up a program, then walked into the broad lawn where the tents had been set up, Rick and Rascal were already in line next to one of the rings.

Ring seemed the wrong word, even though that's the way they were labeled. It was more like a rectangle, with all the equipment set up inside. I'd seen all the stuff at Rita's, but somehow it looked more impressive under the sprawling white canvas tent, with dozens of dogs around. As I watched, a woman led her whippet up a ramp, across a flat plank, then down. Ahead of her, a borzoi was climbing the A-frame while a Sheltie was on the teeter-totter.

I checked out the program. The events were divided into four classes by height; Rascal was in the third category. The loudspeakers competed with the barking of dogs and the whir of portable fans that cooled the area. I couldn't see how the dogs could concentrate on what they were supposed to do. I kept Rochester on a short leash by my side, and sometimes I had to hold him back if he wanted to sniff another dog or take off in search of Rascal.

We skirted the main performance ring and walked between two rows of vendor tables. Fortunately most of the merchandise on display was for little dogs—pink plastic carriers with mesh windows, rhinestones collars and tiny leather jackets with upturned cuffs—or I'd have ended up buying Rochester something I'd regret later, like a pair of felt moose antlers or a big rubber clown nose. I did like the harnesses at one booth, and if Rochester didn't already have a couple of beds I'd have been tempted to buy him another from a vendor with wide variety of beds, cushions and dog blankets. There was even a booth selling clothes for the humans accompanying their dogs around the course.

All around us were dogs on platforms being groomed, dogs practicing their jumps, dogs on leather leashes and plastic cords. The biggest seemed to be the giant Schnauzer, down to a couple of teacup Chihuahuas that I could hold in the palm of my hand.

I spotted Carissa, the elegant Latina who had trained her dog at Rita's. She wore a pair of cream-colored pedal pushers and a sleek V-necked athletic shirt made of some kind of expensive microfiber. It clung to her in all the right places, and it was decorated with tiny rhinestones which matched the ones on the collar worn by her Chihuahua, Tia Juana. I introduced myself to Carissa.

"Oh, Rita," she said. "How terrible. When I heard the news I was so upset. So was Tia. Sadly in my country we are too familiar with violent death."

That was interesting. How did she know Rita had been murdered? As far as I knew the papers had only reported her death, not the crime behind it. "Did you know Rita well?"

"I bought Tia from her and she convinced me to start training her. I wouldn't say I was her friend, but I've been investing with her for years."

Rochester leaned down to sniff Tia Juana. "She didn't seem like the type to make friends," I said.

"Well, you won't find many people here who liked her," Carissa said.

"Really? Why not?"

"She was a very fierce competitor and she had no self-control when it came to telling people what she thought of them and their dogs. As if she was the only reputable breeder around."

"That must have made a lot of people angry."

Carissa nodded toward a forty-something Asian man in pressed khaki slacks and a military-style shirt festooned with pockets and epaulets. As I watched he pulled a treat out of one of those pockets and fed it to the fluffy white bichon he had on a bright blue leash. The dog's haircut made his face look round as a dinner plate.

"That's Jerry Fujimoto," Carissa said. "He raises bichon frises and trains them for his owners. Rita was always bad-mouthing him and his methods. I heard he lost a number of clients because of it."

"But she didn't raise bichons herself, did she?"

"No, only doxies and Chihuahuas. But she definitely

had her own way of doing things, and if you didn't agree with her she'd let you have it."

Tia Juana yelped as Rochester's nose got too invasive, and I jerked back on his leash. "Sorry. He still has a lot of puppy in him."

She looked at her diamond Rolex and said, "We need to get ready anyway. I want Tia to get some practice at the long jumps."

"She does long jumps? But her legs are so tiny."

"They adjust the distance for the size of the dog," she said. "And you'd be surprised at what my Tia can do."

They trotted off, Tia Juana leading the way, and Rochester and I meandered toward Jerry Fujimoto. He was a whirlwind of activity, chatting up owners and dogs alike, and I knew I'd never get a word in with him as long as the show was on. As I waited, a boy of about eight with a bichon on a jeweled red leash said, "Can I pet your dog?"

"Sure. Rochester, sit."

The boy tentatively placed his palm in front of Rochester's mouth so he could sniff, then patted him on the head. The boy's hair was a golden red similar to Rochester's, and he was missing his two front teeth. "Is your dog competing?" he asked.

"Today we're watching. How about you?"

"We already did. Puffball came in second in his height class."

Puffball. What a name for a boy dog, I thought. Then I remembered that name from the list of Rita's ex-clients. "I'm Steve," I said, sticking out my hand to him. "Do you train with Mr. Fujimoto?"

He shook my hand limply and nodded. "My name is Pippin but people call me Pip."

"From the Broadway show? Or *The Lord of the Rings*?" I asked. Puffball was completely disinterested in Rochester, instead straining toward another bichon, probably a female.

"I'm a hobbit. Yeah, my parents are big geeks. My sister's name is Meriadoc."

I laughed. I guess Puffball wasn't too bad then. And that explained why I hadn't been able to find anything about Pippin Forrest online. "He a nice guy, Mr. Fujimoto?"

"Not really. He yells at the dogs a lot and he scares me sometimes. But we used to train with this other lady named Mrs. Rita and she was even meaner. When my dad said we were switching she called him a really bad word. At the last show, Mr. Jerry and Mrs. Rita were yelling at each other. He told her he hoped she died and went straight to – a bad place I'm not supposed to say out loud."

Interesting. But did Fujimoto mean that enough to kill her? I couldn't ask Pip that question, but it rolled around in my head.

Pip petted Rochester some more and said, "Your dog is really sweet. I wanted a big dog but my parents said no."

I leaned down to his level. "I'll tell you a secret," I said. "It's not the size of the dog's body that matters, but the size of his heart. And I'll bet Puffball has a really big heart."

Hearing his name, the dog turned around and returned to Pip's side, sprawling on his back and waving his little legs in the air. Pip stroked his stomach and said, "Yeah, he's a good boy."

I heard the announcement of Rick's class and said goodbye to Pip and Puffball. Rochester and I found a place along the side of the ring. I stood, and Rochester sat beside me as if he was observing and taking notes. It was quite comical to watch the owners scurrying alongside, waving their hands, whistling and making clicking noises as if it was an event for sufferers of some obscure mental syndrome.

Some of the dogs ran right through the course like pros; others were more tentative, and a couple disregarded some of the obstacles. "That's a weave fault," the announcer said, as a border collie entered the weave poles from the wrong side. He called a refusal when the Sheltie stopped short in front of the tire and wouldn't jump through it, and a time fault when a Viszla took too long to complete the course.

Finally it was Rick and Rascal's turn. I couldn't help snickering as Rick, normally the tough cop, babied Rascal up the A-frame, through the tunnel, then over the jump. He ran next to the dog like a crazy person, and I thought I'd get a lot of teasing out of it.

Though Rick looked nervous, Rascal performed like a champ, and he ended the event in third place, winning a yellow ribbon for his trouble.

The four of us strolled past the vendors again. "Late yesterday I heard about a woman who wasn't on the spreadsheets," Rick said. "Cora Straw. Apparently she left her dog with Rita when she went on vacation, and when she came back the dog was dead."

I stopped in front of a display of walking sticks with dog heads. "That's terrible. What happened?"

"Rita gave her some story about the dog having a heart attack on the course. But she had already disposed of the body before Cora came home."

"That would drive me crazy," I said. "Oh, look at the golden retriever bookends!"

A pair of resin dogs looking a lot like Rochester sat on their haunches with their backs against imitation books. "And those yard stakes with little dogs on them!"

"Step away from the display," he said, in his most stern voice. "I'm doing this for your own good."

I cast a glance back at the kitchen towels and garden flags as Rick grabbed my arm and moved me along. We bought some rubber toys and rawhide chews for the dogs, then headed back toward the parking lot.

"When I checked in, I picked up a list of all the

breeders who were showing," I said, pulling the paper out of my pocket. "I thought maybe you could call them and ask about Rita."

"You forget who's the detective around here," Rick said, pulling an identical list from his pocket. "I do have a few skills, you know."

"Yeah, yeah." Rascal and Rochester jumped eagerly into the back of the truck, then sprawled out next to each other and went right to sleep.

"Remember that list you emailed me yesterday?" I asked Rick, as we pulled out of the campus. "The people who trained with Rita? While you were competing, I met one of the ones who dropped her today."

"Which one?"

"Pippin Forrest. But he's only a kid. I think we can knock him off the list, because I doubt an eight-year-old can get his hands on Rohypnol."

"Parents?"

"What do you mean? Does he have parents? I guess so."

"And one of them could have been pissed off at the way little Pippin was treated, right? After all, we're going on the assumption that someone didn't like the way Rita handled a dog. A kid just ups the ante."

"I didn't get that vibe from Pip," I said. "He said that Mrs. Rita yelled a lot, but it seemed like he accepted that from adults. He did say he's training with a new guy, named Jerry Fujimoto, who Carissa told me had a beef with Rita."

"Didn't everyone?" Rick said. He handed me his copy of the trainers' list. "Make a note on the sheet for me, will you?"

I did. "I didn't see any of the other three people who stopped training with Rita, but we both know one of them—Mark Figueroa. From the antique store in the center of town."

144

"Hmm," Rick said. "How about the others?"

"Just did a quick search. Paula Madden owns a shoe store at the mall. I thought I'd get Lili to go over there with me and scope it out. And Sal Piedramonte lives in River Bend. Rochester and I met him and his dachshund last night. He was pretty angry about the way Rita dissed his dog when she found out Blue was deaf. Wanted to give him a different one and put Blue to sleep."

"That seems pretty hard," Rick said. "I mean, being deaf isn't something fatal."

"He said Rita treated her dogs like merchandise."

"It's an attitude. But is it a motive?"

"Hey, as you pointed out earlier, you're the detective."

"So you do listen to me sometimes."

"Asshole," I said. He laughed.

"Lili's finishing up grading her students' projects," I said, as Rick drove up to the River Bend guard house. "You doing anything for dinner?"

"Got a date," he said. "Loser."

He waved to the young female guard on duty, who smiled and opened the gate for him. He dropped Rochester and me off at my house, and I thought about driving into town to look for Mark Figueroa, but he probably had a date, too.

I microwaved a frozen dinner and poured Rochester a bowl of kibble. When he finished I gave him one of the new rawhide chews and he settled down with it, his back against the sliding glass door.

While I ate I grumbled about having a girlfriend and still being home on a Saturday night, but then Rochester came over to me and slumped next to my feet. Then we watched a movie together. I thought it was pretty stupid but Rochester seemed to like it.

Sunday morning Rochester woke me when the sun was just peeking over the rooftops across the street and we went for a long walk. A bluebird darted between the fronds of the weeping willow at the end of Sarajevo Court, and all around us were signs of nature waking up. I was looking forward to spending the day with Lili. We'd been talking about going down river to the flea market in Lambertville, and I thought it was a perfect day for that kind of aimless browsing. But she called me around ten and asked if we could change plans.

"This guy I used to work with called me last night," she said. "He's hot on a story and he needs some background from me. He asked if I could meet him for brunch."

"Background for a story? On what? Art?"

"All he would say is that it involves Eastern, and I'm the only person he knew with any connections to the College."

"It's not like you need an in. He can call the public relations office. Or hell, he could call me."

"Good. So you'll go up to Summit with me to meet him?"

"Summit? Where's that?"

"Ritzy suburb of Newark. About an hour, I think."

"Isn't that an oxymoron? A ritzy suburb of Newark?"

"Since we're heading north you can drive up here to get me, and then we'll go in your car." She hung up.

19 – Peter Pan

I shook my head. How had I let myself get roped into spending my Sunday with my girlfriend and some guy she used to work with? What if he was still interested in her, and using this as an excuse to get together?

And what kind of story was he writing about Eastern?

I rushed through a shower, got dressed, and pacified Rochester with a hard rubber squid he'd already torn one tentacle from. As I pulled into Lili's driveway she stepped out the door, locking it behind her. She wore what I had come to see was her standard casual outfit; skinny jeans, a man's button-down shirt, and bright red high-topped sneakers that matched the rectangular frames on her eyeglasses. She had a couple of cameras on straps over her shoulder. Her auburn hair cascaded in waves down to her shoulders and smelled great as she hopped into the car next to me.

She leaned over and kissed me, then carefully slid the cameras onto the back floor of the car. "Thanks for doing this. I don't have any idea what Van wants but it sounded very hush-hush. If there's something strange going on at Eastern I thought you'd want to know about it and figure out the PR implications."

"How well do you know this guy?" I asked, as I backed down her driveway.

"We worked a couple of stories together when we were both freelancing. She leaned back in the seat, stretching her legs. "Our biggest was an expose for the *New York Times* about child soldiers in Nicaragua. That was a bad story."

"He still works for the *Times*?"

She shook her head. "*The Wall Street Journal.*"

"What would the *Journal* want with Eastern?"

"Beats me. How was your day at the dog show

yesterday?"

I noted the quick shift away from Van, whoever he was, but I went with it. I told her about watching Rick and Rascal compete as we drove downriver to Yardley. We picked up I-95 at the Scudder's Falls Bridge.

"You know these roads pretty well," Lili said, as I exited 95 at New Brunswick, where I picked up US 1.

"My dad grew up in Newark and had family in the area," I said. "So we used to go up this way a lot when I was a kid. But most of the people from his generation are gone and I lost touch with the few who are left."

"Really? That's sad."

"My dad was an only child, so most of those people were his cousins. I can't say I was that close to any of their kids."

"I wish I lived closer to my family," Lili said. "When I was looking for a job I tried to get something near my brother and his kids in California, but nothing came through. I have a few cousins scattered around the country, but the closest to here is one in New Hampshire."

We turned east on I-78 just beyond Newark Airport, and Lili called her friend's cell to get directions to the diner where we were meeting him. "He says to stay on 78 to 24. Then take the Morris Avenue exit. The Peter Pan Diner is right there."

"Got it." We pulled up in front of the diner a few minutes later. A rangy blond guy in jeans and a fisherman's shirt was leaning on a BMW convertible and talking on a cell phone, and Lili hopped out of the car and ran up to him. I followed her, watching as they embraced.

"This is Van Dryver," she said, presenting him to me. "My boyfriend, Steve Levitan."

At least she made our relationship clear. That was a plus.

"I didn't realize you were bringing someone," he said, and I wondered if "bringing" really meant "dating."

"Steve handles PR at Eastern," Lili said. "I thought he'd be more help to you than I could. What's this all about, Van? Why all the cloak and dagger?"

"I'll tell you inside." He led us in, and we sat at a peeling vinyl booth in the front window. The place looked like it had been around since Jesus wore short pants, with a vinyl tile floor, Formica tabletops, and a small jukebox at each table. Around us, teenagers in polo shirts with popped collars ate burgers and fries and joked around.

"What's good here?" Lili asked Van, picking up the menu.

"No idea. Never been here. But I had an interview this morning in Summit and the guy recommended the place."

After the waitress took our order, Van said, "The story I'm looking into is about a woman with connections to your college. Started out as a regular obit, but I've been turning up some strange things."

"Whose obit?" I asked. "Not Rita Gaines?"

He turned to me. "You knew her?"

"Steve's an amateur detective," Lili said dryly. "His friend is the policeman investigating the murder, and he's been trying to help out."

I winced. "Ouch. Trying?"

"He's been helping," Lili said. "Better?"

"Better. Are you looking into her murder?" I asked Van.

He pushed a blond curl off his forehead. His face was tanned and lined, even though he probably wasn't much older than Lili or me. And yet he still had a boyish enthusiasm which came through when he talked.

"In a way. There's something funky going on with her investment business."

The waitress delivered our platters and I had to wait til she was finished to ask, "Funky how? Anything that might bounce back and hurt Eastern?"

"I'm not willing to say anything right now. Just

149

investigating. But I understand she was a member of the board of directors at Eastern, and the College invested some of its capital with her. You know anything about that?"

"I knew she was on the board, but I didn't know anything about investments," I said.

"And I barely knew the woman," Lili said. "Met her at a couple of parties. And then she made that fuss at the exhibition."

"What kind of fuss?" Van asked.

As we ate, Lili told Van about Felae's painting and Rita's complaints. Van took a couple of notes, but it was clear from his demeanor that what we had to say didn't matter to his article.

Lili finished her eggs and pushed the plate away from her. "Is that all, Van? We drove all the way across New Jersey for this?"

"Can't blame a guy for trying."

"Uh-huh. Well, thanks for brunch." She scooted next to me with a gentle push.

I took the hint and stood, then pulled a card out of my wallet. "If you need a formal statement from the College or you want to talk to anyone else, give me a call," I said, handing him the card.

"Will do. Take care of Lili. She's a treasure."

When we were out in the car, I said, "You certainly cast your spell on him."

"Oh, please. This Peter Pan diner was the perfect place to meet him. He's an overgrown boy. He won't settle down and act like an adult; he just wants to keep chasing stories around the world."

"And you outgrew that?"

She looked over at me. "Yeah, I did. Don't get me wrong. If somebody offered me the chance to go somewhere for a great story, I'd probably jump, as long as it didn't interfere with school or anything else. But I like my life now." She took my hand and squeezed. "You think we can still make the flea market?"

"We can try." I backed out of the space and hopped back on the highway. But I wasn't going to let Lili off the hook too easily. "How long did you and he date?"

She looked out the window. "I told you, we just worked together."

I waited.

"We had a fling, all right? When I was married to Phillip, the magazine editor, I knew he was cheating on me, and when Van pursued me, I didn't say no. Philip and I were already living separate lives by then anyway."

I wasn't sure how I felt about that. I had never cheated on Mary, and I was pretty sure she had been faithful to me. But I knew enough not to pry into the state of anyone else's marriage. I could only hope that Lili wasn't going to make a habit of cheating.

"What do you think he found out about Rita Gaines?" Lili asked as we got onto I-78 to cut back across the state.

"No idea. But she was definitely a nasty piece of work, so I wouldn't be surprised if she screwed a few people along the way."

I regretted that choice of words but knew if I called attention to the comparison to Lili's relationship with Van I'd only dig myself in deeper. "She probably cheated some of her clients or something."

"You think one of them might have killed her?"

I shrugged. "I'm only 'helping' with the investigation. I don't know the ins and outs."

Lili turned to look out the window again.

Oops. That was something else I shouldn't have said.

The highway sped past us, miles of farmland interspersed with the occasional office building or suburban development. Even though almost nine million people were crammed into about 200 square miles of the Garden State, big swaths of farmland remained in the middle of the state with little access to the big cities.

Neither of us spoke much. Lili plugged her iPhone into the car's speaker system and played Springsteen tunes, and we both rocked out to "Dancing in the Dark" as we sped along. When we finally hit the Delaware, we took the slow road along the river, enjoying the blossoming of nature. We made it to the flea market in Lambertville by mid-afternoon.

The sun was shining, and the tall sassafras and oak trees along the edges of the parking lot were budding. Senior citizens, families with kids fresh from Sunday School, and forty-something hipsters like Lili and me were browsing the aisles. Lili got her cameras from the back floor and once again slung them over her shoulder. She stopped periodically as we walked, taking pictures of little kids playing – always with their parents' permission, of course.

She also took shots of things I thought were weird—a soda can with flies buzzing around it, a rock with a jagged edge, the leaf of a maple tree with a single drop of water on it. "Think of it like stock photography," she said, when I asked her. "You know what that is?"

"Kind of."

"I merge the images together sometimes. Layer them. Fuzz the edges. Just play around. I never know what will inspire me." She found a guy selling used camera equipment and bought a couple of lenses for her lab at the college. "You never know what camera kids will come in with," she said. "I like to have a variety of lenses for them to play around with."

It was late afternoon by the time we finished at the flea market, but I knew that the stores at the Oxford Valley Mall would be open until six. "You mind making a brief diversion with me?" I asked, as I pulled out onto the River Road on the Jersey side.

I told her about Paula Madden and her shoe store. "I'm

not really a shoe gal, as you can probably tell," she said, pointing to her red sneakers. "But I can fake it if you want."

She leaned back in her seat. "Running around after stories, you realize you need comfortable shoes. It used to kill me when I had to get dressed up and put on heels." She turned to me. "Does it bother you, meeting a guy I used to date?"

I shook my head. "We both had lives before we met. All that matters is what's ahead."

"We've only known each other a couple of months. We both still have a lot to learn. But any time you have a question about my past you can always ask me."

"Me, too," I said.

"Well, there is one thing."

I looked over at her. Her posture was relaxed, but there was something wary in her eyes. "Ask away."

"How come you ended up in prison for computer hacking? Isn't that one of those white-collar crimes they slap you on the wrist for?"

The question wasn't much of a surprise. I had told Lili only the barest facts about my unfortunate incarceration, not wanting to scare her off. I guessed it was time for the details.

"I hacked into three major credit bureau databases. Those companies are very strict about their security and it freaked them out that I could get in. So they all got together and made sure I was prosecuted as fully as I could be."

"Three credit bureaus? What did you do?"

"All I wanted to do was make sure Mary couldn't run up more bills on our plastic," I said. "I know, I could have called and cancelled the cards, but I didn't want her to know what I was doing. And she had a bunch of cards in her own name that I couldn't have done anything with legally, even though I would have been responsible for her debts."

I took a deep breath. "So I got into her records and

lowered her credit limits, then set a couple of flags that would make it tougher for her to get new cards."

"How did you do that?"

I let go of the steering wheel for a minute and waved my hands, as if I was typing. "Magic fingers. And luck. I found a back door no one had exploited before. Honestly, they should have thanked me for finding a weakness in their security systems."

"But they didn't see it that way."

"Nope. But you know how they say, you do the crime, you do the time. I did mine."

"And that's when you got divorced?"

"Mary started the proceedings as soon as I was arrested. She didn't appreciate that I was looking out for her, and frankly, our marriage had been falling apart for a while. The second miscarriage was the end."

Lili wrapped her arms around her and I couldn't help wondering if she had some pregnancy problems in her own past.

"You think you would have gotten divorced even if you hadn't been arrested?"

"I think so. But my head was screwed up then. I mean, those were my kids, too, but the support isn't available as much for fathers as for mothers in those situations."

Lili was quiet as we drove south, past the stone quarry and the now-deserted ski area. I didn't often think of myself as a father; after all, I had no children, just Rochester. But Mary and I had conceived two babies together, even if neither lived to be born. I guess that made me a father in some way.

"I had an abortion," Lili said, as we crossed the narrow bridge in Washington's Crossing. "My marriage to Adriano was over, and I knew I had to leave Italy and come back to the States and finish my degree. My period was late, but it was irregular back then and I didn't think anything of it. Then I got terribly sick on the plane home, and I was nauseous every day for a week."

I didn't say anything, didn't even look over at her. I had no qualms with abortion; I believed it was every woman's right to decide if she wanted to bear a child, and that every child deserved to be born to loving parents. But every time I heard about an unwanted child, I couldn't help but think of the two Mary and I had wanted so badly.

Lili's voice was quiet. "I had no resources to take care of a child, and I knew Adriano didn't want a baby, either. And frankly, I didn't want anything more to do with him. I went to the Student Health clinic and got a referral to a women's health center."

She turned to me, and her voice was stronger. "It was the right decision at the time. My mother was dead and my father was remarried and living in Thailand. I was on financial aid and I didn't have anyone else to rely on. I would have had to drop out of school and I had no skills to get a job."

"Everyone has to make choices," I said.

She took a deep breath. "I dove into my work. My photographs became my children. It wasn't until my marriage to Phillip was ending that I woke up and went into therapy." She smiled. "It's funny how things work out. My students accuse me of being too motherly sometimes. Everything comes around in a circle, you know?"

"I know." I signaled for the turn into the mall, and then reached over and took her hand.

20 – Lush Life

Lili checked her phone and found that Madd About Shoes was next door to Macy's, and I parked in the adjacent lot. "You know, for years I wouldn't go in this entrance of the mall," I said, as we walked up.

"Why not?"

"A girl I went to high school with was killed in the parking lot here. Really tragic—and very mysterious. They never found out who killed her, or why."

"What happened?"

"It was early winter, I think, and I remember she had been in the mall buying stuff. Someone shot her, though they didn't steal her wallet or anything she'd bought. Apparently she dragged herself back through the parking lot until someone found her on the curb. They called an ambulance but she didn't make it. I keep thinking someday someone will figure it all out."

"That's terrible. And that was when you were in high school?"

I nodded. "Senior year. We had a big class, you know, and a lot of people died."

She stopped at the entrance to the department store. "Died? How?"

I started ticking them off. One boy had hung himself, and another had shot himself with his father's rifle. A third had been in a car with his girlfriend, stopped at a grade crossing as a train approached. They had argued, and he jumped out of the car and stood on the tracks. "He said he would stay there until she said she was sorry," I said. "She didn't say it fast enough."

"My god—how awful!"

I pushed the door open and continued my list. Another girl had suffered a brain aneurysm at a speech tournament in Pittsburgh. "Then this girl named Kim, was one of the first in our group to drive," I said. "She liked to pull this trick on people. She'd start to drive away without you, and you had to jump on her car hood to get her to stop and let you in."

"That's dangerous."

"You bet. Another girl pulled that on Kim, and she slipped off the hood and hit her head on the pavement."

"And this was all in Stewart's Crossing?" Lili asked, as we walked through the store. "It's so sweet and pleasant."

I shrugged. "At the time, we took all that death for granted. Though when I got to college and told people I had been a pallbearer at four different funerals they were kind of surprised."

"No wonder you have this morbid interest in dead bodies and crimes," Lili said. "Oh, look, there's the shoe store."

If I hadn't already known that Paula Madden was mad about her little dachshund, I'd have guessed it as I walked up to the store. The window was full of the same kind of pictures I'd seen on her website, only life-sized. Lush was the star of the show, and looking inside I saw the real dog sitting on his tiny haunches next to a woman who was being fitted for what Mary called "do me pumps," glittering red high heels that forced the woman wearing them into a seductive walk.

"Don't even think about getting me in shoes like that," Lili whispered as we walked inside. Instead, she went right to a display of ballet flats painted with splashes of color.

The sales clerk stood up, and I saw she was wearing a T-shirt with a picture of a dachshund on it and the words "I Know a little German" on the back. Her name tag read "Paula."

The little dog came over to us and sniffed. He didn't want to leave me alone; he must have smelled Rochester on me, and he kept nosing against my pants and my shoes. Lili browsed until Paula had finished with the customer and rung her up. "Sorry, I just got back from a buying trip yesterday, and I discovered that one of my salespeople quit while I was gone, so I'm short staffed," Paula said, coming over to her. "How can I help you?"

"Do you have these in a seven?" she asked. I gave up on ignoring Lush and sat down on the floor, so the little dog could climb into my lap.

"You must be a dog lover," Paula said to me.

"Guilty as charged," I said. I tickled Lush behind his ears, and he stretched his tiny legs and yawned.

Paula went into the back and returned with a box, and Lili sat down in one of the upholstered armchairs. "We both love dogs, but I like doxies in particular," Lili said to Paula. "I've been thinking of getting one myself. Do you know a good breeder?"

I realized that if Paula had been out of town, she probably didn't know that Rita was dead. Lili kicked off her sneakers and offered her right foot to Paula, who slipped the ballet flat on. "All I can say is don't get your dog from the woman who sold me my little Lush," Paula said. "She's an awful witch."

"Who's that?"

"Her name is Rita Gaines. She bred Lush—but you should have heard her criticize him when I took him in for training!"

Lush turned on his back and I rubbed his belly. Rochester was going to be very jealous when I got home.

"That must have made you mad," I said. "I hate it when anyone criticizes my dog."

"I was livid. I swear, I could have killed her." Paula slipped the other shoe on Lili's foot and asked, "How do they feel?"

Lili stood up. "I love them. That's foam in the sole, isn't it?"

"Yes, they're made in Argentina, and I'm the only local distributor."

Lili walked a few feet then turned to face us. Then, hand on hip, she stalked back as if she was on a runway. I couldn't help laughing.

"I'll take them," Lili said. "So this woman, Rita. Stay away from her?"

"You bet. And if you buy a dog somewhere else, don't even think about going to Rita for training. Not only is she a bitch, but the dog owners who train with her? They're as nasty as she is. You couldn't pay me to set foot on her farm again. And if I tried, she'd probably chase me away. We didn't end on the best of terms."

I considered telling Paula that Rita was dead as she rang up the shoes, but at that point I thought it was too late to spring that on her without seeming dishonest.

"So what do you think, Sherlock?" Lili asked as we walked back out of the mall. "Guilty or innocent?"

"Well, Dr. Watson, she said Rita wouldn't let her back on the farm," I said. "Whoever killed Rita had to get close enough to her to drop the Rohypnol in her iced tea. I'm going to put her in the innocent column, at least for now."

We drove back to Stewart's Crossing, stopping at Genuardi's to stock my freezer. Rochester greeted me as if I'd left him on his own for days—first jumping around my legs and barking, then slumping in the corner and ignoring me except when I called him over with a treat.

Lili and I made a stir-fry with chicken breasts and the vegetables from Hugo Furst's farm, and then took Rochester on a long walk down by the canal in the lavender twilight. Back in the early nineteenth century, mule-drawn barges used to transport coal from the mines upriver down to the deep water port at Bristol on the Delaware Canal, but now the towpath is a park and the only commerce on it is the kitschy mule-barge rides in New Hope.

The canal banks were blossoming with wildflowers,

fiddlehead ferns and daisies, black-eyed Susans and the tiny pansies we called Johnny Jump-ups. Rochester loved the wide range of smells, darting from the base of a pine tree to cattails at the water's edge to a patch of four-leaf clovers.

I let Rochester off his leash, and he bounded ahead. Lili and I held hands and walked along quietly together, both of us smiling. I was reminded of what an amazing thing a life was, and I felt sorry for Rita Gaines, whose life had been tossed away like a bag of dog poop.

Lili spent the night, and the next morning I dropped her at her house on my way to work, then drove through Leighville up to the employee parking lot on the side of the hill.

As Rochester and I crossed the lot, heading towards Fields Hall, I caught sight of Dustin De Bree. "Hey, Dustin!" I called. "Wait up."

He stopped, but I could tell he was in a hurry from the way he shifted from foot to foot. Considering he was the one who needed my help, I figured he could wait a minute. "You know a guy named Oscar Lavista?" I asked. Rochester pulled on his leash, eager to sniff something, and I had to rein him in.

"Oscar? Sure. He's Mrs. Parshall's assistant."

"I'd like to talk to him. You think you could introduce me?"

He shook his head. "No way. I don't want him asking me how I know you. Because if anybody finds out I saw that check I'll get fired and I really need to keep my job."

"But Dustin, if you want me to help you..."

"He doesn't even leave the office much. And you wouldn't want to talk to him there."

The shifting increased, and I wondered if he was that nervous—or just had to go the bathroom.

"Hey, wait. He's got a meeting later today, with Dr. Shelton in Harrison Hall. I heard Mrs. Parshall say that

Oscar would have to go because she thought Dr. Shelton was an ass and she wouldn't talk to him."

"Cool. Thanks, Dustin."

I let Rochester go sniff what he wanted to, and Dustin hurried off. When I got to my office I turned my computer on, and while I was waiting for it to boot up, I unpacked my briefcase. I had brought in all the paperwork I had collected on Saturday at the dog show, and I hoped I'd get some time that day to look into it.

The computer was still booting when I finished that, so I called Jim Shelton. "I've been looking into the problems with Freezer Burn," I said. "I think this guy named Oscar Lavista might have some information."

"Interesting. I got fed up with going to the help desk with a computer problem I've been having for weeks, and I called President Babson's office. An hour later I got a call from this Oscar guy and he made an appointment to come to my office at eleven to fix things."

"You mind if I come over then? I'd like to talk to him and apparently he doesn't get out much."

He told me I was welcome, as long as I didn't distract Oscar so much that he didn't fix Jim's computer. Mine was finally booted up by then, so I logged into my email account to check for messages.

Instead of the program opening, though, I got an alert that my account had been corrupted and the program needed to restart. For a moment I panicked that someone in IT had discovered I'd been hacking on Friday afternoon— but then, almost by magic, the message disappeared and the email program started normally.

Another Freezer Burn screw-up. I answered some email queries from reporters about graduation and played with Rochester for a few minutes, and at a few minutes after eleven I walked over to Harrison Hall. When I got to Jim Shelton's office, a portly guy with slicked-back dark hair was sitting at Jim's computer. Jim was leaning against a wall of shelves mixed with old hard-cover texts with dusty bindings and brightly-colored newer ones.

"Hey, Steve, come on in," Jim said. "Oscar here's trying to fix my computer."

"The problem is with your printer driver," Oscar said. "The system keeps trying to update the driver, but Freezer Burn won't let it, and so things freeze up."

"Can you fix it?" Jim asked.

"I have a way around Freezer Burn, but don't tell Mrs. Parshall." He bent over the computer and started typing.

I slid into the chair across from Jim's desk. When Oscar finished, he pushed the chair back. Before he could stand up, Jim said, "Steve and I are both on the graduation committee and we've been hearing lots of bad things about software problems with the Registrar's office. You think those are coming from Freezer Burn?"

"Don't have to think," Oscar said. "I know what the problems are."

"So you can fix them?"

He shook his head. "That's too much of a hack. Mrs. Parshall would find out and she'd have a cow."

"Why?" I asked. "Doesn't she want the computer systems to work properly?"

He stood up. "I've really got to go. I have a lot of work back in the office."

"Something strange is going on, Oscar. Are Verri M. Parshall and Freezer Burn connected somehow?"

"Mrs. Parshall is my boss. You'd have to ask her if you have any questions."

"Or we could go to President Babson," I said. "And then when he fires Verri, she'll probably take the department down with her."

"I don't have anything to do with Freezer Burn. It was her decision to buy the product in the first place, even though I recommended against it. She talks to them directly, too, whenever there's any problem."

He lowered his head and hurried out of the office.

"He's scared," Jim said.

"I would be, too, in his position. Verri's a powerful woman around here. She could fire him in a heartbeat if he challenged her."

"So what can we do?"

"Not sure right now. But at least we have some independent verification that Freezer Burn is the problem, and that Verri's in deep with the company." I told him what I'd discovered in my research about Freezer Burn—the newness of the software, and the range of complaints I'd found online about it, both from Eastern and from students at other colleges that used it.

"We have to get this fixed before graduation," Jim said. "I spoke to Dot Sneiss this morning and her office is still in chaos."

His phone buzzed. "It doesn't help that this is final exam week. I'm up to my ass in alligators as it is."

"I'll keep thinking," I said, as he picked up his phone.

I walked back to my office. We had a week before graduation, and I had the feeling that removing Freezer Burn from every computer on campus, installing a replacement program, and troubleshooting the process, would overwhelm even an efficient department. And we couldn't even start that process until we proved that something was wrong with Freezer Burn, and that Verri M. Parshall was behind the problem.

Back in my office, Rochester had gotten into the pile of dog show paperwork I had left on my desk, and when I tried to clean up I discovered he had the list of trainers under his right paw, with a big splat of drool over Jerry Fujimoto's name.

I tugged the paper out from under his foot, and he rolled onto his side. I scratched his belly for a minute, then sat up. I did want to talk to Fujimoto, so I looked up his website and found his phone number.

"I saw some of the dogs you trained at the agility show in Bethlehem on Saturday," I said, when he picked up. "I have a golden retriever I'm interested in showing. You think I could bring him over for an evaluation?" His kennel was in Doylestown, about a half-hour inland from Stewart's Crossing, so a pretty easy trip.

"Some goldens are pretty dumb," he said. "Yours have enough sense for training?"

As if Rochester knew I was talking about him, he looked up. "I think so," I said. I wasn't about to gush about his crime-solving abilities, though.

"Bring him over late this afternoon, and I'll let you know what I think," he said. "Five o'clock?"

I agreed, and hung up. I thought about scooting out of work early and taking Rochester for some practice on Rascal's course, but as I looked at him, I figured he'd do fine without the prep work. Besides, I wasn't really interested in training him—I just wanted to talk to Fujimoto about Rita.

I ran through the suspects I'd already looked into. I doubted that Pippin Forrest or his parents had killed Rita because she'd been rude. Paula Madden had walked out on Rita and it was doubtful, given what I knew of Rita's personality, that Paula would have been able to get close enough to Rita's iced tea to dose it with the Rohypnol. Sal Piedramonte was angry at Rita, but again, I didn't think he could get in to see her.

That left Mark Figueroa. If I eliminated him, I'd have to start on the list of Rita's current clients.

A Hardy Boy's work is never done.

21 – Student Records

As I was finishing a salad I'd brought from home for lunch, an email came through reminding all faculty, full-time and adjunct, that our grades were due in the computer by Wednesday at 3 pm, so I took the opportunity to log in to the mainframe to enter mine while I thought of it. Most of the grades were As, with a couple of Bs and a single F, for a student who'd dropped out right after spring break.

As Jim Shelton had predicted, I ran into trouble. The first time through, I only got a couple recorded before the system generated an error message and kicked me out. My second and third attempts wouldn't even let me into the mainframe. Fortunately, the fourth time I was able to get in, enter all the grades, and log out before the system crashed. To be sure, I logged back in and checked, and they were all recorded.

I used the last few minutes of my lunch hour to check out Pip Forrest's parents, on the off chance that one of them had a criminal record for homicide—or anything else that might convince me to leave them on the suspect list. His father was a high school guidance counselor, and his mother taught social studies in middle school. They didn't fit my internal profile of people who could dope up a woman then shoot cobra venom into her veins.

Dot Sneiss called as I was finishing. "Any chance you could help us out over here?" she asked. "I wouldn't even think of asking, but we're desperate. The students are lined up all the way out the front door of Fields Hall, and I need a couple of bodies with computer access I can recruit to run graduation audits."

"If you show me what to do, I can help."

"I'll come right over to your office with the instructions."

She arrived a few minutes later, and waved a hand distractedly at Rochester, who remained against the french doors. "I'll get you logged into the student database. Then you follow these steps to retrieve and print the students' transcripts. You compare them against these degree requirements. If they've met everything, you go into the database and check this field. Then you save everything, and move on to the next student."

"Sounds simple. I used to be a computer guy so I think I can handle it."

"You're a lifesaver. Everyone else I've called is busy with final exams and their own messes." She stood up. "I'll be back with a couple of students, and we'll keep sending them down your way for the rest of the afternoon. If you have to stop just let me know."

The first senior arrived a couple of minutes later. She was African-American, with her shoulder-length dark hair in elaborate dreads.

"This is my first go-round with this system, so it may take some figuring," I said, as she sat down across from my desk. She was getting a bachelor of science in biology, and she thought she had satisfied all her requirements. I printed her transcript and we went over it together, and it looked good to me. I checked the box on her record and set her receipt to print.

"Thank you so much!" she said. "I've been waiting since seven o'clock this morning."

Rochester sat up and barked once, and I saw a line of students was already waiting outside. The next four cases were fine. Rochester got accustomed to the in and out traffic, and I got comfortable with the clunky, DOS-based student records system. Then it crashed.

"Oh, my god," the student I was working with said. "Does this mean there's something wrong with my record?"

"I doubt it. Just the crappy program." I rebooted my

computer, and while we waited, Rochester got up and walked over to the boy, who was fidgeting. Rochester stuck his head under the boy's hand, and he started rubbing his hand down Rochester's back. By the time my computer came back up, the kid was calmer, and I signed off on him for graduation.

The parade of students continued. My back ached from sitting hunched over the computer for so long, and I itched to get up and stretch or take Rochester for a walk.

While the next student walked in I called Dot Sneiss. My call went to her voice mail, and I asked, probably more plaintively than I meant to, how long she needed me to work that afternoon. It was almost four and I had an appointment in Doylestown at five with Jerry Fujimoto.

I helped another four students before Dot called back. "Sorry, things are still crazy here," she said. "Though they're getting better. I'll stop directing students your way, so if you can finish up with those you have, that would be great."

I told her that was no problem—until I ran into Harryette Caffey.

She had to spell her name twice for me before I got it. "My dad's name is Harry," she said. "But my friends call me Yeti."

"You mean like the…" I couldn't think for the moment. I knew a yeti wasn't a monster, but… Then I remembered. "The abominable snowman?"

She looked at me. "I spell it Yetty. Not the other way."

"Okay." I pulled up her file and found she was missing one of her requirements, a computer proficiency class. "How come you didn't take it when you were a freshman?"

"They told me I didn't need to because I had taken computer courses in high school." She pushed her chest out a bit, and I wondered if that was a strategy she often used with male faculty.

"You remember who told you that?"

She looked at me like I was crazy. "It was four years ago."

I called Dot again, and once more I got her voice mail. I left the message with my question. "Sorry, but can you wait while I get through the rest of these kids? As soon as Mrs. Sneiss calls me back I'll be able to finish up with you."

"I've been waiting all day," she said.

"Let's recap," I said. "You haven't taken a required course so I can't certify you for graduation. If you wait around until I get a call back, I'll see what I can do for you. If you want to leave, you can take the computer course this summer and graduate in August."

Yetty leaned forward in her chair. "I can't do that. I'm going to Europe next week."

"Then you don't have much choice, do you? Wait out in the hall."

Maybe I was abrupt, but I had three more students before I could leave for Doylestown, and I was tired after spending the afternoon with this crappy program and a series of nervous kids.

She went to the end of the line, and I got through the rest of the students. Dot still hadn't called me back, and Rochester was getting antsy. I didn't know what to do.

"Have a seat," I told Yetty. I went online and looked at the course outcomes for the computer class. Students had to be able to use a keyboard and a mouse, exhibit basic familiarity with the Microsoft Office suite of programs, and be able to use an Internet browser to search for information and visit websites.

I closed down the student database program, then stood up and stretched. I turned the keyboard so Yetty could access it. "I'm going to give you a quick proficiency exam. If you pass, I'll certify you."

I made her go through a series of steps, and she managed them all easily. "That's all?" she asked.

"Yup. Whoever you spoke to back then probably didn't mark down that the class had been waived for you."

I took the keyboard back from her, logged into the database, and certified her to graduate. "Have a good time in Europe," I said.

Then I grabbed my dog and got the hell out of the office before any other crisis could come up.

* * *

I was a half hour late to Jerry Fujimoto's spread—a low-slung ranch house with a series of wire cages along one side. Just as at Rita's place, the yipping and yelping was deafening. Rochester didn't even want to get out of the car, and I had to grab his collar and manhandle him out.

The air smelled like cedar chips, mixed with the fragrance of blossoming lilacs from a hedge along one side of the property. Jerry stepped out of the front door as Rochester and I walked up the flagstone path. "I was about to feed the dogs," he said. "I can give you ten minutes. Follow me."

He'd ditched the perfectly pressed clothes I saw him wearing at the agility show for jeans and an Armani Exchange T-shirt. He had the lithe build of a martial arts star, but that was probably just stereotyping on my part.

He led us over to a practice ring like the one at Rita's. Rochester knew what to do, tugging me toward the starting line. I tried half-heartedly to rein him in but he was too excited. Or maybe he just wanted to get this visit over with and get away from the yappy little dogs, whose barking was nearly constant. It seemed like when one took a breath, another one chimed in to create a canine cacophony.

I put Rochester through his paces, hurrying around the course with him the way I'd seen Rick do. He still had some trouble with the weave poles, but he did the rest of the course like a champ.

Not in Fujimoto's eyes, though. He went back over what we'd done, pointing out mistake after mistake—half of them mine, half Rochester's. "I can see he's got some talent," he said finally. "But he's undisciplined. It's clear that he thinks he's the boss."

"I've been working on that. I'm waiting to feed him until after I eat."

"That's only part of it. If you're going to train with me, you've got to be strict."

"I can do that. At least you think he's got potential. Rita Gaines thought he was a waste."

"Rita was a waste herself," he said. We began to walk back toward the driveway. "Not to speak ill of the dead, you understand, but the woman was a bitch with a capital B. And I've forgotten more about training dogs than she ever knew."

"You didn't get along with her?"

"The dog show world's a small one. You've got to play nice, even when other people are assholes. Rita and I used to argue all the time, and it gave me a lot of pleasure to pick up clients who couldn't work with her, and then beat her in the ring."

"You ever go over to her place?"

He shook his head. "She probably had an alarm set to notify her if my truck got within ten miles of her farm. And I wouldn't set foot there unless I had a sick dog and she had the only medicine."

Spoken like a true dog person, I thought, as Fujimoto left us and I ushered Rochester back to the car.

22 – A Woman's Weapon

It was after six, and I didn't feel like rushing home and making dinner. I tried to get hold of Rick to see if he wanted to meet up or share a pizza, but he wasn't answering his cell. Instead I drove to The Chocolate Ear.

Gail had a couple of biscuits for Rochester, as always, and she was able to rustle up a homemade croissant loaded with chicken salad, with a green salad on the side. Things were slow, so she came outside to sit with me as I ate. She did all the baking for the café while her grandmother, Irene, ran the front with the help of a part-time waitress, and I could see she was tired. Wisps of blonde hair escaped from her ponytail, and she had a smudge of dried flour high on one cheek.

"Has Mark Figueroa been around lately?" I asked. "I need to ask him about his dog."

"It's not his, it's his ex's," she said. "I don't think Mark liked it very much."

"I didn't like dogs at all before I got Rochester."

Gail looked at her watch. "His store is open until eight and it's around the corner. If you want to take a run over there Rochester can stay here with me."

"He doesn't let dogs in the store?"

"Think about it, Steve. Rochester. Antique store?"

"Yeah, you're right." I reached down and scratched behind Rochester's ears. "I'm going away for a few minutes. You stay here with Aunt Gail and behave, all right?"

He yawned, showing rows of white teeth and exhaling a doggy breath.

"And when we get home I'll brush your teeth." I finished the last bite of my croissant, then stood up. "I'll be back for dessert."

Traffic was backed up on Main Street as I approached the corner of Ferry, the only red light in the downtown area. The light was green, but no one was moving. Cars began honking, but nothing moved until it turned yellow.

Looking ahead, I saw the problem. A white-haired woman in a housecoat was moving slowly through the intersection on foot. She had to be at least three hundred pounds, and she moved as slowly as a snail. The lead car at the light was politely waiting for her to cross before moving on.

By the time I walked up to the corner, the light had cycled back to green again, and I was astonished to see the woman step back into the crosswalk. A Land Rover SUV zigged around her and sped through the intersection, but the next car, a Toyota sedan, came to a stop and waited for her to cross. Only two cars made it through on that light, and there was another cacophony of horns.

I turned down toward the river, and walked the half block to Mark Figueroa's antique store. A bell over the door jingled as I walked in. Mark, looking even taller and skinnier than I remembered, came out from behind the counter.

"Hey, Steve. Long time no see. You looking for something special?"

"I'm shopping for information."

I saw a bit of disappointment on his face, but he covered it. "How can I help?"

"You know a woman named Rita Gaines?"

"Yuk. Nasty bitch."

"Yeah, that's what most people say. You have a dog?"

He shook his head. "I was dating a guy who did. Awful little dachshund with the worst name ever."

I tried to remember but couldn't. "What was it?"

"Judy's Last Song. You can't get gayer than that. A dachshund, and Judy Garland." He shook his head. "It's a wonder we lasted as long as we did."

"So how did you meet Rita? Through this guy and his dog?"

"Yeah. Judy hated me, and every time I came over she peed. He thought it would be good for the two of us to bond—me and Judy, I mean, not me and Rita. We went to the farm a couple of times for training lessons, but I couldn't stand her, and I couldn't stand the dog. Eventually I couldn't stand the guy either."

"You know somebody killed her, right?"

"We didn't stay in touch. But I'm not surprised. I hope someone sicced a Rottweiler on her, or a pit bull."

"Poison," I said.

"Ooh, a woman's weapon. I always wondered if she was a dyke. Maybe some disgruntled lover. I know I might have poisoned the guy I was seeing if I hadn't broken up with him."

That was an interesting idea. Had Rita had any romantic connections, either male or female? I made a note to ask Rick.

It didn't appear that Mark had much of a motive to kill Rita Gaines. At least he was one more suspect knocked off my list. I thanked him, and started walking toward the door. As I went, I noticed a framed photograph leaning up against an old table, of a couple in the rain standing on a street in what looked like Paris. I stopped to look at it.

"The photographer's name is Francois Regaud," Mark said. "He was a French photojournalist of the same era as Cartier-Bresson. Nowhere near as well known, though."

I liked it and thought Lili might, too. "How much?"

He leaned the picture forward and looked at the back. "I have $250 on it, but I'll give it to you for $200."

I gulped. "You think it's too expensive for a first real gift?" I asked. "We've only been dating a couple of months."

"I think it's perfect. She likes photography?"

"She's a photojournalist herself."

"Then this is just right for her. It's romantic, it's beautiful, and she'll connect to the photographer. I'll even knock off another ten percent because I know it's going to a good home."

I paid for the picture and walked back out to Ferry Street, carrying it under my arm. Traffic was still backed up, and up ahead I saw the flashing red and blue lights of a squad car parked in the Drunken Hessian's lot. My first thought was that someone had sped through the intersection after waiting too long, and caused an accident.

A young officer, probably no older than my Eastern students, was on the sidewalk talking to the heavyset woman who'd been lumbering across the street. As I approached I heard him saying, "Bethea, I've told you this before. You need a different hobby. You can't just walk back and forth across the street, stopping traffic."

"I got rights," the woman said. "I can cross the street. There ain't no law against it."

"Get in the car, Bethea. I'm taking you home."

Traffic was finally moving smoothly through the intersection as I walked up to the curb. A couple of cars honked at Bethea as the cop forced her into his back seat, and she waved at them.

When I got to the café, Gail was sitting out front with Rochester, with a big piece of carrot cake on the table in front of her. "You bought that for Lili, didn't you?" she asked, as I rested the photo against the wall of the café.

"Yeah. You think she'll like it?"

"How can she resist? Paris, lovers, the rain? I wish I had a boyfriend who bought me pictures like that." She petted Rochester once more, then stood up and went back into the café. I ate the carrot cake she'd left for me and paid my bill, then took Rochester and the photograph home. When I was settled, I called Rick again, and this time I reached him.

"I've been doing my Joe Hardy routine, like you

asked," I said. "Pip Forrest's parents are school teachers, and I think any parent who names his kid after a hobbit doesn't sound homicidal to me."

"You'd be surprised. But go on."

I told him about visiting Madd About Shoes with Lili, and then about my trip to Doylestown to meet with Jerry Fujimoto. "We can knock both of them off the list. I don't think either of them could get close enough to Rita to poison her. Paula left Rita on very bad terms, and Jerry told me Rita wouldn't let him on her property."

"Yeah, I'm hearing a lot of that."

"Then on my way home, I stopped by Mark Figueroa's store. The dog he was training wasn't even his, and he broke up with the guy anyway."

"So nothing you did panned out."

I guess I got defensive. "Mark asked a good question -- did Rita have any disgruntled lovers?"

"Not that I've heard. I've talked to a couple of her friends, and some cousins in New York, and none of them mentioned any romance in her life."

"Oh, one more thing. Lili dragged me out yesterday to meet this ex-boyfriend of hers, an investigative reporter for the *Wall Street Journal*. He's looking into Rita's death."

"The *Wall Street Journal*? What the hell for?"

"He said there are some problems cropping up with her investment funds. You know anything about that?"

"Not at all. He give you any clues?"

"Not a one. Except he mentioned that he knew the college had invested some money with her."

"I can't see any connection," Rick said. He paused for a minute. "So. An old boyfriend, huh?"

"Yeah. Not my favorite way to spend a Sunday morning, I can tell you."

"How was she with him?"

"Not very happy," I said. "Which made me happy."

"Well, that's good."

"What do you want me to do now?" I asked. "Keep going with people who bought dogs from Rita?"

"Hold off on that," Rick said. "I'm going back full tilt on Rita first thing tomorrow morning."

"What happened? You nabbed the orchid thief?"

"Not exactly. I reached out to this national organization of orchid breeders, and they put out some feelers for me. Turns out there's an epidemic of orchid theft up and down the East Coast, and the FBI is on the case. I turned over my files to an agent from the Philly office."

"Wow, look at you. Consorting with the FBI."

"At least I'm on the right side of them," Rick said.

That stopped me. Of course Rick knew everything about my rap sheet—what I hadn't told him, he'd figured out on his own.

"Hey, I didn't mean anything," Rick said. "Just tossing shit. You know."

"No worries," I said. "Listen, I'll type up my notes and email them to you."

"Thanks, Steve. I mean it."

"The name is Joe. Joe Hardy," I said, before I hung up.

After I sent Rick the email, I brushed Rochester's teeth, as promised, using a new chicken-flavored toothpaste he liked. Then I took him out for a long walk—or rather, he took me, since he led the way the whole time, pulling and tugging impatiently when I couldn't keep up. I had to agree with Jerry Fujimoto—Rochester knew he was in charge.

Tuesday morning was gray and drizzly, so Rochester got a quick walk and we drove up to Leighville, where the weather wasn't much better. I barely had time to go through my emails and answer the most pressing ones before I had to leave for a meeting of the graduation committee. "Try to stay out of trouble, all right?" I said to Rochester. He looked up from gnawing a rawhide, and I scratched him behind his ears before I walked out.

There was still a line at the Registrar's office as I

pushed and squeezed my way into the conference room. I spread out the information I had on Freezer Burn, preparing for a private confab with Dot and Jim after the meeting was over.

Once everyone was in place, Dot began by telling us that the credentialing situation was still very serious. "We got a lot of help yesterday, and that cleared some of our backlog. If we don't get this computer situation resolved quickly, we may be faced with huge problems. Verified transcripts for graduate schools and transfer applications, financial aid audits, summer school registrations… it boggles the mind."

Suddenly the room was filled with the theme from the *Indiana Jones* movies. "Sorry, I have to take this," Dot said. She turned away from us, but a moment later said, "I'm afraid I have to cut this short. I've got an emergency." She hurried from the room before I could tell her what I'd learned about Freezer Burn, and Jim Shelton was right behind her.

I began to put my papers together as the rest of the group scurried out. By the time I finished Phil Berry and I were left alone. He was punching some keys on his phone as I stood up.

"Now that I'm on the administration side, I have a whole different attitude toward graduation," I said. "When I was a student, and even as an adjunct, it was a big milestone. Now it's just another day in the calendar." I looked over at him. "That the way you see it?"

He looked up from his phone. "Right now I'm grateful for any day that doesn't involve me getting fired."

I sat back down. "Fired? Why?"

"I got a heads up last night that one of our investment positions is in trouble," he said. "You ever meet a woman from the Board of Trustees named Rita Stanville Gaines?"

"Sure. You know she was killed, right?"

"Yeah, I read her obit in the *Journal*. Rumors are

going around now that at least one, maybe more, of the companies she invested in might be going under, and that's causing shares in her high-tech fund to tank. That's dragging down the rest of her funds."

"What does that have to do with you getting fired?"

He sighed. "I invested some of the college's funds with Rita." He sat back in his chair. "StanVest laid out capital in two ways. First, as an angel—putting money into startup businesses. But Rita also ran limited partnerships for seed funds and incubators, which is essentially like being a second-tier angel investor. That's where I put some of Eastern's money—in those seed funds."

"Isn't that kind of risky?" I asked. "I mean, Eastern's a conservative institution."

"In the investment business, there's a tradeoff between risk and return. If you put everything you have in very safe places, like federally insured bank savings accounts, you get a very low return on your money. If I did that for Eastern, I wouldn't bring in enough interest income on our endowment to bridge the gap between what we earn from tuition and what it actually costs to run this place."

"So you have to make some riskier investments to bring in higher returns."

"Exactly. Because Rita was our alumna, and she was on our Board of Trustees, I thought that balanced some of the risk in investing with her. After all, she wouldn't steer her alma mater wrong, would she?"

I was an English teacher, so I knew a rhetorical question when I heard one. "But now she's dead, and her company is in trouble," I said. "So that means Eastern is, too."

"Because nobody knows right now which of the startups she funded are in trouble, all of them are suffering, and so is StanVest. And that means everybody who invested with StanVest is, too."

"And because you're the guy who put Eastern's money

with StanVest, you're under the gun."

"Yup. And you know what's ironic?"

I shook my head.

"I have this stock gossip program that pops up alerts for me. It had the rumors about StanVest before anybody else. But I can't get it to work on my college computer because Freezer Burn blocks it."

"What's ironic about that?" I asked. "Freezer Burn blocks everything."

"The company that makes Freezer Burn is one of the ones StanVest invested in—using college money." He held up his BlackBerry. "The program is meant to run on a desktop PC, so I had to run it on this. I've been having problems getting the BlackBerry synched to my office computer so I was using my wife's phone for a while. She saw the alert but never mentioned it to me."

"For want of a nail," I said.

Phil looked confused.

"Sorry," I said. "It's an old proverb. "For want of a nail, the horseshoe was lost, for want of a shoe the horse was lost, and so on, down to for want of a battle the kingdom was lost. Supposed to mean that one little thing can trigger a whole avalanche that can have major consequences."

"Jeez, don't go saying things like that," he said, standing up. "You're going to freak me out."

I was already freaked out, I thought, as I walked back down the hall to my office. As I'd already figured out, if problems with faculty entering grades cascaded into financial aid and accreditation troubles, Freezer Burn could end up causing us major trouble. If you added in financial losses and damage to the college's investment portfolio, then Eastern could really be in danger of collapse.

When I got back to my office, Rochester jumped up and yipped sharply twice. "Yes, I know, I left you," I said. "Come on, I'll take you out." Fortunately the sun had come out, though the grass was still wet. As soon as he peed, I tugged him back indoors.

I had to grab a roll of paper towels and dry Rochester's paws before he tracked mud all over my office and I had to deal with an irate cleaning staff, who were already cranky about the amount of golden hair that showed up in their vacuum cleaners.

Rochester considered any kind of canine maintenance a game. One that included paper was his favorite, so half my effort went into keeping him from chewing the towels.

Once that ordeal was over, he relaxed on the floor for a nap and I turned to my computer to look for the article Phil had mentioned. I could only read the first paragraph, because the rest was behind a paywall—you had to have a subscription to read it. But I could see the byline was Van Dryver, which meant I already knew what it said.

I dug around until I found the business card Van had given me on Sunday. I'd assumed he'd be the one calling me for information, not the other way around. I hoped he might know which of the companies Rita had invested in was in trouble, and if it was one of the ones Phil had put some of the College's money into as well. I wasn't sure what I would do with that information, but I always believed that knowledge was power. I dialed Van's number and left a message.

Then I called Rick. This was information he ought to have, too. Perhaps the motive for Rita's murder was in her investment business, not among her neighbors or her dog-training clients. I had to leave him a message, too.

Frustrated, I considered what other sources I had for information.

I looked at my dog, who was staring up at me from the floor. "Why didn't I go to business school, Rochester? If I had an MBA maybe I'd be able to make sense of this."

He woofed once, and then I knew what I had to do. I called my old graduate school friend Tor.

23 – Estate Planning

Tor was probably the busiest guy I knew, yet he answered his cell phone as soon as I called. "Hello, Steve! You are well, I hope?"

"Yeah, doing pretty good. Do you have a minute for some questions?"

"Of course. The market is slow today."

Tor was a Swedish exchange student in business school when I was in studying for my MA in English at Columbia, and we were roommates there, and then for a few years after, until we both married and our lives diverged. He was a successful investment banker, married to a former model, with two kids in expensive private schools.

"You know anything about a company called StanVest?" I asked.

"Ah, you are up on the latest news, even though you are far from Wall Street. Yes, I knew Rita Gaines. She was a savvy investor, but she took many risks."

"Can you tell me why her company is in trouble, in layman's terms?"

"That may take more than a few minutes, my friend." Though his English was almost perfect, he still had the slightest hint of a Swedish accent. "Perhaps you will come up to New York this weekend?"

It was Tuesday, and I had a feeling things might break out faster than that. "Any chance you might be free for dinner tonight?" It was an hour up to the city, and I thought it would be worth making the midweek trip, if Tor could meet me.

"Your timing is excellent! Bjorn and Lucia are away this week, on a trip to Washington, DC with their school. I will see if Sherry can join us. You must get yourself a wife again, Steve!"

"Well, I have been dating someone," I said. "I might be able to convince her to come with me."

"Good, good. Can you make a seven-thirty reservation?"

"Lili's favorite restaurant in the city is Donatello's on West 45th. If we go there I think I can persuade her to join us. You feel like Italian?"

"No, I feel like I am Swedish. But I can eat Italian food. I will call them."

I agreed to meet him and Sherry at Donatello's when I got to the city, confident that Tor could secure the table, and then called Lili. "Think I can tear you away for dinner in New York tonight? At Donatello's?" I gave her a quick rundown on StanVest and Tor.

"I have two more portfolios to grade, then I'm free, at least for now," she said. "Car or train?"

Even two round-trip train tickets would be cheaper than bridge and tunnel tolls and an evening's parking in Manhattan. I pulled up the schedule online. "There's a six o'clock from Trenton. Can I pick you up about four, and we'll make a pit stop at my house to drop off Rochester?"

"Sounds great. It'll be fun."

"By the way, I called your friend Van to ask if he knew anything more about Rita Gaines than he put in the article. I'm hoping he'll call me back."

"He doesn't take calls unless he wants something," she said. "But he'll take mine." I didn't love the sound of that, but it was what it was. Like I'd told Lili on Sunday, we both had pasts.

I hung up and began considering lunch options. Mike MacCormac stuck his head in my office door. "You free for a powwow with Babson about this Rita Gaines situation? He's paying for La Sandwicherie."

"Sounds good to me." I stood up, gave Rochester a treat and promised him some leftovers. Then I locked the door behind me and hoped he wouldn't get into trouble.

Mike and I drove into downtown Leighville, where we met Babson and Phil Berry at La Sandwicherie, a quasi-French storefront café, a step up from the usual student-oriented food in town. I was the only one at the table not wearing a tie and I felt a bit out of place. Babson and Phil looked like they were ready for a power lunch, and even Mike, whose neck always looked constricted by his collars, could have passed for a corporate type. If I'd had advance notice of the lunch I'd have worn a button-down shirt, though I'd have waited to put the tie on until we were ready to leave the office.

"I'll get right to the point," Babson said, when we had put in our orders for soups, salads and sandwiches. "This Rita Gaines business is turning into a nightmare."

"So far Eastern hasn't come into the press reports," I said. "I spoke with the reporter from the *Wall Street Journal* on Sunday. He was fishing around for information but I didn't have anything to give him. I have a follow up call into him to see what I can find out."

I neglected to mention that he was my girlfriend's ex; it didn't seem relevant to the conversation.

"Good." Babson turned to Phil. "What's our financial exposure?"

"It's still fuzzy," he said. "No one I've spoken to knows exactly what's going on with StanVest. Just that trading has been suspended in the master fund."

"What does that mean, the master fund?" Mike asked, as the server brought us a basket of french bread and butter, and tall glasses of ice water.

"StanVest is a complicated entity," Phil said, when she had gone. "It's a general partner as well as the main entity that disburses funds to individual projects. Take MDC, for example. It's a small business startup, created by an Eastern alum named Matthew Durkheim. Rita created a limited partnership to act as a second-tier angel investor for his company."

Something about the name MDC rang a bell, but I had to push that aside. I could see that Babson and Mike were having trouble following all the financial jargon. I was barely hanging on myself, and only because I'd spoken to Phil before.

As a PR guy, I was accustomed to framing my message. I thought I might be able to throw Phil a lifeline—shifting the situation so that the blame appeared to fall on those Wall Street wolves rather than on Phil or Rita, at least for the moment. "Basically, Eastern invested part of the college endowment with Rita's company, and now that she's dead, some bad rumors are circulating on Wall Street about StanVest, and she's not around to defend herself," I said. "So the share price of the StanVest funds are going down. Is that a fair statement, Phil?"

He looked relieved. "Yeah, that's about it."

"Could StanVest recover from this?" I asked.

"No one knows the extent of the situation," Phil said, as the server returned with our crocks of onion soup. "If the companies that the fund invested in are sound, and based on the financials I've seen they are, then I think the overall exposure will be minimal. But there are certainly going to be some short-term losses."

We shifted the conversation to talk about the capital campaign, the $500 million fund-raising operation Mike headed. Money was coming in, though not at the pace he hoped for. "I've been having a lot of problems with the alumni database," he said. "Half the time when I log into it and try to enter information, it tells me I don't have the right privileges. I have to turn my computer off then reboot, sometimes two or three times. And I can't get in from my home computer no matter what I do."

"I've had the same problem with my investment ticker," Phil said, and I remembered he had complained to me about a similar problem he was having. "I called the help desk to complain and they told me that it's not supported. I've tried explaining that I need it to do my job, but I get nowhere."

"Talk to Verri," Babson said. "She'll get you sorted out."

"I've tried. She keeps telling me her job is to support academics, not play around with wish lists from staff."

I suppressed a smile. If Phil married Verri, she'd be Verri Berry. I doubted that would happen, though.

"I think she's got her hands full right now," I said. I described the problems Dot Sneiss had been having. "I spent all yesterday afternoon helping her out with graduation audits because the online system has been down for days."

"No one told me," Babson said. "I'll have to have a word with Verri."

"Talk to Dot first, sir," I said. "So you can be clear on the problem."

We all cleaned our plates at lunch, so I had no leftovers to bring back to Rochester. Fortunately, I kept a bag of his kibble on a high shelf in my office closet, and when I got back to the office I poured a bowl for him. He gobbled it up as if he was in a speed-eating contest, then passed gas.

"Rochester!" I waved my hand in the air and then took him outside, where he dilly-dallied around finding just the right place to leave his poop. I picked it up, then deposited it in an outdoor trash barrel on my way back to the office.

I called Rick and left another message for him, telling him that Lili and I were going into the city to find out more about the failure of Rita's business. "If I get a chance I'll call you. But we may not get back to Stewart's Crossing til late."

A few minutes before four, I hooked Rochester to his leash and led him across campus to Lili's office in Harrow Hall. "I'm so glad you invited me to dinner," she said. "I've been jonesing for a dose of urban culture, even if it is just for a couple of hours."

"You mean our trip to North Jersey on Sunday didn't do it for you?"

"When I say urban culture I mean a place with pedestrians, cabs, and gridlock," she said. "Not a suburban diner along the highway."

"I'll try not to disappoint," I said.

"Let me send one more email." She began typing, and halfway through the message her computer made a grinding noise, and the blue screen of death popped up. "This is the third time this week," she said, backing away from her computer. The power was still on, so it wasn't a surge. "Forget it. I'll send it from my phone while we're on the train."

As we walked out of Harrow Hall, we heard cursing coming from the secretarial station. "Guess yours wasn't the only computer to go down," I said.

"We're going to have to stop at my house. I can't meet your friends for dinner in jeans."

"I think you look beautiful no matter what you wear."

"Smooth comment. But I still need to change."

We drove over to the apartment Lili rented, in a converted Victorian a few blocks from campus. The owners had restored it to its former glory, cleaning the small stained-glass windows, refinishing the pine floors, and painting the crown moldings. Art-quality photographs shared space with pen-and-ink drawings by undiscovered geniuses but I didn't see any of her own work. She had decorated with an artist's eye, and the apartment was simple and uncluttered, with classic Craftsman-style furniture and hand-knotted wool rugs from Mexico.

I took Rochester for a walk around the block while Lili changed. The hundred-year-old maples, broad front porches and ample space between the houses was quite different from the zero-lot-line townhouses and youthful pines of

River Bend, but to Rochester I guess it was all the same. He sniffed and peed as much there as he did back home.

By the time we got back to Lili's house she was wearing a form-fitting black dress with a scoop neck and her new ballet flats. She had pinned her luscious hair up with some vintage Japanese combs decorated with crayfish. "You're going to show up every woman at the restaurant," I said.

"Your friend's wife is a New York City woman. I'm sure she'll be dressed to the nines."

We zipped downriver, dropped Rochester at my house with a bowl of kibble and one of cool water, and made it to the station in Trenton with a few minutes to spare. "Tell me about these people," Lili said, when we were settled on the train.

"Tor was my roommate when I was in graduate school. He's a big Swede with a good heart and a brain for business. Usually we get together ourselves, so I haven't seen Sherry in a few years."

"What's she like?"

I shrugged. "She's a real estate broker. Very sharp. They have two kids."

"Did they know Mary?"

"Yeah, we double-dated before we were married. I don't think either of them liked Mary."

"Really? Why not?"

"Don't know. They just never jelled, you know?"

She looked at me like she expected more to the story, but honestly, I didn't think there was. The four of us had been young together in New York, and we hung out with a lot of people we didn't love, just because we knew them.

Lili's phone rang as we were pulling into the Newark station. "Van! I'm glad you called. Steve and I are on our way into the city."

She listened. "I know. Can we meet up with you? A drink, maybe?"

He had time to return her call, but not mine. Jerk.

"I see. Well, call me later. Maybe we can do a nightcap."

She hung up. "He's on deadline. But if he finishes early enough he'll call me."

I was torn. I did want to talk to Van Dryver, to see if he had any inside information on the failure of StanVest, and anything that might shed light on her murder. But at the same time I didn't want to see him with Lili. I knew their fling had been years before, and that it shouldn't bug me, but it did.

24 – Dinner at Donatello's

When we arrived in New York, we had some extra time before our reservation, so Lili and I walked from Penn Station down Eighth Avenue. It was twilight, and the city seemed magical—headlights and streetlights and people on their way home or to dinner.

"You ever want to move back to the city?" Lili asked.

"I don't think so. I love coming in for dinner or theater or shopping or whatever, but I don't think I could take the frantic pace full-time. I like having a car, heating in the winter and air conditioning in the summer. How about you?"

"I'm torn. On the one hand I love all the artistic ferment—the little galleries, the museums, the artists struggling in Brooklyn now that SoHo and Tribeca are too expensive. But it's almost harder to work when there's so much going on."

I knew that Lili still took a lot of photographs, though I rarely saw any of them. "You think you'll have a show soon?"

"Not for a while. I got so accustomed to having my subjects thrown at me that I've been lost. It's hard to go from photographing rebel soldiers in Darfur to taking nature photos in Bucks County – to figure out where the middle ground is—something I care about photographing, where I can make a difference, while still staying grounded in one place."

She turned to me as we waited for a light to change. "Does that make any sense?"

"Of course. I'm not an artist, but I had to remake my life when I got out of prison, and I had to look for balance myself. Feeling like I belonged, like my life had a purpose."

"And you found that in Stewart's Crossing?"

"It's still a work in progress. Rochester helps. I mean, I have to feed him and walk him and play with him. That gives me some structure. And getting a full-time job at Eastern helped, too. Last year I was so worried about paying my bills and figuring out what kind of career I could have."

As we arrived at the restaurant, a Lincoln Town Car pulled up and Tor stepped out, then extended his hand to Sherry behind him.

Every time we met I couldn't help considering the different directions our lives had taken. He was a couple of inches taller than I was, and his hair was many shades lighter, a blond that was almost white. We dressed the same way back then—jeans and T-shirts and running shoes. I had graduated to khakis and polo shirts and penny loafers, but Tor looked like a real grown-up.

He had grown a bristly blond mustache, his hair was thinner, and he looked like a prosperous investment banker. He wore a dark suit that probably cost more than my old car, a purple and white striped shirt, heavy on the starch, and a matching purple tie embellished with tiny gold crowns. His shoes were made specially for him in London. But he was as warm and friendly as he'd always been.

"Steve!" he said, enveloping me in a big bear hug. Then he turned to Lili. "You must be Lili. A pleasure to meet you!" He hugged her, too, as I kissed Sherry's cheek.

She was almost as tall as I was, a shade under six feet, still as slim and immaculate as when she was a working model. She and Lili air-kissed, and we all walked into the restaurant, where the hostess recognized Lili and led us to an excellent table.

Donatello Nobatti himself, a rotund, gray eminence, came out to see us when we were seated, kissing Lili's hand and promising to send us out a special antipasto platter. "It's like this everywhere we go," I said. "Lili has men falling at her feet."

"I know what you are saying," Tor said. "We both have selected well, eh? The two most beautiful women in the restaurant right here at our table!"

Sherry gave him an aggrieved look but Lili just smiled.

Our waitress, an elegant young woman who moved with the cat-like grace of a dancer, delivered our cocktails and a platter of cheese and flash-fried vegetables and calamari. We discovered that Sherry had sold an apartment to a photographer Lili knew, and they bonded over a shared obsession with the delicacies of bald chocolate-maker Max Brenner.

Tor turned to me. "But you have a reason to come to New York," he said. "You want to know about StanVest?"

I nodded. "Rita Gaines was a member of our Board of Trustees, and the guy who manages Eastern's endowment portfolio invested in some of her funds. He heard there might be problems with her company."

"He is hearing correctly," Tor said. "I met Rita many times at investment conferences. She was a smart woman who took big risks. Sometimes they paid off, and sometimes they didn't. But she was usually clever enough to hedge her bets. I am surprised at a scandal now. Maybe because she is not here to move the chess pieces around the board."

It was funny to hear Tor's speech patterns once again, after having lived with them for so long. For the most part he spoke clear, unaccented English, but occasionally he reminded me of the Swedish Chef on *The Muppet Show*. The mustache only helped solidify the resemblance.

"Is that why her business is in trouble?"

Tor nodded. "I made a few calls for you this afternoon, and because I was curious myself. There is a fund called StanVest Hi-Tech Seven. You have heard of it?"

I shook my head.

"This was started by Rita two years ago. It is a seed fund for second-tier angel investing in high-tech companies."

"I have a basic idea what that is."

"The rest of us don't, my love," Sherry said. "But can you explain in words of one syllable, in less than five minutes?"

Tor did so, with great grace, I thought, then continued. "Rita invested in six companies, from one that promises to make a better, faster jump drive to an online community that connects expectant mothers to doctors, babysitters, and other services."

I resisted the impulse to glance at Lili, keeping my eyes fastened on Tor. The waitress returned and we switched our focus to the entrees.

Lili had the most experience with the menu, and she guided our choices. For Sherry, who was always watching her weight, the grilled snapper with a citrus beurre blanc and a side of roasted asparagus. Lili had the same. For Tor and me, she recommended the Tuscan grilled steak with potatoes Donatello.

When the waitress had wafted away, Tor resumed his story. "Last Monday, anonymous comments began to appear in online forums about three of the companies in which this fund invested. Very pointed, specific details about operations issues, leadership troubles, and so on. Things only an insider would know."

"Rita?" Lili asked.

"She is the prime suspect," Tor said.

"But why would Rita want to sabotage companies she invested in?" I asked.

Tor picked up a piece of crusty Italian bread and buttered it. "As you know, Rita was not a nice person. Sometimes she let her temper get in the way of her business judgment. Perhaps she was angry at someone."

"I've seen clients make that kind of mistake," Sherry said. "I can understand with one company, but not three. She can't have been that stupid."

"There was a case," Tor said, speaking slowly, as if he was thinking about each word. "Some years ago. A senior vice president with one of the big investment banks, in municipal finance, creating complicated loan packages for development somewhere in the Middle

East."

We were all looking at him. "Forgive me, I don't remember the details, but a series of deals went bad. At first no one suspected anything. He was a very smart man, from one of the best schools, an excellent track record. But the losses mounted and an investigation was launched. It was discovered that he had deliberately sabotaged this series of deals because he was in collusion with a relative of the sheik, and every time a deal failed, they both pocketed an obscene default fee."

"You think that could be the case here?" I asked. "How?"

Tor shook his head. "I have no idea. But high finance is very complicated. Look at the way some very smart people can lose millions of dollars overnight on a bad wager—and others can steal millions without anyone noticing for years. Who knows what was going on in Rita's mind?"

We all considered that for a moment. I'd seen Rita in action—the way she could shift from anger with a human to adoration of a dog in the space of a heartbeat, the way she'd been so open to expressing her every opinion. I'd never witnessed her intelligence, but enough people had testified to it. She was clearly a very complicated woman.

"What happened once those anonymous comments appeared online?" I asked.

"Any piece of negative information can trigger an avalanche of trading on Wall Street—especially something like this, which smells like inside knowledge. Suddenly everyone wanted to sell StanVest shares—in every fund, not just the high-tech one. The exchange had no choice but to suspend trading."

The waitress delivered our entrees, and we began to eat, with many comments about how delicious the food was. "This was a wonderful choice, Lili," Sherry said. "We'll have to come back here again."

"I love this place," Lili said. "It's convenient to Penn Station and to Broadway, and Donatello does a great pre-theater dinner, too."

Sherry reached into her tiny scallop shell-shaped

purse and pulled out her card. "If we depend on the boys nothing will ever happen," she said, handing it to Lili. "Call me and we'll set something up."

Lili retrieved her own card from her shoulder bag and handed it to Sherry.

"Isn't it sweet," I said to Tor. "They're like real businesspeople."

Tor laughed. "You are playing with fire, my friend," he said.

Lili smiled sweetly at me, and in a perfect imitation of Margaret Hamilton, said, "I'll get you, my pretty. And your big dog, too."

Everyone laughed, and we went back to our food. Then Lili turned to Tor and asked, "What happens to the companies Rita invested in?"

"I don't know the specifics of their agreements with StanVest," Tor said. "Usually in such cases, the company has a milestone schedule they must meet in order to receive the next disbursement. Of course, if the fund no longer has the money to meet its obligations, then the companies must look elsewhere for financing. If they are unable to find it, then..." He shrugged. "But then, such companies are always a high-risk proposition. For everyone involved."

I thought of Rita, whose risk – in whatever way—had ultimately led to her death.

"When on Monday did this start?" I asked. "Do you know?"

Tor pulled out his Blackberry, and Sherry groaned. "I made him promise to put that away during dinner. But you had to ask him."

"Only a few minutes, my love," Tor said. While he punched a series of keys, I pulled my own phone out and dialed Rick Stemper.

"Boys and their toys," Lili said.

When Rick answered, I asked, "Did you ever get Rita's time of death? And do you know what time her body was discovered last Monday?"

"Why?"

"I'll explain it to you later. Right now I just want to know."

194

He huffed out a breath that I'm sure was intended to demonstrate his irritation with my Hardy Boy antics. "Coroner puts time of death at approximately six p.m. Sunday. She had a kennel assistant who came in at seven on Monday morning to feed and clean up after the dogs in the barn. When she hadn't come out of the house by eleven, he went inside to look for her. He called 911 then. What have you dug up?"

"Nothing concrete. But I'll let you know once I put the pieces together." I hung up as Tor looked up from his Blackberry. "The first comments were actually posted Sunday night at a few minutes after eleven o'clock. Could they have been made by Rita herself?"

"No. She was dead on Sunday evening. But if the killer had invested with her, and knew the fund was going to fall apart with her death, they might be connected."

"Enough death," Sherry said. "This was supposed to be a nice dinner so we could meet Lili."

Lili looked over at me and I knew I should have given her more of an indication that she'd be under a microscope. "I wanted to talk to Tor about StanVest," I said to her. "I can't control if he told Sherry this was going to be about meeting you."

"Now, you are going to get me in trouble, Steve," Tor said.

Sherry finished her grilled snapper and pushed the plate away from her. "We're multi-tasking here. But I can already tell Lili is a thousand times better for you than Mary ever was."

"Tell me about her," Lili said. "Steve is very diplomatic."

"Because Steve and Tor are such good friends, we spent a lot of time with Mary while they lived in New York," she said. "Mary always had – issues."

I looked at her. "Really? What kind of issues?"

"Steve," Sherry said. "Have you forgotten her already? How she was always sniping at you to get a better job, to work out at the gym, to have your hair cut or wear nicer clothes?"

I did remember, but I hadn't realized it was so

obvious to everyone else.

She turned to Lili. "Steve is a sweetheart, but you have to have a high tolerance for goofy. Mary didn't."

"Goofy!" I said.

"I can see that," Lili said. "Have you seen him with Rochester?"

"Ah, the famous Rochester," Tor said. "We have heard a great deal about this mythical character but never met him."

"Excuse me, I'm sitting right here," I said.

They trampled over me. Before dinner was over, we had made plans for Tor and Sherry to come out to Stewart's Crossing the following weekend so they could meet Rochester. "Do you like flea markets?" Lili asked.

"Absolutely!" Sherry said. "I'd love a good antiquing afternoon."

The waitress reappeared and we ordered a round of cappuccinos. "And dessert?" Tor asked.

"I couldn't eat another bite," Sherry said, dabbing her lips with her napkin.

"It's always like this," Tor said mournfully. The edges of his mustache tipped down and he looked like a basset hound.

Lili came to his rescue, turning to Sherry. "If you like chocolate, you must try Donatello's *baci d'alassio*. They're little hazelnut chocolate kisses. So tiny, they have almost no calories, but they're full of flavor."

"Excellent!" Tor said, slapping his hand on the table. "Bring us a plate of them!" He shooed the waitress away before Sherry could complain.

Lili's cell phone rang. "It's Van," she said.

She answered, and told him where we were. "He says he can come by, if that's all right?"

"I'd like to talk to him. You don't mind, do you?" I asked Tor and Sherry.

"Go right ahead," Tor said.

Sherry and Lili talked about antique hunting while we waited for Van to arrive.

"Can you get me a list of the companies in that high-tech fund of Rita's?" I asked Tor. "I'd like to know which ones had the bad comments posted about them.

You said only three, right?"

Tor nodded.

"I wonder if there is anything special about those three—or the other three that didn't have anything posted. I'd also like to see if I can make any connections to the people my friend Rick has been investigating—the ones who had access to Rita's barn and to the poison that was used to kill her. If Rita was already dead by the time those comments were posted, then someone else put them up. And if only Rita had access to the information that went into those posts—then maybe the killer took the material from Rita after killing her."

"That's a big jump, Steve," Sherry said.

"I agree," I said. "And I know I'm not a cop. But my friend is one, and if I can provide him with some information, then maybe he can use it to make an arrest." I looked back at Tor.

"It will take a little research, but I can put my assistant onto it tomorrow morning," he said.

"That would be great." I took a sip of my cappuccino. I felt like I was finally on track to help Rick find out who had killed Rita. Even though I hadn't liked her, she was a human being, and she deserved justice.

I looked up and saw Van Dryver at the hostess stand, and waved to him. He pulled a chair up at the end of the table, next to Lili, and slid into it. She introduced him to Tor and Sherry.

"We've spoken on the phone," Van said to Tor. "Pleased to meet you."

"Van wrote the article for the *Journal* about StanVest," I said to Tor, though I was pretty sure he already knew. Then I turned to Van. "Are you still investigating?"

He caught the ballerina waitress's eye and ordered himself a cappuccino, then returned his gaze to me. "Yup. I just finished a story for tomorrow's paper."

"Any chance of getting a heads up?" I asked.

Tor took over before Van could answer. "Let me guess," he said. "You are focusing on the rumors about the companies that StanVest Hi-Tech Seven invested in."

Van eyed him carefully. "You're very good," he said.

Tor picked up his cappuccino and took a sip. "Yes."

He waited. I waited. The entire table seemed to be holding its collective breath to see who would break first.

Van shrugged. "It'll be in the paper tomorrow morning. I spoke to each of the companies involved about the rumors, and for the most part, they're true."

"I assumed so," Tor said. "They had that ring of authenticity that only an insider could have provided."

"Take the Baby Connection," Van said, and I winced. Why had he chosen that example? Did he know about Lili's background? Or was I too sensitive because of my own?

Van picked up a sugar packet and shook it as he spoke. "I spoke to the CEO and she admitted everything. But she swore the only people who knew that stuff were her executive team, her attorneys, her investment bankers, and Rita Gaines. Same thing with each of the companies I talked to. The only common thread was Rita."

The waitress delivered Van's cappuccino as if she were Salome serving up John the Baptist's head and then fluttered away.

I asked Van, "So you believe Rita is the one who made those posts?"

"Had to be her," he said. "Every person I spoke to mentioned her bad disposition, and her irrational tirades. She made a lot of enemies on Wall Street, and there's no shortage of people who are willing to say that her behavior might have verged on dementia. My article is going to chop her into little bits."

My eyes met Tor's. The edges of his mustache moved up a fraction. Who knows? Maybe Rita did have a touch of dementia. "Well, she wasn't a very nice person," I said.

"That's what everyone told me," Van said.

His phone buzzed, and he answered. He turned away to take the call, and when he had finished he said, "Sorry, I've got to run. I have an opportunity to talk to a source."

Everyone said their goodbyes. When Van was out the door, Lili said, "Source my ass. Van's going to hook up."

"You caught that?" Sherry asked. "I thought it was just me."

Tor and I looked at each other, both of us baffled. "He's meeting a source," I said.

"Men," Sherry said.

Lili looked at me and Tor. "Why didn't either of you tell Van that Rita was already dead by the time those online comments were posted?"

"She probably set those comments up to post automatically," I said. "I know bloggers who do that. She didn't know she was going to get killed. Maybe she wanted it to happen while she was asleep."

Tor shook his head. "I think you can only do that when you control the site."

"Then who posted them?" Lili asked. "And why?"

Tor and I looked at each other. We both shrugged. "When I get the information from Tor, I'll try and find an answer to that."

"Van's going to look awfully stupid when the truth comes out about the time of Rita's death," Lili said. She looked at her watch. "If we're going to catch the 11:00 train, we'd better get moving."

So. Lili believed that Van was going to make a big mistake in print, and hadn't said anything when she had the chance. I guess I didn't have to worry about her leaving me for him.

Tor and Sherry wanted to drop Lili and me back at Penn Station, but we had time to walk, and we both wanted to soak up a bit more city atmosphere. "I like them," Lili said as we strolled past an endless row of electronics stores with perpetual going-out-of-business signs in their windows. "Sherry's a hoot. And did you see that Judith Leiber purse?"

"The scallop shell? You could tell who manufactured it?"

"From a mile away." She patted my arm. "Don't worry. It's a girl thing."

"If you say so. I didn't realize how much she

disliked Mary."

"I didn't get the feeling she hated her. Just didn't think she was right for you."

"And how about you?" I asked, putting my arm in hers. "Are you right for me?"

"We'll get a further report from Sherry next weekend," she said.

25 – Blind Spot

It was nearly midnight by the time we got back to Stewart's Crossing. Rochester was eager to see us both, hopping and jumping around so much that I had to order him to sit three times before he consented to let me put his leash on. We took him for a walk around the block, and I considered how nice it was to have Lili with us. She and Rochester had bonded, and I knew it was his influence that had opened me up to love again.

When we returned to my house, Lili and I got in bed and kissed good night, and even though it was late we slid into each other and explored the possibilities of our romance. When we had spent ourselves, she turned on her side to go to sleep. I sat up for an extra couple of minutes, thinking about Mary again. Lili was a very different woman. Then I fell asleep myself.

I left Lili in bed Wednesday morning while I walked Rochester. The rainy weather had moved on, and the air was crisp, the sun sparkling on the lake at the center of River Bend. Rochester was frisky, and I let him off the leash to rampage around the lake for a few minutes, chasing ducks and squirrels. By the time he galloped back to me his tongue was hanging out and his eyes were shimmering with delight.

When we got back to the house I toasted a couple of English muffins for breakfast. I had discovered Lili liked the cinnamon raisin kind, so I always kept a package in the freezer. I was pouring the orange juice when she walked downstairs, rubbing her eyes.

"Sleep well?" I asked.

"Yes. Nice evening last night."

"Yeah, Tor and Sherry are great." As she sat down, I saw the framed photograph I'd bought for her leaning against the wall in the living room. While she helped herself to a muffin, I picked it up and brought it to her.

"I saw this the other day and thought you might like it," I said.

She turned and saw it. "Oh!" She looked from the photo to me. "It's wonderful." She kissed me, then took the photo from me. "It's a Francois Regaud!"

"You know him?"

"Not him, but I know his work. How did you know I'd like this?"

I shrugged. "I saw it and it spoke to me."

"I know just where I'm going to put it. This is the nicest gift! Thank you so much." She kissed me again, and it took us a couple of minutes before we got back to our English muffins.

"Are you marching with the faculty at graduation?" she asked.

"I'm planning to," I said. "I was thinking I'd walk in the parade of classes first, then join the faculty at the stadium."

The parade of classes was an Eastern tradition. About an hour before graduation was to start, the alumni present would organize themselves into their classes on the broad lawn in front of Fields Hall. Each class was led by a student carrying a banner with that year emblazoned on it. The old guard – those alumni whose graduation occurred more than fifty years before – rode in golf carts at the head of the parade.

"You're not going to wear your cap and gown in the parade, are you? That would look weird. Everyone else will be in street clothes."

"I guess I could carry it with me. I hadn't thought that far in advance," I said.

"Why don't you give your stuff to me now," Lili said, as we stood up to clear the table, Rochester underfoot as always, looking for scraps. "I'll keep it at my office and then meet you at the stadium with it."

"Good idea. I've got it upstairs airing out." I ran up the stairs, Rochester right behind me, and pulled my black master's degree gown off the hanger. With it was the hood—light blue with a white chevron, and with a white lining signifying my master's in English. The plain black mortarboard that went with it was on the shelf above the gown.

I hurried back downstairs, Rochester once again underfoot. By then Lili had cleaned up and we were ready to go.

Rochester didn't seem to mind climbing in the back so Lili could ride shotgun, but as soon as I dropped Lili at her house he wormed his way up front. I drove the few blocks to the Eastern campus, already buzzing with preparations for graduation. Workmen were posting directional signs and erecting tents on the back lawn. I parked in the faculty-staff lot, already emptier as the faculty began filtering away, and walked Rochester to my office.

While my computer was booting up, Rochester settled into his customary place by the french doors, his head resting on his paws. I emailed Rick to apologize for not calling him the night before, and to tell him what I'd learned about the rumors surrounding the companies Rita had invested in—and the timing of their posting.

My office phone rang. "Eastern College, Steve Levitan."

"It's Van Dryver. I need some help and I'm hoping you can give me a hand."

"Depends," I said, sitting in my chair with my hand on the top of Rochester's head.

"I'm looking for an address and phone number for a guy named Matthew Durkheim, who graduated from Eastern."

"Sorry, can't help you. I'm not authorized to release any information our students or alumni."

Rochester got his blue rubber ball between his paws and settled down to gnaw on it. "Come on, Steve. I know about you. You've broken the rules in the past."

"You know what, Van? You don't know anything about me."

"Yeah, but I know about Lili," he said. "Here's a piece of advice, between you and me. I wouldn't expect Lili to stay in Podunkville much longer. She's got big dreams, that girl, and she loves to see the world."

I remembered Lili's action the night before—not telling Van about the huge mistake he was about to make. He didn't know me, and he didn't know her as well as he thought.

I hung up the phone without saying goodbye. I wasn't sure which I was more angry about—his assumptions about me, or about Lili. Either way, I wished he had been in front of me, because I'd have loved to punch him in the nose right about then. Instead I banged my fist on my desk, startling Rochester awake.

"What?" I asked him. He lowered his head onto his paws and gave me a baleful stare.

A few minutes later, I got pulled into a series of meetings, and put my personal cell phone on mute. When I finished the meetings and checked the display, I noted that Van hadn't bothered to call me back.

Before returning to my office, I detoured to the library, hoping they had a subscription to the *Wall Street Journal*. They did, and I was able to read Van's latest article. As he'd said to us, he put the blame for the rumors on Rita Gaines. I read the whole article, then checked the comments. So far, no one had figured out that she was already dead by the time the rumors had been posted.

Should I stir the pot? Be the one to show Van up as an idiot? Nope. I'd leave that to some other enterprising reporter. I wouldn't spit on him if he was on fire. Or provide any other bodily fluids either.

On my way back to my office, Jim Shelton buttonholed me. "Hey, Steve. President Babson wants to talk to us about these computer problems. Seems like he's finally woken up to the dimensions of the problem and he's going to crack down on Verri."

I looked at my watch. It was almost noon, and Rochester would be expecting lunch. But I couldn't ignore an executive summons; my dog and I both needed me to keep my job at Eastern.

When Jim and I walked into the President's office, Dot Sneiss was already there, sitting across from his big wooden desk. Jim sat beside her, and I stood behind his chair.

"I wish you'd told me about these problems sooner, Dot," Babson said. "Do you think that if we remove this Freezer Burn from all the campus computers, we can get back on track in time for graduation?"

"I'm no computer expert. But I can tell you if we don't get rid of it ASAP, things are only going to get worse," Dot said.

He turned to Jim and me. "Dot says you've been meeting about these issues with Freezer Burn and that you have additional information on the situation."

"I got involved through Lou Segusi, one of my students," I said. "Lou tutors at the Writing Lab, and one of the kids he works with has a work-study job in the IT department. This student, Dustin, was scared, and his fear was getting in the way of his class work. Lou asked me to speak to Dustin and see if I could help solve his problem so Dustin could concentrate on his schoolwork."

"What was this Dustin frightened of?" Babson asked.

"I met with Dustin, and I could see he very upset. It took me a while to worm it out of him. But eventually he told me that he was doing some filing in Verri's office and he saw a check that had slipped out of a folder on her desk. The check was from the company that makes Freezer Burn, and it was made out to Verri personally. For twenty thousand dollars."

I waited a moment for that to sink in. I knew that Babson had a blind spot when it came to Verri, so I thought I'd better lay it on thick. "At first I didn't believe him. I know what a dedicated employee Verri has been. I couldn't imagine that she'd take a bribe from a vendor."

I stole a glance at Babson's face. It was stony, but I couldn't tell if he was angry with me, or with Verri. I shifted from foot to foot behind Jim's chair, then said, "I had been having some problems with the software myself, and as I spoke to other people on the faculty and staff, they confirmed that they had been having issues, too."

"Hear, hear," Jim said, and Dot nodded.

"I knew you were busy with graduation, sir, and I didn't want to bother you without some concrete proof. I did some checking with a guy from Verri's office, and he confirmed that there were a lot of problems with the software, and that he had complained to Verri multiple times and that she shut him down every time. I planned to come to you next week with all the information."

Babson's face was still a mask of anger. Crap. I had only done what I thought was right. I didn't want to get fired because of someone else's incompetence.

"What's this staffer's name?" Babson asked.

"Oscar Lavista."

He buzzed Bernadette and told her to have the man come to his office immediately. Then he shook his head. "Verri has been a member of this community for decades," he said. "I can't believe she would do anything to jeopardize our mission. But you never know. Jim, you've seen these problems among your faculty?"

"Absolutely. I've had them in my office, with my support staff, and I've had reports from my department faculty, and through the Faculty Senate."

I started to feel better. Babson wasn't mad at me. He

had to be angry with Verri. I leaned back against the wall as Jim went through a recitation of all the issues he had experienced or heard about—computers locking up in faculty offices and in classrooms; secretaries unable to use purchasing office systems to order supplies; emails not being sent or received. Every aspect of college operations that depended on computers had been affected.

As he was finishing, Bernadette knocked on the open door and announced Oscar. Then she turned and ushered him in. Oscar looked surprised to see so many people in the President's office. "I was told you were having a problem?" he said.

Oscar looked younger than I'd thought before, no more than thirty. Probably the moon face and the extra weight added a few years. A moment later Bernadette was behind him with two extra chairs, one for Oscar and one for me.

"Have a seat, son," Babson said, pointing to the chair Bernadette had placed behind him. "Do you have something you want to tell me about this Freezer Burn program?"

Oscar and I both sat down. He pulled a white handkerchief from his pocket and wiped sweat from his forehead. "Are you having problems, sir?"

Babson leaned forward and smiled. "You aren't in trouble, Oscar. I know you've been trying to point out the difficulties with the software, but you haven't gotten any attention. I'm ready to listen now. Just take it slowly. I'm not much of a tech wizard like you younger guys."

I could see Oscar start to relax. "There are so many viruses out there, sir, and lots of students, and some faculty, aren't real careful about the programs they install on their computers, and the files they download. So most companies, and Eastern is like a big company, you know, they install software to control what gets access to our network."

"I can understand that," Babson said. "All you have to

do is pick up the newspaper to read about the latest attack."

"Exactly. It's our job in IT to protect the College. When we upgraded to Windows 2010, the program we'd been using to monitor the network couldn't keep up, so we had to shop around for a new one. Mrs. Parshall asked me to handle the requests for proposals and meet with the vendors."

It was clear he was proud he'd been handed the responsibility. Then he frowned. "I thought I chose the best one. We have a lot of legacy equipment here—older computers in some buildings, specialty software in departments like math and science, unique equipment for research. I tried to negotiate the cost down as far as I could. But Mrs. Parshall overruled me and went with Freezer Burn even though it was clearly an inferior product."

"Did she give you any reason for her decision?" Babson asked.

Oscar shook his head. "She got really mad. You know how she gets sometimes when you challenge her. I was afraid if I argued too much I'd get fired. My wife has MS and we really need the health insurance."

He turned to looked at me, Jim and Dot. "I tried to contact the company myself, to see who I could send a list of bugs to. The president of the company called me and told me that no one from the college other than Mrs. Parshall was authorized to contact them, and that if I continued to bother them he would see that I got fired."

He was shaking, and I reached out and put my hand on his shoulder.

He took a couple of deep breaths and turned back to Babson. "That's such a weird thing that it made me suspicious, so I looked through all the files on Freezer Burn. There was nothing in the contract about tech support or authorized contacts. So I looked to see if there was anything from MDC—the company that makes Freezer Burn. Nothing there either. I looked online, too. They don't have much of a website, not even an 800 number for a help desk or anything."

He took another deep breath.

"I was about to give up when I remembered the name of the man who owned the company—Matthew Durkheim. I found a separate folder in Mrs. Parshall's filing cabinet under his name, and there was a rider to the contract that didn't go through the college purchasing office—or at least it wasn't stamped by them. The rider said Mrs. Parshall would get a referral fee if the college signed the deal." He took a breath. "Twenty thousand dollars."

My brain started to buzz. Matthew Durkheim. That was the name Van was chasing down. He owned MDC, the company that made Freezer Burn? What was going on? But I had to pay attention to what was going on in Babson's office. I'd think about Durkheim and MDC when the meeting was over.

"Do you have a copy of that rider?" Babson asked.

"Unless Mrs. Parshall took it out, it should still be in the folder under his name," Oscar said.

"I'm going to ask you a question, Oscar, and I want you to think about it carefully before you answer," Babson said. "Can you remove Freezer Burn from every computer on campus?"

"It's a two-part answer, sir," Oscar said. "The first part is easy, but the second part is time-consuming and labor-intensive." He looked over at the computer terminal on Babson's desk. "Do you turn your computer off every day?"

Babson shrugged. "Not usually."

"That's the problem. See, every computer on our network goes through a series of setup instructions. I'm sure you've seen the routine as you wait for your computer to warm up. The easy part of removing Freezer Burn is that we just remove the command that executes the program from the startup routine."

"That's all?" Dot asked.

Oscar turned to her. "The difficult part is that the change won't take effect until you turn your computer off and reboot. Since not everyone does that every day, we'd have to send a technician out to every on-campus computer in order to make sure that all traces of Freezer Burn disappear. That could take some time."

"What if we prioritize critical systems?" I asked. "Registration, mainframes, servers, and so on. And we send a college-wide email notifying faculty and staff of the problem. Tell them if they're experiencing problems, all they have to do is reboot. Then over the summer you can come up some kind of diagnostic and isolate any computers that still have problems."

Everyone looked at me. "I thought your background was in public relations, Steve," Babson said.

"I used to work in high tech," I said. I turned to Oscar. "How about it? Would that work, as a band-aid?"

"Sure," Oscar said. "We could probably have something like that in place by midnight, at the latest. But I couldn't do it without Mrs. Parshall's approval."

"That won't be a problem," Babson said. He looked at Jim, Dot and me. "I'll take this from here," he said. "Thank you all for bringing it to my attention."

The three of us walked out. "I'm glad we didn't have to talk to Verri ourselves," Dot said. "I'd suggest we all stay away from the president's office for a while, too. I've seen her temper, you know. I saw her throw a glass ashtray at one of her techs once when he couldn't fix a problem right away."

"She was the assistant director of student life, back when I was a new faculty member," Jim Shelton said. "The brothers of Kappa Sigma were serving grain alcohol in their punch when they weren't supposed to. Verri set out to prove they were. She walked into the middle of a party with one of those remote lighters you use for a barbecue and used it on their punch bowl. The bowl went up in flames and then so did the living room of the frat house."

"You're kidding," I said.

"Cross my heart with a Maidenform bra," Jim said.

"I heard that story," Dot said. "She had to move to Physical Plant after that. Babson put her in charge of renovating the frat house."

"Were any students hurt?" I asked.

"A few singed eyebrows," Jim said. "Nothing more serious. But it did mark Verri as a force to be reckoned with."

"No wonder Babson's been treating her with kid gloves," I said. "I hope he has the Fire Marshall standing by when he talks to her."

"Or the police," Dot said.

26 – Wrong Directions

When I got back to my office, Rochester attacked me. I didn't blame him; after all, I'd ignored him all morning, between phone calls, meetings and library research. I wrestled him into submission, hooked his leash, and took him out to empty his bladder.

As we walked downhill toward the lunch trucks, I called Rick. "Get the email I sent you this morning? About the six companies Rita's fund invested in, and the three of them that were getting trashed online?"

"Haven't had a chance to check in yet. I've been busy running around the county. I interviewed every person who trained a dog with Rita, current or past. You were on target with the people you talked to—I eliminated them from my list."

"I think we're going in the wrong direction. Somebody had insider information about the companies Rita invested in—stuff only Rita could have known—and posted it online only an hour or two while after her death."

"Why would somebody do that?"

"I haven't figured that part out yet. But you should read the article in today's *Wall Street Journal*. The reporter lists all six companies, and what the rumors were. He thinks Rita made all the postings because she was nasty and starting to have dementia, but she couldn't have, because she was already dead by the time they were posted."

"That's why you wanted to know the time of death." Then it sounded like he had turned away from the phone. "Jesus Christ, not Bethea again." He came back. "Listen, Steve, I've gotta go. Crazy lady on the premises."

"The woman who keeps crossing Main Street? I saw her the other night."

"Yeah. She's been doing that for a while, but last night

she made the mayor late for a meeting of the Knights of Columbus, and I've got him and half the business leaders in town complaining."

I ended the call and slipped the phone in my pocket as we reached the food trucks. I got a sandwich and gave Rochester part of it as we sat at one of the stone tables outside the Cafette. I could finally focus on what I'd learned in the meeting with Oscar Lavista.

Matthew Durkheim, who had trained his dog Calum with Rita, owned a company called MDC, which made the Freezer Burn software. But where else had I heard the name MDC? I puzzled over it all the way back to my office.

I wanted to do some online research, but I had college work to do. I was busy answering emails when my cell phone rang, and I saw from the display that it was Tor.

"Hey," I said. "Great dinner last night."

"Yes, very excellent. Lili is very beautiful, very intelligent and charming. Sherry thinks she is perfect for you."

"I'm relieved. Especially now that I know what she really thought of Mary."

He laughed. "Sherry is very clear about her opinions."

"I know you didn't call just to tell me what Sherry thinks of Lili. Did you find out anything about the companies in Rita's funds?"

"I am emailing you the list. You should have it now."

Sure enough, my email program popped up a little ghost window in the lower right side of my screen that indicated a new message from Tor. "Thanks," I said. "We'll see you this weekend."

"Absolutely." He hung up, and I opened the message. The answer to the question that had been bothering me was right there—MDC was one of the companies that Rita's fund had invested in. So Matthew was ultimately behind that twenty-grand check to Verri Parshall that Dustin De

Bree had accidentally seen.

I looked up Matthew Durkheim in the alumni database. All we had was an office address and phone number in Manhattan. Because I was curious, I dialed it from my office phone. A woman with a throaty, sexy voice answered.

When I asked to speak to Matthew, she said he wasn't in.

"Do you know when he'll be available?"

"This is the main reception desk," she said. "I don't have a copy of Mr. Durkheim's schedule. But I'd be happy to take a message for him."

"No thanks," I said, and hung up.

I dialed Rick and got his voice mail, where I left him the information about Matthew. I went back to Tor's message. Rita's fund had invested in six companies, and negative information had been posted online about three of them. MDC and two others had escaped.

I did some quick searching and read the rumors. To my untrained eye they weren't that serious. There were production problems with one company, server issues at another, and at the third, the baby company, the CEO's son had been diagnosed with autism.

Yes, all three could cause trouble for a new company. But were they enough to derail a whole investment fund? If Rita were still alive, could she have talked her way through them? And why were no rumors posted about MDC, and its crappy Freezer Burn software? Surely Rita, with her Eastern connections, must have heard something about the problems, even if Matthew had been shielding her from any other client complaints.

I was puzzling those questions when Mike buzzed. "Do you have any time to help out?" he asked, and his voice was plaintive. "We're getting swamped here."

I left Rochester enjoying his squeaky ball, and spent the next hour printing check-in lists for every reunion class, making sure that we had flagged all our top donors and prospects for special attention. Then Mike asked me to take a walk along Fraternity Row and make sure all the on-campus frats had cleaned up their yards.

I was happy to take on any assignment that got me out of the office, and I hooked Rochester up for the walk downhill to a cluster of faux-Colonial buildings that housed Eastern's alphabet of fraternities. Rochester snagged a loose frisbee from a couple of Alpha Tau Epsilon brothers, and romped on the grass with the sisters of Zeta Beta Theta. Everything looked clean, and by the time we had patrolled the entire area it was time to head for home.

From my car, I dialed Lili's cell, but the call went direct to voice mail. All the way down the River Road to Stewart's Crossing, I kept looking at my phone, but it never rang.

"Nobody loves us today, Rochester," I said, and he pulled his head back from the open window to look at me. "Rick doesn't call. Lili doesn't call. I guess it's just you and me."

He woofed once and nodded his golden head.

27 – Twelve Steps

When I got home, I took Rochester for a long walk, made dinner, ate, played with the dog—but still felt unsettled. I knew what was wrong. I wanted to know more about Matthew Durkheim and MDC, and the only way to find out was by hacking. It's like an addiction to me—sometimes I can't help myself. My adrenaline starts to flow and my brain buzzes with all the neurons jumping around, eager to be used.

I felt almost like a guy in some twelve-step program. My fingers itched and my pulse raced. Should I call Santiago Santos and have him talk me down? Or should I give in and go online? I was in the service of a greater good, after all. I was trying to find out who killed Rita Gaines, and what was going on at Eastern College, which threatened to bring down my alma mater—and the place that gave me a paycheck that supported me and my dog.

Rochester knew what was up. He brought me his foam boomerang, and I tossed it. He scrambled down the tile floor and retrieved it, but while he did, I went upstairs and crawled into the back of my closet, where I kept the laptop that had belonged to his former owner, Caroline Kelly.

While Rochester and I were investigating her murder, I had discovered her laptop, and installed some hacking software on it that I had used to find information that helped expose her killer. Since my own laptop had my parole officer's tracking software installed, I couldn't use it for illegal purposes, and I'd kept Caroline's around and hidden.

Rochester saw what I was doing, and he gave up trying to distract me and settled back on the floor, with a reproachful look on his face. I'll bet that if he could have, he'd have barked loud enough to summon Santiago Santos.

I didn't know where Matthew Durkheim banked, or where he kept the accounts for MDC. Where the company was incorporated, who his attorney was or his accountants. It was frustrating, but I had nowhere to start.

Nowhere except with Rita Gaines. I closed my eyes and concentrated, running through everything I knew about her and her connections to Matthew Durkheim. I couldn't concentrate, though, because Rochester had begun running around the living room like a wild dog.

I opened my eyes. "What in the world are you doing, you crazy mutt?" He was on all fours, scrambling between the legs of the dining room table as if they were weave poles. Then he darted across the room to the coffee table, and jumped on top of it, scattering a pile of Eastern college magazines, then holding his pose.

"This is not an agility course!" I said. "Get down from there!"

I stood up to chase him away, then sat down hard on my chair. Agility training. Rick had forwarded me the schedule of Rita's sessions, and I remembered she had used a notoriously unsecure online email host. Had I saved the message with her address?

I scrambled over to my own computer and waited impatiently for it to boot up. I'm very anal about my own filing system; I had a folder called "Rochester," and the message was right there. Her address was rita.gaines@mymail.org.

Back at Caroline's laptop, I let my fingers do some walking. The folks at mymail weren't quite as dumb as I remembered; they had put in new security that took getting around. I had to pull a few old tricks out of my bag, and make up a couple of new ones, before I had access to the user directory for rita.gaines.

By then it was eleven o'clock and Rochester was nosing me for his late-night walk. "Rochester," I whined. "I just got where I wanted to go. Can't you hold it?"

He pushed his nose to my knee and sniffed, his wet black nostrils huffing in and out.

I sighed. "I guess not." I stood up, and he jumped up and down on all fours.

We hurried through our walk and even though I cheated him, he was sweet enough not to mind. I slid back into my chair and flexed my fingers. "This is going to be fun," I said.

It wasn't. Rita was as disorganized with her email as Oscar Lavista. "Doesn't anybody manage their inbox these days?" I grumbled. I ended up creating a massive zip file of Rita's inbox and downloading it to the laptop's desktop. Then I did the same thing with her sent messages folder. As soon as I could, I logged out of the mymail server.

I unzipped the files, then ran a couple of basic searches, one for each of the companies the fund had invested in. I wanted to check her emails for clues to the online comments.

All I could find that related were a couple of questions about the health of the baby company's CEO's son, the one who had been diagnosed with autism. But there was no indication in those emails that Rita had any concern that his diagnosis could impact the company or its finances.

MDC, however, was another matter. Starting about a month before her death, Rita began emailing Matthew comments about Freezer Burn she had heard from people at Eastern. It appeared she was a lot more connected to the college than she had let on when she spoke to me. She talked to secretaries, faculty members and students at meetings, social events, and as she walked around the campus. Everywhere she went she heard complaints about the software.

Matthew reassured her that yes, the program had a few bugs, but his programmers were working them out. In one message she wrote that she had made an unexpected visit to his office in New York when he wasn't there, and discovered only one programmer in the office, though that guy mentioned others in India who could be hired on a per-project basis. "That is not the way you presented this company," her message read. "We need to discuss this, Matthew. Immediately."

In his response, he tried to soothe her, without success. He appeared to be ducking her phone calls, because her emails got increasingly angry in tone. Finally he agreed to bring Calum to her training yard, and meet with her after the session was over.

I looked at the date of the message. That would have been the day Rick and I saw him, the Sunday she was killed.

It was well after midnight by the time I finished reading the messages, too late to call Rick. I couldn't forward the emails to him; I didn't want an electronic trail that would lead back to me and provide documented evidence that I had violated my parole. That clear evidence would send me right back into the California penal system.

I'd lose my job. My relationship with Lili. Rochester.

I couldn't allow that to happen, even if it meant letting a murderer go free. I wasn't returning to prison just to see Matthew Durkheim behind bars, too. It wasn't worth it. I'd have to call Rick in the morning and figure out how to get him the information.

I shut down the laptop and returned it to its hiding place, then went to bed. I had two long days of work ahead of me, culminating in Eastern's graduation on Friday. I'd think about how to prove Matthew's guilt after everything was over.

* * *

Thursday morning I pulled onto Main Street in Leighville, only a couple of blocks from the entry to the college parking lot. Then I got stuck in a long line of cars, waiting for a huge wire-framed sun encrusted with thousands of lights to rise over Fields Hall.

219

Eastern's logo is the rising sun, and President Babson's wife is a devotee of modern art. The two combined in a commission for a pop-art sun that would be attached to the bell tower of Fields Hall, and be illuminated at the start of the parade of classes on Friday afternoon.

Hanging the sun was huge process, involving a tractor trailer, a crane, and enough workers in red pinneys and hard hats to man the construction site of a new high-rise. Rochester got antsy at the delay, leaning out the window with his front paws on the windowsill, and I kept having to tug him back into the car. Finally I put the car in park, and Rochester remained with his head out the window to supervise what was going on.

While I was waiting, Rick called. I almost didn't answer, because I was afraid somehow he knew I'd been hacking the night before and he was ready to challenge me. But that was silly, I thought. No one had me under surveillance.

"Hey," I said.

"Hey. Thanks for that tip on Matthew Durkheim and his company. It's definitely one of the ones Rita Gaines invested in. He was at the farm on Sunday, and he was familiar with her barn and the way she handled dogs. So he's got means and opportunity, and if there's something hinky going on with their business dealings he'd have motive. I've been trying to find him, and I discovered that he boarded his dog and his neighbors haven't seen him in a couple of days, so I think he might have done a runner."

"Good work. You know, Rita and Matthew might have exchanged some emails about problems with MDC, or at least confirming their meeting on Sunday," I said. "You should see if you can get a subpoena for Rita's email account. You have the address—you forwarded a message from her account to me."

Rick was quiet for a long couple of seconds. "Are you suggesting that there might be incriminating information in those emails?"

"As a matter of speculation, of course," I said.

"Of course." If his voice had been any drier he'd have been in the Sahara. "I'll look into it. Thanks for the tip."

"Any time. Let me know if I can help—after graduation."

"Will do."

He hung up, and the workers finally lifted the sun off the truck, and it pulled away. Traffic began to creep ahead, and I drummed my fingers impatiently on the steering wheel. "It's just a sun, people," I said. "You can see one of them every day."

Rochester settled back into his seat and looked at me.

"I know, I know," I said to him. "You think I should relax. But I've got a million things to do today."

Once we reached the college, the day became a chaotic maelstrom of graduation planning. At least Freezer Burn had disappeared from my college computer; when I booted it up, it whirred smoothly through its startup routine, and every program I tried worked without a flaw.

In between phone calls and emails, though, I kept worrying whether I should tell Rick what I had discovered about the trouble between Rita Gaines and Matthew Durkheim. Was I impeding his investigation by not revealing what I knew? Or did it matter? Matthew was already Rick's primary suspect. Anything I knew was only hearsay, and improperly gained. Accountants would have to sift through the real evidence anyway.

Mike had pizzas brought in for the staff, and Rochester was delighted to snarf down his share of crust along with a few choice bits of sausage and pepperoni. After lunch, I had to meet with representatives of the student honor societies, who would be manning tables on Friday, handing out tassels and cords to graduates, and lapel pins to alumni. Once I was confident they knew what they were doing, I grabbed Rochester and we joined one of the maintenance supervisors to walk the entire route of the parade of classes, making sure everything was prepared for the next day.

Ford was an older black guy with his name on an oval patch on his work shirt. "Ain't supposed to have dogs on campus," he said, when he saw Rochester.

"I have permission," I said.

"Still, ain't supposed to be here."

"Let's get this walk going," I said. "Where does the old guard meet?"

"Over here towards the tents." He turned his back and started walking toward a big open area where the college had set up party-style tents for each class or group of classes.

Security had installed portable bollards painted bright yellow to block cars and trucks from driving through the main roadway. As soon as we reached them, Rochester began darting around them as if they were weave poles, dragging me with him.

"Rochester!" I stumbled and clutched his leash as he rounded the last bollard. Then he sat down and opened his mouth wide, expecting a treat.

"Something wrong with that dog," Ford said. It wasn't a question.

"Nothing is wrong with him. Let's keep going."

Eastern's graduation was also the kickoff for our reunion weekend. We invited all alumni to join us for a big lawn party before the ceremonies, then hang around for individual class picnics afterwards. We sponsored campus tours and faculty lectures open to all alumni and their families on Saturday, as well as formal dinners for each reunion class.

Ford, Rochester and I circled around the tents, each one marked with a banner proclaiming a reunion slogan, like "We're making do: Class of '72" and "On our way to heaven: Class of '57." I had to keep Rochester from investigating each tent in search of food or playmates.

We turned right and headed toward Fields Hall. Most of the trash receptacles on campus had been freshly painted, but we spotted one the painters had missed, and Ford called it in on his radio. Rochester and I kept on going, until he startled me by dashing forward to a wood-and-wrought-iron bench. As I stumbled behind him, he jumped up on the bench and assumed his "sit" position.

"Jesus, Rochester, this is not an agility course," I said, tugging the leash.

"People gonna sit on that bench," Ford said, coming up behind me. "Gotta have it cleaned now."

Rochester hopped down and tried to jump up on Ford. I jerked back on the dog's leash. "He was up there for five seconds," I said, pulling tightly.

"Need to have a bench cleaned," Ford said into his radio. I groaned and kept on walking. We passed Fields Hall, and Rochester managed to intercept a passing frisbee, then submit to being petted by a couple of adoring female students. As we walked downhill toward the football stadium, we neared a beer delivery truck with a ramp up into the back. I held a strong grip on Rochester's leash as he strained to dash up it.

As soon as Ford and I reached the stadium, I said, "Looks like everything's okay."

"Except for the dog," Ford grumbled.

Rochester tried to jump up on him again, and this time I didn't pull him back until he'd already placed his big furry paws on Ford's groin, and the older man had reared away in horror. I smiled and said, "Have a great day!"

28 – The Things You Can Do

After finishing the walkthrough, Rochester and I slogged back up to Fields Hall. I hadn't been to an Eastern graduation since my own, so many years before, and I was astounded at how much planning went into one. Rochester seemed to be as exhausted as I was, after all his jumping, playing and tugging.

I was too tired to think about talking to anyone else, or making dinner. I stopped at a drive-through on the outskirts of Stewart's Crossing, and fed Rochester bits of a plain hamburger as we drove through River Bend. "You know, Uncle Rick says I'm spoiling you," I said, as I pulled into the driveway. "I should have eaten my dinner first, and then given you yours."

He looked at me.

"Yeah," I said. "What does Uncle Rick know?"

I let him out of the car, and he peed. We went inside, and at least I sat down and ate my dinner before I poured out his kibble. He was chomping noisily as Rick called my cell. "Want to grab a burger?" he asked.

"Already did. I stopped at a drive-through on the way home. I'm beat, anyway. Graduation's tomorrow and things are crazy up at Eastern." I told Rick about Rochester's antics at the walk-through with Ford.

Rick laughed. Then I told him about my conversation the day before with Van Dryver, and how I'd hung up on him. "That guy needs to get his nose out of this," he said. "He's muddying the waters. Can't Lili call him off?"

"You want me to get my girlfriend to call her ex and ask for a favor? What planet are you from?"

"Planet Cop. You want to play Hardy Boys? This is how we operate. We lean on people to talk—or to shut up."

"He's not some cub reporter for the *Boat-Gazette*," I

said, citing our local paper. "He's an investigative journalist for the *Wall Street Journal*. I could ask Lili to give him a blow job in exchange for dropping the story and he'd still say no."

"You'd ask her that?"

"Of course not, asshole. I was speaking metaphorically."

"Never heard of a metaphorical blow job," he said. "But then, I don't have a master's degree in English. They teach you that kind of stuff up at Columbia?"

I took a deep breath. We were both stressed and I could see that arguing wasn't going to get either of us anywhere. "Sorry. I'm beat," I said.

"I know how you feel. I've been going at this case hard and I'm not getting anywhere. I wish Matthew Durkheim would just turn himself in."

"Good luck with that." Rochester had finished his bowl, and was still looking like he hadn't been fed. "Listen, I'm falling down on my feet. I'll talk to you tomorrow after graduation is over."

I went upstairs and lay down on my king-sized bed. Rochester clambered up next to me, and I leaned back against the headboard. I kept expecting Santiago Santos to show up for a surprise visit—he always seemed to pick the worst times. Instead, when my phone rang, it was Lili. "Steve? You busy?"

"Just chilling. What's up?"

"I've been driving around. Feeling weird. Do you mind if I come over?"

There was something strange in her voice. I sat up and even Rochester raised his head. "What's the matter?"

"I'd rather talk in person."

"Sure, come over. I'll call the gate and let them know you're on your way."

"Okay. I'm not far—a couple of miles up the river."

I hung up, then dialed the guard house and gave them

Lili's name. I wondered if it was time to put her name on my permanent guest list.

But then I had a terrible thought. What if Van was right? He had said that Lili wouldn't stay out in the middle of nowhere for long, that she had big dreams and she was determined to see them fulfilled. What if she was coming over to break up with me?

It was the end of the academic year, and maybe she'd gotten a better offer, either from a bigger college, or from a magazine or newspaper. Suppose she'd been driving around trying to figure out how to tell me she was leaving. I sat back, and Rochester crawled over to put his head on my lap.

Then I took a couple of deep breaths. I was letting my imagination get away from me, as I often did. For all I knew, Lili was upset about failing a student, or a leaky roof, or something else totally unrelated to our relationship.

Whatever it was, I was going to need some coffee to deal with it, because I was exhausted. I went downstairs and started the cappuccino machine, and by the time Rochester heard Lili's car pull up in the driveway and started barking, I had the espresso ready, chocolate syrup already mixed in, and was steaming the milk.

"Hi, sweetie," I said, greeting her at the door with a kiss.

"Something smells heavenly," she said, after she kissed me back.

Well, that was a relief. Whatever was bothering her probably was not about me.

She reached down and petted the dog as I walked back into the kitchen to finish the coffee. "Must be Rochester's new shampoo," I called behind me.

She followed me into the kitchen, the dog on her heels. "Have anything to go with that coffee?" she asked. "Suddenly I'm starving."

"Cookies in the cabinet." I poured the foam over the

espresso, then whipped cream, more syrup, and chocolate shavings. I had been massing my chocolate artillery in case Lili wanted to break up with me, because I wasn't going down without a fight. Now I could just enjoy the coffee.

She opened up a package of chocolate thumbprint cookies and brought them to the kitchen table. Rochester sprawled at her feet as I carried the cups and joined her.

"So what's up?"

"I spoke to Van. Something he said really upset me."

"Let me guess." I stirred my café mocha. "He said you'd never be happy out here in the middle of nowhere. That you needed a life of action and adventure."

Her eyes widened with surprise. "How did you know?"

"He said the same thing to me. I hung up on him."

"I should have done the same thing. You don't think it's true?"

I took her hand. "I hardly know you, Lili. We've only been dating for a couple of months. But I've seen some things that matter to you." I used my other hand to hold up my thumb. "Your students. You genuinely seem to care about them and about helping them explore their talent."

She smiled, then picked up her coffee and sipped.

I held up my index finger. "Your talent. You look at the world as an artist, and you bring that vision to everything you touch—your clothes, your apartment, the things you create with your camera and your computer."

My third finger went up as she ate a cookie. "Your heart. You have the ability to open yourself up to love—from me, from Rochester. You care about people—look at the way you stood up for Felae."

I let go of her hand and picked up a cookie. "You've already been around the world. I know you enjoyed it, that you learned from what you saw, and that you were moved by it. Do you need that kind of stimulation on a constant basis? Only you can say that."

I bit into the cookie. It was Lili's turn to talk.

"You're a smooth talker, Steve Levitan," she said. "I didn't realize you had gotten to know me so well so quickly." She reached down and petted Rochester. "And obviously, in a way that Van never did. You're right. Those <u>are</u> the things that matter to me the most. And I have them all right here."

She shook her head. "I don't know why I let that jerk get under my skin."

"He has a talent for that. He said some things about me, too." I picked up another cookie and ate it. The caffeine and the sugar were working their magic, and I felt more alive. If we were delving into Lili's psyche, it was time she got a look at mine as well. "He said he knew me. That he knew what I'd done."

"The hacking? That's old news." Lili picked up her mocha again and sipped.

"Not exactly."

She cocked her head a bit, almost the way Rochester does. I resisted the urge to smile. "You know I'm on parole, right? That if I do anything illegal I could go back to prison in California."

"But you wouldn't do anything like that? Would you?"

She looked at my face and then took my hand. "Steve?"

"I don't know how to explain it," I said. "I could say it's an addiction, like drugs or alcohol. But that would be a cop-out. I could put the blame on Rick Stemper and say he knows what I do, and he doesn't stop me. But it's not his problem, it's mine." I took a deep breath. "I could justify myself by saying I only do things for a good cause, like to help figure out who killed Rita. But that's just sad."

I slumped back in my chair. Even Rochester stayed by Lili's side. "I won't blame you if you walk out now."

"I don't understand," Lili said. "What did you do?"

I told her.

"You can do that?" she asked, when I was finished.

"Break into someone's e-mail account?"

"Yeah."

"That's amazing. But you don't do it to steal anything or get people in trouble?"

I shook my head. "Absolutely not. And since I've been out of prison I've only hacked a few times, to help Rick with investigations."

"And he knows about it?"

"It's kind of like that program the military used to have. Don't ask, don't tell," I said. "I pass the information on to him, or give him leads, and he doesn't ask me where I get the information."

"Did you tell him this stuff, about this insider information?"

"I gave him a sort of back-handed hint that he should subpoena Rita's email records. But he understood what I was saying."

I was still waiting for Lili to chastise me, to back away, at least to say that knowing I couldn't suppress those criminal instincts made her want to reconsider our relationship. I felt like that guy in the comic strip, the one with the cloud that always follows him. Instead, Lili reached over and took both my hands in hers.

"You showed me tonight that you've gotten to know who I am over the past few months," Lili said. "Well, I've gotten to know you, too. I know that you're smart, and funny, and you're good with words. That you have the ability to love and care about people, too. Tonight you've shown me one more of the things you can do. That doesn't change anything else that I feel about you."

She pulled me close, and her kiss left me no doubt about what those feelings were.

29 – Class Consciousness

Lili didn't stay the night, but we did go upstairs together after we finished our coffee. Rochester dozed on the kitchen floor until Lili left, when he returned to his customary place beside my bed.

As I got ready for work on Friday morning, the day of Eastern's graduation and the kickoff of reunion weekend, I remembered I wasn't just an employee—I was an alumnus, and I had to dress the part.

Every Eastern class came up with a clever clothing item so that classmates could identify each other at reunions—which was important, as the years passed and we all looked less and less like those skinny, fresh-faced undergrads we'd once been. Some chose ball caps, some windbreakers, some T-shirts. If you came to a graduation, you wore your item, even if wasn't your reunion year.

For our my class's twentieth reunion, we'd hired a graphic designer to create a white polo shirt with the slogan "Class of 89: We're Just Fine!" splashed across the back in Eastern's sky blue. I'd worn it to work a couple of times since then, and had to dig through the closet to find it.

I debated leaving Rochester at home. It was going to be a wild and busy day and I wouldn't have much chance to check in on him. But knowing him, he'd be better off in my office than home alone all day. I tied a blue-and-white Eastern bandanna around his neck so that the rising sun logo rested on his shoulders. The colors looked jaunty against his golden fur.

I tried to take him for a quick walk before leaving home, but he was very agitated, tugging me left and right, chasing a squirrel and a duck and trying to eat a crushed can of Red Bull. There was a horrifying thought: Rochester on an energy drink.

I managed to drag him home and into the car for the drive upriver. When I got to work, Mike MacCormac was pacing around the reception area that led to our offices. His navy suit hugged his broad shoulders, and his white shirt looked uncomfortably tight around the neck. His Eastern college tie, light blue with a pattern of yellow sunrises, wasn't long enough to reach all the way to his waist.

"There must be something we forgot," he said. "What is it?"

His secretary said, "If we knew what we forgot, it wouldn't be forgotten."

"Get everybody in my office for a meeting," he said. "Everybody except Rochester, that is."

He leaned down and scratched the scruff of Rochester's neck, and his tie dangled in front of the dog's face. "You're the only one who can relax today, boy."

I wanted to check my email and voice mail, but I had to spend the next hour in Mike's office as he obsessed about everything that could go wrong with the graduation festivities. It wasn't even his responsibility—but any screw-up could lead to a dip in alumni contributions, and reunions were one of the best times to solicit donations.

I got back to my office at ten. Rick called while I was struggling to answer at least a few email messages before the graduation festivities began. "Hey, I know that Matthew Durkheim is an Eastern alum," he said. "You think there's any chance he'll show at the college this weekend?"

"No idea," I said. "But if you hold on I can see if it's his reunion year." I checked his record in the college database, then returned to the call. "It's not. But I remember him saying something about getting together with his buddies at reunions."

"I'll head up, just in case."

"All right. I'll keep an eye out for him, but I'm going to be pretty busy."

I hung up, and spent the next hour scrambling to finish

whatever I could before I had to leave the office. Just before eleven, I took Rochester out to pee. I had to keep him on a short leash because there were so many people milling around outside Fields Hall, and he was acting wild—he wanted to go up to every person and say hello and I kept having to rein him in. I was grateful to get back through the french doors into my office, pull off his leash and toss him a rawhide chew. "Stay out of trouble, boy," I said. I realized that was becoming my mantra with him.

The campus was jammed with students and their family groups. Beaming parents, elderly grandparents, younger brothers and sisters in their special-occasion best. Eastern's colors were everywhere, white and the light blue of a summer sky. Graduates wore custom gowns in slate blue, and many of them had decorated their black mortarboards with the letters of their fraternity or clever messages in masking tape. Loudspeakers placed throughout the campus were playing a brass-band version of Eastern's fight song, complete with the "rah, rah, rise up Suns" chorus.

Had I ever been that young? That enthusiastic about the future?

I recalled my own graduation. My father took a million pictures—most of which my mother and I never saw. I did remember a photo of my mother adjusting the hood of my gown, showing off the rising sun crest imprinted on the fabric. My mom had it printed and framed, along with my diploma, with matting in light blue and white. I wondered where that picture was—probably in one of the boxes of my parents' stuff I had never unpacked, still in my garage.

As I hurried toward the tent area, I started to sweat in the heat. There was no breeze to speak of and I felt sorry for the graduates in their heavy gowns, and the college administrators, like Mike, in their coats and ties. I only escaped the formal attire because I could wear my reunion shirt.

I paused for a moment in front of a roped-off play area where slim, pony-tailed moms in Eastern polo shirts gossiped and watched their kids play with future classmates. As I did, I felt a sharp pain in my side. Was I still so hurt by Mary's miscarriages that seeing little kids playing was painful? By the thought that I probably wouldn't ever have kids of my own?

Then I realized it was a physical rather than metaphorical pain. "Ow!" I said, rubbing my flank. My skin hadn't been pierced, but an ache radiated just above my waist.

A boy no older than twelve or thirteen, holding his pants up with one hand, had poked me in the side with a long pointed stick he carried in the other. A congratulatory banner hung from the end of it, the bottom dragging in the grass.

A gym-toned blonde whose taut skin belied a face lift rushed up behind him. "I told you to wear a belt, Justin!" she said. "And to watch where you're going with that thing!"

She looked at me. "I'm so sorry. Are you okay?"

Rubbing my side, I tried to smile. "It's all right." Justin trooped on ahead, followed by a legion of family members. "Try and hold the point up, Justin," I called after them, as his mother hurried to catch them.

I threaded my way past red-faced alums already hoisting beers, alert for any more errant jousters. Every class seemed to be playing music from the era when it had gone to school; Jan and Dean competed with Nirvana, The Who with Katy Perry. It was enough to give you a headache if you listened too closely.

A group of twenty-something former lacrosse players tossed a ball back and forth as I passed. Then I heard a loud bark and looked to my right. There were my people, I thought. A group of dog lovers had thrown together their own makeshift puppy park, using one wall of Harrow Hall, a couple of folding tables laid sideways, and a row of picket fencing it looked like someone had been carrying in their trunk. I wished I had Rochester with me; he'd love to play. But he was locked up back in my office.

A rhythmic knocking sound drew my attention to the left. Another group of alums, this one from a class a few years before mine, had obviously been on the crew team together. As they beat their paddles against each other they began to chant. Right in the middle of them was Matthew Durkheim.

Like many of his former teammates, he was wearing a class outfit of running shoes, cargo shorts and a muscle shirt with the Eastern logo. Even from that distance, I could see they all had matching tattoos on their upper arms. I flashed back to that moment at Rita's farm when I had first noticed Matthew's. If only I'd been able to have Rick arrest him then, Rita would still be alive.

But he hadn't committed a crime then, so there was nothing to arrest him for. Such are the questions philosophers obsess over.

The sound of the chanting and knocking grew in intensity and volume, drowning out everything else. I had to keep walking backwards, glancing around me to avoid knocking into anyone, yet keeping Matthew and his buddies in sight, until I got somewhere quiet enough to call Rick.

"I knew it," Rick said, when I told him I'd spotted Matthew. "I knew he'd be there. God damn it."

"Where are you?"

"Still in Stewart's Crossing. Bethea's tying up traffic again. I was supposed to be out of here a half hour ago but I just hit River Road."

"Get here as fast as you can," I said. "The parade of classes starts in an hour. I'll bet he cuts out before then."

"The parade of what?"

I explained that groups of alumni organized to march

into the stadium for graduation. "I'll do my best," Rick said. "Keep an eye on him."

He hung up and I looked around. Though plenty of people were in the area, they were all with their class groups. Mine, unfortunately, was too far away, and since I was wearing a shirt with my class slogan on the back, I couldn't easily fit in with any other.

Matthew and his pals mercifully stopped banging their paddles and I could hear the rest of the crowd again, including the barking dogs. I realized the puppy park had a perfect view of his class tent. I'd have to get Rochester and use him as camouflage.

But I didn't want to leave Matthew unattended. What if he slipped out while I was gone? What could I do? Call Lili? Someone else from my office?

Then I spotted Yudame, my tech writing student, wandering aimlessly through the crowd. He was hard to miss, with his huge dandelion puff of curly blondish-brown hair. Today's T-shirt was a flag in the shape of the island of Puerto Rico, with its single white star against a blue pennant, with a little tree frog, called a *coqui*, perched in the corner of a field of red and white stripes. Underneath was the slogan, "Hire me, I'm a *Boricua!*"

Don't ask me how I know all this stuff. Years of trivia quizzes, watching Jeopardy! on TV, and reading student papers. I waved him over to me. "Can you do me a huge favor?" I asked.

"No probs, my Prof. What you be needing?"

"See that guy?" I pointed to Matthew. Because his classmates were dressed so much alike, it was hard to identify him. I had to wait until he picked up a plastic beer mug, tilted his head back, and drained it. "There," I said. "That guy, pounding back the brew."

Yudame laughed. "You old guys talk funny, my Prof. Yeah, I got eyes on him."

I filed the 'old guy' comment away, in case Yudame

was ever in my class again. "I've got to run back to my office for a minute. If he starts to leave, will you give me a call?"

"So I gots a requestion, though. Who is he? Some rich alum?"

"Exactly. We're going to ask him for a big donation later and I'm supposed to know where he is." I pulled my business card out of my wallet and scrawled my cell phone number on it, then handed it to him.

"Coolio." He nodded and accepted the card, and I took off for Fields Hall, dodging between crowds of people.

It was slow going, and even slower returning with Rochester, because kids wanted to pet him and old people wanted to take his picture. I should have taken off the stupid bandanna and left it at the office, but Rochester loved it.

I kept checking my cell phone to make sure neither Yudame nor Rick had tried to call. By the time I had Yudame in sight I was drenched in sweat and my heart was racing. I made a brief detour to buy two bottles of cold water—one for me, and one I'd pour out for Rochester once we got settled.

Then we walked over to Yudame. "Your man's still there," he said, nodding toward Matthew's class tent. "He's totally crunked. I bet he be giving you whatevs."

"Hope so," I said. "Thanks." I took the bandanna off Rochester's neck, though he jumped on me and tried to take it back, then used it to wipe the sweat from my brow. Then I opened up one of the water bottles and took a long drink. It was so good.

Yudame reached down to scratch behind Rochester's ears. "No probs, Prof. Keep on chillaxin'."

"Will do." I tugged on Rochester's leash and led him over to the makeshift puppy park. He began jumping up and down, and I had to make him sit before I could pull open a space in between the picket fence and one of the tables and let him in. He immediately went wild again and started romping with a Rottweiler. I smiled at the other doggie dads and moms, and checked once again to make sure Matthew was with his friends.

I couldn't see him.

I dodged around. Were those his shins? His lower arms? What if he'd already taken off? How could I explain that to Rick?

Then I got a better view, and yes, that was him. Relief. But where was Rick?

30 – End of the Parade

Rochester jumped and rolled with the other dogs, and I made casual, if distracted conversation with their moms and dads. It was hot, with only the shade of a single spindly elm, and eventually people rounded up their dogs and left. Time ticked on.

The marching band struck up the chords to begin the parade. I called Rick's cell. "Where are you? The parade's about to start."

"The campus is parked up. I had to leave my car a couple of blocks away, and I'm on foot. Where are you?"

"Right now? There's a whole bunch of tents set up on the flat area on the south side of the campus. But once the parade starts, we'll be marching up the hill, past Fields Hall, and then back down the other side toward the football stadium. Your best bet is to stay on Main Street and call me when you get to the campus."

"Roger that." He hung up and I noticed Matthew's class beginning to move into place for the parade. I had no choice but to leash up Rochester and follow them. I couldn't join the parade, because I had the dog with me. I had to stay on the outskirts as a spectator, struggling to keep Matthew in sight.

The crowd was loud and boisterous, and kept moving and shifting, and I had to dart and elbow and push. Fortunately I could pretend that Rochester was just dragging me along, and apologize as I followed him.

I also wasn't going to be able to march into graduation with Lili and the rest of the faculty as she and I had planned. When Rochester and I reached a relatively clear area along the parade route I called Lili. "I can't march in with you. Something's come up."

"Are you sure? I can wait until the very end of the

procession."

"No, you go on and walk with your department. We'll walk together next year."

Assuming we were both still at Eastern by then, I thought, as I hung up. My job in the alumni relations office was only a temporary one; if the campaign faltered, or money otherwise got tight, I'd probably be among the first to be let go.

But I couldn't worry about that; I had to keep an eye on Matthew Durkheim. It was tough to keep track of him, because he looked so much like his former teammates. A half dozen of them had all maintained their figures, and all wore identical sleeveless Ts and cargo shorts. A couple had lighter hair than he did, and a couple were balding, but those were small differences in a moving crowd.

The light played tricks on my eyes, too, as the parade moved in and out of shadows, under the shade of ancient elms and maples and then out into the bright sun. The guys had all had a lot to drink, and they were laughing and knocking into each other, hugging, improvising dance steps, even forming a kick line. The class behind them, a somber group of typical Eastern bankers, doctors and lawyers, looked disapproving.

Just as their section of the parade approached the entrance to the football stadium, Matthew began to shake hands with his teammates. After a lot of hugging and shoulder punching, he turned and walked in the opposite direction from the campus.

Rochester and I remained in the shadow of a giant maple, watching to see where he went. As his class marched through the stadium's arched gate, he rounded the corner of the building. We took off after him, staying higher up the hill and maintaining a vantage point.

Matthew crossed the driveway and headed toward the brick field house, where the coaches and trainers had their offices. Rochester and I began to descend the last bit of hill, keeping Matthew in sight.

Rochester was a model dog, keeping pace with me, his head up and alert. No deviations to sniff or dig or act crazy. I wanted to praise him but I didn't want to create any distractions, either.

Once we got down to ground level, and had the solid bulk of the field house between us and the stadium, we left the clamor of the parade behind and it was almost quiet around us, just the low rumble of applause and music from the ceremonies.

I held Rochester's leash loose so that his tags and collar didn't clank together and make noise, and I put my cell phone on silent and looked ahead. The soccer field itself had been marked off limits, but the grassy area beyond it, where I had played the occasional pickup game of touch football as an undergrad, had been converted into a temporary lot. Chalk lines on the grass indicated row after row of spaces, now filled with SUVs and luxury cars of every make and model.

Matthew walked straight down the center of the field as if he owned it. If we followed him, he'd only have to turn around to see us and it was going to be hard to pretend I was just out walking the dog. Instead, I turned right and guided Rochester behind the bleachers.

My phone buzzed, and I answered, putting it up close to my mouth so I could speak in a low voice. "I'm following Durkheim. He just left the parade, and he's on his way to the temporary parking lot below the stadium. There's also a big student lot beyond it. I don't know which lot he parked in."

As I spoke, I reprimanded myself in my head for ending a sentence with a preposition. Once an English teacher, always an English teacher. Even in a dangerous situation.

"I just got to the campus entrance," Rick said. "I can see the stadium from here. I'll head that way and meet you at the temporary lot."

"Better get there soon."

He disconnected, and I kept moving parallel to Matthew's path, watching him through the gaps in the bleachers. It was awkward having Rochester with me, trying to make sure that neither of us stumbled over the rough grass. I worried that he'd start barking, or see a squirrel or something and take off, and blow my cover. Could I tie him up under the bleachers? Probably not. He'd make a huge fuss.

Matthew came to the end of the field, and I was nearly abreast of him. The entrance to the temporary lot was only a few feet away. The lot was eerily quiet; alumni, faculty, students and families were all gathered at the stadium for the graduation.

I lagged for a moment to let Matthew get ahead of me. I was just about to step out of the shelter of the bleachers when Verri M. Parshall appeared from the other side. I stayed under cover to see what would happen.

Though she wasn't a fashion plate, she'd always been neat and well put together when I'd seen her, in her pants suits and sensible foam-soled shoes, but now she wore a polyester track suit and sneakers. Her brown and gray hair was tousled and there was something odd about the way she moved.

"I knew I'd find you here," she said to Matthew. "You said you came to every reunion but you never stayed for graduation." Her voice was unnaturally loud, and her words slurred. She pointed her index finger at him. "Your check bounced!"

I assumed that Verri had either been fired, or at least suspended, after Babson confronted her. I could understand how she might drown her sorrows for a while, and look for someone to blame for her situation. But to come on campus drunk? That was a really stupid move.

Matthew turned to face her. "You're an idiot, Verri.

You couldn't keep your staff quiet about the problems with Freezer Burn. People blabbed to Rita Gaines and she cut off my funding. That's why the check bounced."

He turned and continued walking into the parking lot. I knew that once he reached his car, he'd be gone. I had to do something to stall him until Rick arrived.

I stepped out from my side of bleachers, still holding tight to Rochester's leach. "Is that why you were meeting with Rita that Sunday, out at her barn?" I asked. "To talk about your company's funding?"

Matthew stopped again, and this time turned in my direction. "Who the fuck are you?"

"Steve Levitan. You don't remember me? I guess I'm not that memorable. But I'd think you'd remember Rochester. We were there that Sunday." I shrugged, trying to keep Matthew talking until Rick could arrive. "My friend Rick and I brought our dogs up to train with Rita that day. Rochester really took to the agility course."

I leaned down and scratched under Rochester's neck. "Didn't you boy? You're a natural for that." He nodded his big head up and down.

I took a brief glance toward the street. Still no Rick.

"How did you know I stuck around to talk to Rita?" Matthew asked me.

"Rick and I took the dogs out for a drive," I said, improvising. "We circled back past Rita's later and Rick noticed your car was still at her house. He's a cop in Stewart's Crossing, you know. He's always paying attention to little details like that."

"That's nothing," Matthew said. "So I hung around Rita's afterward. That doesn't prove that I had anything to do with her murder."

Oops, Matthew. I hadn't said anything other than that I knew he'd stuck around to talk to Rita. And there had been nothing in the news to indicate that the police were considering her death a murder.

"She was murdered?" Verri asked. "Rita Gaines? She'd been coming around my office all the time over the last few weeks, snooping around about Freezer Burn. I told you that, Matthew. You said you'd get her out of my hair."

Before Matthew could answer, she stepped up until she was right next to him. "You didn't kill her, did you?" she asked.

Now I was sure. Verri was drunk. Only a fool or a drunk would step that close to someone and accuse them of murder. I'd seen Matthew slugging back beers, and now Verri was sloshed, too. What a great combination.

Matthew seemed floored by the turn of events, and I didn't blame him. We all stood still and my brain raced to make connections. There hadn't been any negative comments online about MDC, even though Rita knew of significant problems with Freezer Burn, and she had cut off Matthew's funding.

Matthew had stayed at Rita's after everyone else left. If he'd killed her, he could have checked her emails and found the information on the other companies, then made those anonymous posts to shift suspicion from his own company.

I was still processing information when Matthew looked from Verri to me, then shook his head. "This whole college is a waste of space," he said. "Sometimes I'm sorry I ever went here."

Rochester nudged my knee, and I looked down at him. But he wasn't facing me; instead he was looking toward the street, and as I followed his gaze I saw Rick Stemper approaching. He was wearing his uniform, and though he didn't have his gun drawn, I saw his right hand on his holster.

I looked back at Matthew, and saw him turning to head toward his car once again. Then Rick's voice rang out across the lines of cars. "Police! Freeze!"

His voice carried, though he was still a few hundred

feet away. As I watched, Mathew looked in Rick's direction.

Verri was still right beside him. He whirled on her and grabbed her by the arm with his left hand. With his right, he pulled a gun out of the pocket of his cargo shorts and pointed it at her head.

"You've just stepped in a whole pile of dog doo, Verri," he said, once again his voice betraying no trace of the beer I'd seen him drink. "I'm not letting the police arrest me. You're going to be my get-out-of-jail-free card."

He pushed her forward and they began walking down one of the aisles of the lot.

"Mr. Durkheim!" Rick called. "Put the gun down. I just want to talk to you." Rick closed on us, his hand on his holster.

"I'm not talking to anybody," Matthew said. He and Verri continued through the broad aisle, though Verri stumbled and it looked like Matthew was half-dragging her. Rochester and I kept pace behind them, hemmed in on both sides by cars and SUVs. I could see Rick paralleling us on the outside of the lot.

The air was eerily quiet. In the distance I heard something banging, then the faint traces of the graduation march floating up from the stadium.

"You didn't go to Rita's farm with the intention of killing her," I called to Matthew's back. "That'll be good for you. No premeditation. If you let Verri go, that'll be another thing in your favor. Your attorney can use those to negotiate."

"I won't need an attorney, because the police aren't going to take me in," he called over his shoulder.

Matthew and Verri stopped, and I assumed he had reached his car. He was going to kill Verri, jump in and drive away. Rick was a good shot, but he was still too far away, even if he ran, to hit a moving car.

Verri must have had the same idea, because she

twisted in Matthew's grasp. "You cheated me, you bastard!" she yelled. She elbowed him in the stomach. I remembered a self-defense course Mary and I had taken when we moved to New York. One of the things we were taught was to aim elbows and knees at soft spots in the human anatomy.

Had Verri taken a similar course?

If she had, it hadn't worked, because all Matthew did was shoot her in the head, then drop her body to the ground.

I was so stunned I just stood there, my mouth open. Rochester surged forward, jerking his leash from my hand.

"No, Rochester!" I yelled. "Stop!" I took off after him.

I must have been wrong about the car, because instead of jumping into the one he stood beside, Matthew took off running. But he was nearly fifty years old, and Rochester had four legs and a whole load of year-old puppy energy. My big, enthusiastic golden retriever caught up to him, then took a flying leap and landed right on Matthew's back, as if he was on an agility course, just doing what he had practiced.

Matthew fell forward, and he dropped the gun as he tried to brace himself with his hands. I caught up a moment later, and picked up the gun before he could reach for it.

He struggled under Rochester's weight, but the big dog wasn't letting him move. He pummeled Rochester's side with his fist, and the sound of it infuriated me. I wrapped both hands around the grip of his gun and aimed it at his head.

"Get your hands off my dog or I'll shoot you!"

Out of my peripheral vision I saw Rick galloping forward. I took a couple of deep breaths as Matthew made a fist again. "Leave my dog the fuck alone!" I leaned down and pressed the gun against the side of Matthew's head, staying out of his reach. My arm was shaking with adrenaline and I knew it would only take the tiniest pressure to pull the trigger.

Then Rick was right beside me. "I'll take that," he said gently, taking Matthew's gun from my hand.

I leaned down and pried Rochester up from Matthew's back, as Rick cuffed him.

I sat down on the grass and Rochester was all over me, snuffling and licking me. "Yes, I'm all right, boy," I said. "You were amazing. But you shouldn't do things like that. You could get hurt."

I reached up and hugged him, burying my face in his soft neck hair.

We were surrounded by the lights and sirens of the approaching Leighville police, whom I learned Rick had called for backup as soon as he knew for certain that Matthew was on campus.

"I can't believe Rochester took him down," Rick said. "That dog."

I sat with Rochester as an ambulance arrived for Verri. Car-top cop lights strobed and radios blared and uniforms collected evidence and took statements. I sat up and recited everything that had happened, with my hand constantly finding Rochester's fur for reassurance. When Rick and the Leighville cops were finally done with me, I asked Rick, "Any word on Verri?"

He shook his head. "She didn't make it. The shot to her head killed her instantly."

"There'll be a memorial service here, I'm sure," I said. "She dedicated her life to the college, despite the way things ended. Maybe even a joint one for her and Rita Gaines."

"Nobody should go the way they both did," Rick said.

I nodded my head, then stood and walked Rochester back to Fields Hall, slowly, giving him plenty of time to sniff everything he wanted to. I'd never taken my cell off silent, and when I got back to my desk I looked at it and found a message from Lili asking me to call.

"Are you all right?" she asked when I did. "I saw all those cop cars and I was worried you had something to do with them being here."

"I can tell you all about it," I said. "If you're still up for that late lunch. But I'm at my office, and I don't have the energy to drive Rochester back home and then go upriver to New Hope to meet you. Do you think maybe he and I could just come over to your house and we could order out?"

"You bet. I'm here. You sound exhausted. You want me to pick you guys up?"

"I can make the drive."

"I'll throw something together. You just bring yourself and your dog."

"I'll see you soon. I love you."

I realized it was the first time I'd said it to Lili. But after all I'd been through, I knew that I meant it.

"I love you too, Steve. And I'm very glad you're all right."

I hung up, then put Rochester's leash on and we walked outside. A nice breeze had picked up, and the air was fresh with the smell of new-mown grass and humidity from the placid Delaware, just a few blocks away. Graduation was over and the campus had cleared out. My car was one of the few left in the parking lot.

Leighville was crowded with celebratory graduates, their families and their friends. I took a couple of side streets to reach Lili's and was glad to snag a parking space only a block from her apartment.

Lili kissed me as soon as she opened her front door, then stepped back. "What happened to your forehead?" she asked.

I reached up. "I guess I bruised it when I went down after the dog."

"After him how?"

"It's a long story."

"Well, come on in and sit down. Have something to eat, and then you can tell me."

Lili had made us croque monsieurs, ham and cheese sandwiches grilled on thick slices of farm bread, which she served with thick potato chips and bottles of French orange soda. In between bites, I told her the whole story. "Poor Verri," she said, when I was finished.

"I do feel bad for her," I said. "She wasn't a nice person, and neither was Rita Gaines. But both of them made contributions to Eastern, and neither of them deserved to be murdered."

I drank some soda, and we were quiet for a while. "I do wish I'd been at graduation, though," I said. "There were a couple of students I wanted to see graduate."

"Good ones or bad ones? I know I had a couple I'm eager to see move on."

I laughed. "I guess some of each."

I leaned over to kiss her, and while I wasn't paying attention, Rochester sat up and wolfed a couple of potato chips from my plate.

"Go on, help yourself, dog," I said, sitting back and laughing. "You earned it."

* * *

If you've enjoyed Steve and Rochester, and haven't read their two earlier adventures, I hope you'll consider *In Dog We Trust* and *The Kingdom of Dog*.

CPSIA information can be obtained
at www.ICGtesting.com
Printed in the USA
FSOW03n2040240816
24180FS